L[illegible]N

Murder at the Herald

A Polynesia Henman Mystery

First published by Snapdragon Press 2022

First edition

ISBN: 978-1-7391683-0-8

This book was professionally typeset on Reedsy.
Find out more at reedsy.com

For Sam

1

Chapter 1

Polynesia jabbed viciously at the keyboard. She was imagining that each key was one of the mascara-fringed eyes in the smirking face of Alice Smith, and she stabbed at them all mercilessly.

As she typed, she went back over yesterday's events in her mind.

'Thank you, Polynesia,' Joanna, the News Editor, had said. 'We've got one more candidate to see. We'll be in touch tomorrow.'

Joanna and Martin, the newly-appointed Managing Editor, stood up and smiled as she left the room and Polynesia felt a fizz of excitement as she closed the door. The job opportunity – deputy news editor on the *Daily Herald* – was her chance to move her career in the direction she'd always dreamed of and become an investigative journalist. It also meant promotion and a chance to escape the *Herald's* Lifestyle department with its endless articles about trending paint colours and eco-friendly yoga mats. She couldn't wait.

She smiled to herself as she went down in the lift, planning to dash out for a quick, celebratory sandwich before getting back to work.

'It's Polynesia, isn't it?'

Polynesia looked around and saw a woman sitting on the leather sofa in reception. She took in the impeccably manicured red nails, displayed to perfection on the white bone china cup, and the glossy red lips forming a little pout. With a nasty jolt Polynesia recognised those wide, seemingly innocent blue eyes. It was Alice Smith, former class bully at Putney Bridge Girls' School.

'Alice!' she said, trying – and failing – to smile. 'I didn't know you were at the *Herald*.'

'I'm not … yet,' Alice said, with a knowing little smirk. 'I've just come for an interview.'

'Oh, right. Well, good luck,' Polynesia felt it would be churlish not to wish her luck, although she actually hoped that Alice would trip up on her way out of the office and fall under a bus, preferably while Polynesia was watching out of the window.

'Thanks,' said Alice. 'I'm pretty confident, though. Martin said the *Herald* would be lucky to get someone like me.'

Polynesia's heart sank as she headed out of the building towards Arnie's Sarnies. Hiring Alice would be a coup for the *Herald*, would it? Then how come such an avid reader of rival newspapers as Polynesia had never heard of her? Then she gave herself a little shake. It was probably just Alice doing what she did best, winding people up by being Mean Girl Extreme. She mustn't let it get to her. After all, she wasn't an awkward little girl now, she was a thirty-year-old Cambridge graduate working for a national newspaper. And where had Alice gone to university? She perked up even more. Not Oxbridge, definitely – somewhere so nondescript that Polynesia couldn't even remember where. She did remember Alice's entry in their school yearbook though, she'd been voted girl most likely to marry well. Only if she manages to hide her true character until after the wedding, Polynesia had thought at the time. Polynesia herself had been voted girl most likely to become Head of Hufflepuff, which hadn't displeased her.

Surely the *Herald* editorial team would choose someone with head of house potential, rather than a husband hunter? And with that comforting thought, she picked up her smoked salmon and cream cheese bagel and hurried back to work, where she was soon engrossed in her article, *Forest bathing or wild swimming? How to capture the zeitgeist.*

And now this morning, she'd got the phone call. She could tell immediately that it wasn't good news. Joanna sounded uncomfortable and almost apologetic.

'Such a difficult decision ... two strong candidates ... so much potential ... Martin felt some outside blood would benefit the team ... a new perspective ... a fresh pair of eyes.' Joanna got a grip and stopped babbling. 'But we know how keen you are to join us so Martin's arranged a secondment for you. Two days a week in the News team working closely with the new deputy editor.' Joanna's voice had now taken on a pleading quality. 'That way you'll be a shoo-in for the next vacancy.'

Polynesia felt her stomach churn and then sink. 'Who is the new deputy editor?' she asked as calmly as she could.

'Well, actually, it's an old friend of yours. I understand that you were at school together. Her name's Alice Smith.'

Polynesia's heart plummeted and landed somewhere in the

region of her large intestine. She fought to keep her voice neutral. 'We were in the same class at Putney Bridge.'

'Well, we ran it past her this morning. She thought it was a great idea for you to join the team part time.'

I'll bet she did, Polynesia thought sourly. How bloody brilliant! Not only had Polynesia not got the promotion, but Alice Smith was going to be her new boss.

She put the phone down and began her vicious attack on the keyboard. Looking up after several minutes of solid battering she saw Jess, reluctant Lifestyle guru and wannabe travel writer, watching her.

'Bad luck, Pol,' said Jess. 'Let's go out for an early lunch and a debrief.'

'I just don't get it!' Polynesia said, as they settled into a booth with their Bento boxes at Tokyo Express. 'I haven't heard anything about Alice Smith since we left school. How come she's suddenly so shit hot that Martin thinks the *Herald*'s "lucky to get her"'?

Her air quotes sounded so savage that the man in the next booth looked across in alarm.

'I've just googled her and nothing comes up,' Jess agreed. 'Mind you Alice Smith's a pretty common name. But Alice Smith Journalist doesn't bring anything up either. It seems odd that there's no record online of anything she's written.'

'She's devious and poisonous,' Polynesia said. 'And I'm sure she still hasn't forgiven me for winning five prizes at speech day. She didn't even win the Congeniality Cup, even though she'd been sucking up to the teachers for weeks.'

'Surely you didn't win the Congeniality Cup?' Jess sounded amazed.

'No,' Polynesia admitted. 'I didn't get that one. But because I won so many of the others, there were more contenders than usual for the nice but dim awards. You know, good deeds, punctuality, a dazzling smile and whatever else they can think of.'

'So, you think she's been plotting to get her own back for ten years because she didn't win a school prize? And now she's faked a CV in journalism, just to get the job you wanted?'

'I agree. It does sound a little far-fetched,' Polynesia said. 'But there's something that's not right about all this.'

She dipped her last piece of sushi into the soy sauce and then chewed it reflectively. 'I'll talk to Dad tonight and see what he thinks.'

Polynesia unclipped her feet from the pedals with a twist of her heel and wheeled her bike through the gate and up the path to the front door. One of the few advantages, she mused, of not having a mother, was that she could always leave her bike in the hallway; her father agreed that it was the only sensible place to keep such an expensive piece of kit. But she'd noticed, over the years, that other friends who did have mothers, met with a lot of resistance when it came to sensible bike storage locations. Her feet clattered on the tiles as she walked inside and propped the bike up against the wall, vaguely noticing the scuff marks where the handlebars rubbed against the paintwork. Bending down to remove her shoes, she saw a pair of dark green corduroy trousers appear through the doorway from the kitchen and then stop just in front of her.

Straightening up, she managed a half-smile. 'Before you ask – I didn't get the job.'

'Oh Pol, I am sorry.'

'You know me, Dad. I go down hard, but I soon bounce

back.'

'I know you do, love – strength in adversity and all that – one of your strong points. But I know how much you wanted that job. You didn't resign in a fit of pique, did you?' he added anxiously.

'No, Dad, I didn't. I seem to be acquiring wisdom at long last, and cutting off my nose hasn't featured in today's debriefing and regrouping. Not even as Plan B.'

Trevor Henman looked relieved. Polynesia's inclination towards reckless impulsiveness had given him a fair amount of anxiety over the years. He shuffled forwards in his ill-fitting slippers and gave her a brief hug.

'That's my girl. If it wasn't meant to be this time, there'll be lots of other opportunities. Who got the job, do you know yet?'

'Do you remember how I once punched a bitchy little cow at school because she gloated to my face that Mum had been murdered and you were in prison?'

'Yes, I remember your gran telling me about it when she visited.' Trevor gave a chuckle. 'She said the headmistress told her, in not so many words, that the girl deserved a good punch and they wouldn't be taking any further action due to "the extenuating circumstances."' He stopped smiling and looked sharply at his daughter. 'You're not telling me –'

'I'm afraid I *am* telling you. The *Herald*'s deputy news editor is Alice Smith, the Bellatrix Lestrange of SW15. And sadly, I don't think I'll get away with punching her in the face again this time,' Polynesia said.

'Jokes!' she added hastily as she saw the expression on her father's face. 'But seriously, Dad. Doesn't it tell you a lot about someone if they jump at the chance of bullying a classmate when their mother's been killed and their father's been accused of murder? It's like that Aristotle quote we learnt in Classics "show me the child of seven and I'll show you the man." And Alice wasn't seven, she was eleven. She was practically a fully formed psychopath.'

She spoke lightly, because she didn't want to upset her father, but she remembered those dark days before her father's release and how Alice had made everything just that little bit harder to bear.

'So what are you going to do, love?' Trevor asked.

'I'm going to hang in there. My investigative antenna's twitching. I've been seconded to the News team for two days a week as a sort of consolation prize. And I intend to make full use of my time there to investigate Alice Smith.'

'Well, your investigative antenna got me off a murder charge, so I can't fault it,' her father said. 'But promise me you won't do anything rash.'

'Rash? Me? Of course not. What's for supper, anyway? I'm starving.'

Polynesia tucked her cycling shoes neatly behind the front wheel of her bike and followed her father into the kitchen.

2

Chapter 2

On the first day of her secondment to the News team, Polynesia alternately pedalled furiously and braked hard as she made her way eastwards from Putney towards the South Bank. Propped on one leg waiting for yet another set of lights to change, her thoughts centred on the day ahead. Dad had asked her not to do anything rash, and while she didn't intend to, the problem with rash things was that she tended to do them ... well ... rashly.

She allowed herself a brief daydream where she accidentally dropped a banana skin and Alice slipped on it, plummeted headfirst down the stairs, and was carted off to hospital. On hearing the news that Alice was to be immobilised in a full body brace for at least six months, Polynesia immediately volunteered to take on extra work and soon became a highly regarded member of the News team. Her incisive stories got her on the front page with her own byline. Smiling as she accepted an award at a press dinner, she paid a gracious tribute to 'my colleagues, who have always supported me and believed in me.'

A horn sounding from behind alerted her to the green light ahead, and she put the smile and the applause behind her and pedalled on towards the *Herald*'s offices.

The *Daily Herald* had moved from its original Victorian home into a modern block several years earlier. There were bicycle racks in the underground car park to facilitate the daily death dash of the younger staff who a) couldn't afford a car and b) liked to believe that their carbon-neutral commute somehow offset the tonnes of avocados, goji berries and Javanese civet coffee flown in every day to form an essential part of their diet. Polynesia locked up her bike and went upstairs to her desk, where she grabbed a notebook, her water bottle and the jacket she kept on the back of her chair for meetings.

'Well, if it isn't Clark Kent!' Jess raised an eyebrow. 'What are you doing down here slumming it with us Lifestyle no-hopers?'

'Just off to daily briefing now. Thought I'd better wear a jacket to create a good impression on my first day.'

'I know a jacket's supposed to look professional. But I'm not sure that's true if it's a moth-eaten old rag that you wrestled out of the iron grip of a bargain-hunting pensioner at a car boot sale.'

'It wasn't a car boot sale. It was a vintage sale,' Polynesia said crossly. 'And it was a very glamorous pensioner. She looked just like Joanna Lumley. In fact, it might even have been Joanna Lumley, now I come to think of it.'

'Yeah, yeah,' said Jess with a smile. 'Well, I hope you get a stonking good story to cover today. I'm planning a meteoric career rise by clinging to your coat tails. Well, not those coat tails obviously –' she broke off with a meaningful look at the jacket Polynesia was just shrugging into as she walked towards the lift.

Polynesia got into the lift, waggling a middle finger in Jess's direction. She looked down at the jacket; it wasn't exactly Chanel, but it did have a certain class ... didn't it? There were a few stains down the front, but tweed always looked kind of splodgy anyway so she was pretty sure nobody would notice. Perhaps she should have replaced the missing button or, at the very least, cut off the long piece of thread that dangled from the jacket, highlighting its buttonlessness. Oh well, too late to do anything about it now.

She made her way towards the big conference table in the middle of the News office, where the team was starting to gather. She saw Alice in the centre of a group of male reporters.

'You know that's not what I meant,' Alice was saying, as there was a loud burst of laughter. 'All I'm saying is that I can't believe how small my hands are compared to yours.'

And she stretched out one perfectly manicured hand in front of her and held it next to Ross Andrews' meaty fist. There was an inaudible comment from someone in the group and more laughter.

Polynesia remembered that Alice had always been one of the pick-me girls at school, hanging around at the bus stop until the boys' school finished, and keen to sign up for any joint school project that brought the girls into contact with the awkward, nerdy boys at St Jude's. Polynesia gritted her teeth. Behaviour that was annoying but understandable in a fourteen-year-old girl, was frankly nauseating in a thirty-year-old woman. What would Alice do next, put on a pair of ankle socks and start skipping around the office?

'Right, folks, let's make a start.' Martin spoke up over the general chatter.

'Ooh – just one second, Martin,' Alice said and walked across to Polynesia.

Was she going to welcome her, Polynesia wondered? A private word before the general introductions?

'Polynesia. Or are you Polly these days?' Alice asked.

Polynesia shook her head. 'I've never really seen myself as a Polly. I'm still Polynesia. Or Pol to my friends.'

'I see,' Alice paused for a fraction of a second. 'Polynesia, would you mind popping out and getting me a coffee? I'm absolutely desperate and there was a huge queue when I walked past Starbucks this morning.'

Alice gave her a pouty little smile that she obviously believed would melt the hardest of hearts, but Polynesia's heart was made of sterner stuff.

'There's a coffee machine over there,' Polynesia said. 'No need to go out. I'll show you.'

'Oh, I know there's a very basic machine,' Alice said. 'But unfortunately, my allergies mean that I just can't tolerate ordinary coffee. I need a decaf oat milk latte, and Starbucks is my go-to for that. I'm sure the queue will have died down by now and you won't miss much of the meeting. Oh, and ...' Alice smiled sweetly, '... keep the change. Perhaps you could put it towards a new jacket.'

With twenty pairs of eyes watching her, Polynesia took the proffered five-pound note and turned to walk back to the lift.

3

Chapter 3

'So, did you gob in her oat milk latte?' Jess asked, as she and Polynesia settled into their seats in the pub after work.

'For once in my life I've decided to think first and act second. And I promised Dad I wouldn't do anything rash. Besides, revenge is a dish best served cold, as some vengeful genius once said.'

'Are you sure they weren't talking about gazpacho?' Jess said. 'What story did they put you on today? It had to be more interesting than my piece on vegan dog food: T*he perfect solution to eco-trauma for animal-loving millennials.*'

'By the time I got back with the coffee the meeting was nearly over. I've no idea what was top of the agenda. Martin asked me to rewrite a piece about breaches of the planning regulations in local government. I had to take it down to five paragraphs from nine.' Polynesia sighed. 'I wasn't expecting Watergate or anything like that on my first day. But I had hoped for something more than public humiliation followed by sheer mindless tedium.'

Although, if Polynesia was being completely honest with

herself, she had been nurturing a secret hope that her talent would be recognised as soon as she joined the News team. Perhaps Joanna would lean casually over to see what she was writing and gasp in astonishment at the way Polynesia had got to the very heart of a complex story, painting a brilliant picture with pithy epithets and penetrating insights. *'Give this girl her own byline!'* Joanna would cry. *'And from now on, any story of Polynesia's goes straight on the front page!'*

Of course, she would never admit this to anyone, ever, no matter how much Prosecco she'd drunk, but the death of her dream certainly added to her disgruntled feelings as she cycled home that evening. Weaving her way expertly through Battersea and Wandsworth, she wondered why she always allowed herself to get carried away, which only doubled the disappointment when things didn't work out. Too much imagination, she told herself sternly. But that wasn't it exactly – the thing was that she knew, deep down, that she was exceptional and that one day everyone else would recognise it too. She just didn't know when or how that would happen, which was fairly annoying.

Now it was time to bounce back and play down the story for Dad, who was waiting for her with a shepherd's pie and a sympathetic ear. She didn't want him riled up – she'd got him off one murder charge already, and she wasn't keen to see if she could manage it a second time.

The pattern was set, it seemed. Every Tuesday and Friday Polynesia would make her way up to the News Office in time for the daily briefing. Then Alice would remember that her dry cleaning needed to be collected urgently, or she would have a headache that could only be relieved by special pills from a homeopathic pharmacy in Holborn. So, Polynesia would head off, seething, and return in time to be given some boring rewrite that a competent GCSE student could have managed.

'It's not fair!' Polynesia said for the hundredth time, as she arrived back in Lifestyle one Wednesday morning after a particularly trying Tuesday. 'Alice treats me like her personal slave and doesn't miss a single opportunity to show me that she's in charge. And nobody else does anything about it! Martin sits there nodding his head and smiling vaguely whenever Alice opens her poisonous little mouth. As for Joanna, she just pretends she hasn't noticed. Whatever happened to the sisterhood?'

'Either disbanded by the patriarchy or sacrificed on the altar of female ambition, depending on your point of view,' Jess said.

'Well, I'm going to try to reform the sisterhood. I'll go and talk to Joanna and find out what's going on.'

'Alice is also technically a member of the sisterhood,' Jess pointed out.

'And Hitler was technically a vegetarian,' Polynesia said, somewhat obscurely, as she walked towards the lift.

This was not how she'd planned for her career to pan out, she thought crossly, as she got out of the lift. She peered around the corner to make sure that Alice was nowhere in sight, before scuttling across to Joanna's office and slipping through the open door.

Joanna was sitting at her desk and Polynesia thought, not for the first time, how colourless she looked. Everything about her – hair, skin, eyes, clothes – was a bland, indeterminate shade of beige or vanilla. If she stood in front of a magnolia wall, she'd be practically invisible.

'Sorry to interrupt. But do you have a moment?' Polynesia asked.

Joanna looked up. Was there a guilty, shifty look in her eyes, or was that just Polynesia's overactive imagination?

'Oh, yes.' Joanna said without much enthusiasm. 'Come in. Shut the door and sit down.'

Joanna made no move towards the sofa in the corner of the room, so Polynesia sat on the hard chair facing the desk, which was obviously meant for unwelcome visitors. Joanna pushed her own chair back from the desk, picked up a pencil and started twirling it round and round in her fingers. Definitely shifty, Polynesia thought.

'What can I do for you?' asked Joanna. Twirl, twirl, twirl.

Polynesia took a deep breath. 'When you offered me two days a week in the News team, you said I'd gain experience that would help me when the next vacancy came up. But so far all I've done is run errands for Alice and rewrite pieces to make them fit on the page. I've been writing my own copy for years now in Lifestyle. So this is really a step backwards for me, not forwards.'

'I can see that it might look like that,' Joanna continued to twirl. 'But Martin feels that Alice needs to exert her authority a little while she finds her feet.'

While she finds her feet, Polynesia thought. As far as she was concerned, Alice's feet were already very firmly planted on the Newsroom floor. They were normally clad in size 5 L.K. Bennett's, and she used them every Tuesday and Friday to give Polynesia a metaphorical kicking.

'I feel sure that once she's comfortable in her role, she'll ease you into the heart of the News team. Then you'll soon be working on some front-page stories.' Joanna was now rolling the pencil determinedly back and forth between her palms, as though she'd just discovered the secret of fire.

But why is Martin so keen for Alice to ... umm ... "exert her authority"'? Polynesia asked. 'I thought this was a team.'

'You'd have to ask Martin, I'm afraid. He's new – different management style – we all need to be able to adapt and flex. You know – go with the flow - take on new ideas - get out of our comfort zone.'

Polynesia had already noticed Joanna's tendency to gabble clichés when she felt uncomfortable and here she was doing it again. So, Joanna wasn't happy with the situation then? She wasn't adapting and flexing to Martin's new management style, she was simply putting up with it. But why? This definitely required further thought and investigation.

'OK, then.' Polynesia smiled sweetly at Joanna. 'I'll go and ask Martin why he thinks several trips a week to Starbucks is expanding my comfort zone.'

She was gratified to hear a snapping noise as she walked towards the door, and turned to see Joanna gripping the two splintered halves of the pencil, one in each tightly clenched fist.

'Yes,' Polynesia thought to herself. 'Be afraid, Joanna. Be very afraid. Polynesia Henman, investigator extraordinaire, is back!'

4

Chapter 4

Frustratingly, Martin wasn't in his office, which put a damper on the budding investigation. But despite this setback, Polynesia felt much more cheerful as she went back down to Lifestyle to work on her current piece for the Saturday magazine: *Me and my campervan - ten celebrities revel in the freedom of the open road.* Well, pretty minor celebrities, to be honest, but that was only to be expected. You're not going to find Elton John or Victoria Beckham in a car park in Dorset, sitting in a van that the average tortoise would consider cramped, and saying 'Somehow, Pot Noodles never taste this good when my chef makes them at home.'

Campervans, Polynesia thought, cunningly ticked all the right boxes for those who claim to love off-grid, unplanned adventures, but actually prefer a locked door at night, an emergency pint of UHT milk in the glove compartment and a map showing the nearest campsite with electricity and hot showers.

She finished the article and then started to write a plan of action:

1. *Tackle Joanna* ... well, she could tick that off for a start.
2. *Tackle Martin* ... have to wait until tomorrow.
3. *Tackle Alice*

'That's a lot of tackling for someone who claims to hate team sports.' Jess was peering over her shoulder.

'Don't you know that it's extremely bad manners to read someone else's private plan of action? And anyway, why are you here? I thought you'd gone off to spend the day glamping in Essex.'

Jess shuddered theatrically and flicked her long dark hair behind her shoulders. 'It was freezing cold and blowing a hoolie. Just look at my hair!'

It looked immaculate to Polynesia. It was sleek and glossy and very much to be envied by someone cursed with light brown poodle hair.

'And do you know what?' Jess went on. 'A yurt is just a tent with a good image consultant. It's uncomfortable, draughty and not at all what I was expecting. No fire pit, no hot tub, no Mongolian goatherds, not even an ensuite bathroom! My boots got stuck in the mud and the owner's dog tried to bite me. So Dave took some photos, I asked a few questions and we legged it. I'll get the rest of the information off the website for the article.'

Not for the first time, Polynesia reflected that Jess's holiday preferences could stand in the way of a successful career as a travel writer. A fondness for five-star hotels in Mauritius and a deep loathing of self-catering staycations would prejudice her chances with most travel publications. Jess would have to hope that a position came up at *Conde Nast Traveller* sooner rather than later; she was definitely not *Rough Guide* material.

'To get you up to speed,' Polynesia said. 'I've tackled Joanna and she fobbed me off. Martin's out, and I'm not tackling Alice until last. So that's it for today. And I need to leave on time because Dad's taking me out to dinner.'

'Chinese?' Jess asked

'Of course.'

'Peking Palace?'

'Where else?'

Jess laughed. 'Honestly, Pol. You'd think the gastronomic revolution had never happened! There must be a thousand different cuisines in London. You could try Ethiopian or Nepalese. But no! The Henmans only eat at the Peking Palace. You're like salmon, always returning to the same river.'

'It's hardly the same. We're not spawning and then dying in the Peking Palace. We're eating prawn toasts and Szechuan chicken. And you know how much Dad likes it there. It reminds him of when Mum was alive and we used to go every week.'

Polynesia didn't usually play the dead mother card to win an argument, but she was in a hurry, so a low blow was acceptable for once. She grabbed her high vis cycling jacket and helmet and gave Jess a 'no hard feelings, I forgive you for being insensitive' smile as she headed for the lift.

The next morning Polynesia was still fired with enthusiasm over her Plan of Action. She had decided that she would tackle Martin first thing in the morning. Then she could either leave him to talk to Alice, or else she could pin Alice to the floor and tip a large oat milk latte down her newly dry-cleaned Karen Millen pencil dress. It would all depend on how she felt after her meeting with Martin.

She hurried up to the News office, mentally rehearsing her speech as she got into the lift. 'I feel that I'm not being given the opportunity to contribute fully to the News Team. I have so much more to offer than rewrites and errands. If you recall at my interview –'

The lift doors opened and a loud scream interrupted her carefully crafted speech. She rushed around the corner to the News office, but the place was empty; half past eight was a little too early for most of the reporters. She heard the scream again and saw a movement behind the frosted glass of Martin's office window. Oh my God! What should she do? Was this a moment for heroics? She liked to think of herself as courageous, but on the other hand, Martin was pretty solidly built, and she hadn't got as much as a bicycle pump to defend herself if he'd gone berserk in there.

She hesitated for a moment, but then decided that if he had gone berserk, he was doing it silently. This somehow seemed less threatening, and so she ran across to his office. Taking a deep breath, she leaned forward and opened the door, pushing it forwards and then jumping back in case anyone or anything came flying out. There was no movement, just a strange gasping sound. So she stepped forward again and, steeling herself, looked inside. At the far side of the room, beyond the visitors' chairs and the large desk with its computer screens, keyboard, paper trays and telephones, Alice was standing, staring fixedly down at the floor. She didn't seem to have noticed Polynesia and was just opening her mouth for another scream.

'Alice, what -' Polynesia began. Then she noticed that Alice's pale pink dress was marred by several dark stains, and in her right hand, she was clutching a large knife.

Alice moved her head and saw Polynesia. The scream turned into a shriek, 'He's dead! He's dead!'

With a growing sense of dread, Polynesia moved forward, skirting around the desk until she could see the floor behind it. And there, lying at Alice's feet, was the body of Martin Trellis. His head was twisted awkwardly to one side, his tie was spooling onto his right shoulder and there were several horrifying gashes in his blood-soaked shirt.

She stared at Alice, frozen with shock, noticing the blood on Alice's hands and on the knife she was gripping so tightly. Then Alice stumbled towards her and Polynesia, suddenly realising that she was alone in the News department with a murderer, began to back slowly towards the door.

'Where are you going?' Alice shrieked. 'Don't leave me here!'

'Alice, put the knife down,' Polynesia said, trying to sound calm and in control.

She was nearly at the door now – a couple more steps and she'd be out in the corridor. Perhaps she could hold the door closed and trap Alice inside. Although the insane were supposed to have superhuman strength, weren't they? She was sure she'd read that somewhere. If that was the case, then there would be no point trying to shut her in. Alice would force the door open with Polynesia hanging grimly onto the other side, and comfortably within stabbing range. Perhaps it would be better to run for it and hope Alice's stilettos would slow her down.

'Put the knife down,' she repeated, continuing to edge towards the door.

Alice suddenly stared down at her hand, gave a horrified little moan, and dropped the knife on the floor. Polynesia sighed with relief and stepped out of the door.

'Just stay where you are,' Polynesia said. 'I'm going to get help. Stay here and don't do anything that will make things worse for you.'

'But it wasn't me! I haven't done anything! I just came in and found him!' Alice was beginning to sound hysterical again. 'Polynesia, please! I didn't kill Martin. You have to believe me!'

5

Chapter 5

The police arrived and began photographing and measuring. Polynesia and the other three members of the News team who'd arrived before the police sealed off the department, were sent to sit in Joanna's office. Alice had been led away, still hysterical, by a couple of nervous-looking constables.

Polynesia was secretly thrilled to be involved in a murder investigation. At least she hoped it was a secret. She'd hate her colleagues to think she was a ghoulish disaster junkie. But here she was, a potential chief witness – what a bit of luck that she'd decided to come in early. Obviously, it was a shame for poor Martin, but she hadn't known him very well, so after the initial shock began to wear off, it was all pretty exciting.

Pippa, Martin's secretary, was shaking slightly as she drank a glass of water. 'I can't believe it!' she was saying. 'Are they sure he's been murdered?'

'I've heard of people falling on their swords and dying,' Polynesia said. 'But he didn't fall on the knife, he was lying on his back and there were at least three stab wounds on his front. I don't think they could have been self-inflicted.'

Pippa started to cry. 'Poor Martin! And poor Clare! Their baby's due next month and he'll never see it now.'

Polynesia looked at Pippa's tears and realised that she'd never thought about Martin having a family. She'd never thought about him having any life at all outside work, and she began to feel slightly ashamed of herself.

'And it was Alice!' Ross said. 'I can't believe it! Why would she kill Martin? He absolutely worshipped her.'

'What?' Polynesia said. 'Worshipped her? How do figure that one out?'

'It's true,' Will Rowe said. 'You're only up here a couple of times a week, so you might not have noticed. But the rest of us used to joke about it all the time. He was always nipping across to her desk to talk to her or asking her come to his office for some meeting. And in daily briefing, if he's not speaking to the team, he's watching her. Literally all the time.'

'The reason I haven't noticed is probably because I'm out collecting coffee or dry cleaning during daily briefing,' Polynesia said.

'Yes, Will and I talked about that,' Ross said. 'Alice doesn't seem to like you much.'

'It did seem a bit unprofessional,' Will agreed. 'You know, the way she seemed to take such pleasure in humiliating you.'

'Thanks for speaking up for me, guys,' Polynesia said. 'Remember that poem "First they came for the female reporters, and I didn't speak up because I wasn't a woman"? I'm paraphrasing, but I'm sure you get the idea. And by the end, you're the only one left. So there's nobody around to save you when she finally turns on you, brandishing her large kitchen knife. And all because you didn't speak up for anyone else.'

'Yeah, well, we didn't want it to end in a catfight.' Will looked very uncomfortable now.

'A catfight!' Polynesia was suddenly furious. 'You witness bullying in the workplace and justify saying nothing by hiding behind a sexist term like catfight.'

'Look, she has just murdered someone,' Ross said. 'So it's not like we were way off target. Suppose we'd told her that we felt uncomfortable about the way she treated you and then she'd whipped that knife out of her bag and stabbed us? Or even stabbed you?'

Polynesia thought about the neat, little crossbody bag that Alice brought to work every day. Wherever she'd kept the knife, it wasn't in her bag.

'Well, it's too late to be arguing about all this now,' she said. 'But I hope you won't use it as an excuse for cowardice in the future. If you call someone out on their bad behaviour, the probability that it will end in murder must be ridiculously low.'

She turned as the door opened, and Sir Giles Ravencroft, Editor-in-Chief of the *Herald* came into the room. With his well-worn suit, dark-framed glasses, and harassed air, he looked just like an editor-in-chief from central casting. If he ever took his jacket off, Polynesia was sure that he would be wearing those metal armbands over his shirt sleeves.

'This is terrible news,' he said, looking round at them. 'Simply appalling.'

Pippa sniffed loudly and fumbled for another tissue in her bag, while the three reporters sat in silence.

'I wish I could send everyone home for the rest of the day. You know - shock - a mark of respect - mourning. But we must soldier on, I'm afraid. A newspaper has to go to print – we can't just miss a day – not even for a tragedy. Got to keep the cogs of journalism turning.'

A tendency to babble under stress was obviously a common feature among editors, Polynesia thought. She might need to work on acquiring that skill in the future, if she was to move up the ladder, but not right now she decided.

'It's all right, Sir Giles, we quite understand,' she said firmly. 'And if Lifestyle can spare me today, I'll happily stay and help out. I know the News team will be short staffed. Of course we're all ready to start work. Just as soon as the police let us go back to our desks.'

She looked at the others. Will and Ross nodded in agreement, while Pippa sniffed again and gave Sir Giles a look that could only be described as tearfully plucky.

'I think that can be arranged now,' Sir Giles suddenly looked much happier. 'The police have finished photographing and measuring and they've removed the err ... the ... umm. Well, they've removed Martin.'

Pippa gave a little sob and Sir Giles began to look uncomfortable again.

'Oh dear. I'll just go and see what's what and then we'll have an emergency briefing. The rest of the team's downstairs. We can go and –'

Whatever they could go and do was lost as he hurried from the room to secure their freedom. Whatever happens in today's briefing, I will not go back to rewriting council reports, Polynesia vowed.

Joanna led a very subdued briefing and Sir Giles gave everyone an incoherent message of support, very similar to the one he'd given the three reporters earlier. He told them that Alice was currently 'helping the police with their enquiries', but nobody was to say anything about this to anyone else.

Then they all got down to work in silence, with none of the usual hum of excitement and urgency that characterised the News office.

Polynesia had just started on her short piece about an international eel smuggler when the phone rang.

'Good morning, Polynesia. I have Detective Inspector Wilson and Detective Sergeant Knight in reception. They'd like to talk to you. Could you come down, please?'

Polynesia was out of her seat before Susie had finished speaking. It was time to give the police the benefit of her first-hand experience of Alice Smith's narcissistic personality disorder.

D.I. Wilson was a tall slim woman in her forties, with dark hair cut into a severely geometric bob. She was wearing a waterproof jacket and stretchy polyester trousers, and looked much as Cleopatra might have looked had she decided to join the Ramblers' Association, Polynesia thought.

'Polynesia Henman? I'm Detective Inspector Wilson and this is Detective Sergeant Knight.'

A short, plump man of about Polynesia's age nodded his head. His grey suit was too tight and slightly crumpled, but not in a fashionable way, in more of a homeless way.

'Sir Giles has kindly loaned us a room. Let's go through and sit down.' D.I Wilson led them into a small meeting room and shut the door.

'Now,' she went on as they settled themselves in the rather uncomfortable chairs around the table. 'Talk me through what happened when you got to work this morning.'

D.S. Knight got out his notebook and pen and Polynesia launched into her account. Both police officers listened without interrupting as she described the scream, the closed door, and her discovery of Martin's body behind the desk.

'I don't know how long it was since she'd stabbed him. I mean, she wasn't bending over him and there was no blood dripping off the knife.'

'How do you know that it was Alice who stabbed Martin if you didn't see it happen?' D.I. Wilson asked with a frown.

'Well, it was obvious,' Polynesia said. 'There was no one else in the department and she was standing next to the body holding a knife. And I can personally vouch for the fact that Alice Smith is a grade A bully and a manipulative power freak.'

'Strong words,' said D.I. Wilson with raised eyebrows.

'Yes, when we were at school -'Polynesia began.

'I don't think we need go back quite that far at the moment.' D.S. Knight spoke for the first time. 'We just need to know what happened this morning.'

'But surely some background information about Alice's character would be helpful?'

'Just what happened this morning,' D.S. Knight repeated, and looked down at his notebook again.

'OK, then. I saw Alice standing next to Martin's body. She had blood on her dress and she was holding a large knife.'

'And did she say anything?' D.I. Wilson asked.

'She said "I didn't kill Martin." But of course, that's exactly what she would say, isn't it?'

'I don't think we need to be too analytical at this point.' D.S. Knight was proving to be irritatingly resistant to Polynesia's attempts to be helpful.

'We'll need you to come down to the station to make a formal statement,' D.I. Wilson said as she stood up to leave.

'Of course! I can come now if you like,' Polynesia said, ready to jettison the international eel smuggler in favour of doing her duty.

'Oh, tomorrow will be quite soon enough. Sir Giles has impressed on me the urgent need for you all to make up for lost time this morning. Even tragedy mustn't be allowed to silence the newspaper presses of a democracy, apparently.' D.I. Wilson gave a small smile, raised her eyebrows slightly, and went up several notches in Polynesia's estimation.

The two police officers left, and Polynesia had no choice but to return to work on her article.

6

Chapter 6

Of course, Jess was waiting to ambush her at the end of the day as Polynesia went down to Lifestyle to collect her helmet and jacket.

'Oh my God!' she said. 'I can't believe it. Everyone's saying Martin Trellis was murdered, and judging by all the police everywhere, they must be right. What's going on? Nobody's telling us anything.'

'Come to supper,' Polynesia said. 'Don't worry, Dad's cooking not me. I'll call and let him know you're coming. You can jump on the tube and meet me there.'

'Love to,' said Jess. 'Dan's out tonight. So it was going to be a sad snack for me in front of the TV. And I haven't seen your dad for ages.'

Polynesia was just putting her cycling shoes away when Jess rang the doorbell.

'Bloody District Line,' she grumbled. 'Why is there never a train for Wimbledon, except when I want to go to Richmond, and then every train's going to Wimbledon?'

'Oh, that's because the entire London Transport System has been set up to feed Jess Taylor's persecution complex. Didn't you know?' Polynesia took Jess's coat, chucked it carelessly onto the bottom stair and then went through to the kitchen where her dad was busy stirring a pot on the cooker.

'Hello, Trevor. God, that smells amazing!' Jess hurried forward to give him a hug.

'How's my favourite lifestyle reporter?' asked Trevor, putting down his wooden spoon, wiping his hands on his Rick Stein apron and giving her an enthusiastic squeeze.

'Hey! Be careful what you say about favourite reporters,' Polynesia said. 'Just remember who got you that apron free of charge after a photoshoot. And it wasn't Jess.'

'I know. But you see, Jess is my favourite lifestyle reporter and you're my favourite news reporter. So there's no conflict of interest. And now I've got both my favourite reporters coming to dinner tonight. Lucky me!' Trevor beamed at them both.

'Dad, you're such a smooth talker! I'm amazed you weren't snapped up years ago when you can come up with lines like that.' Polynesia said it lightly, but not altogether jokingly. She and her dad had had this conversation before. If only he would find himself a girlfriend, or a significant other, or whatever the older generation called them these days, then she wouldn't feel quite so responsible for him.

'You know me, love,' Trevor said. 'Footloose and fancy free. And quite capable of looking after myself.'

He said this firmly, and Polynesia knew she had to let it drop. Her father would do what he wanted when he wanted. And she had to admit that his feelings were understandable. If your wife was murdered by a psychopath and then you were falsely accused and imprisoned for the murder yourself, it would tend to make even the most ardent marriage-lover think twice before leaping in for a second helping.

'What have you made, Trevor? Jess asked. 'I'm starving!'

'It's my special chilli con carne. Made to my own recipe with a lump of dark chocolate and some ancho chilli powder for colour and depth.'

'God, Pol, you're so lucky! My dad thinks a bit of Worcester sauce with his cheese on toast is the height of gourmet sophistication.'

Jess grinned at Polynesia, who smiled back, grateful to Jess for smoothing over what could have been a sticky moment.

'Let's eat first and talk later,' Trevor said. 'Momentous revelations can wait, but my chilli definitely can't.'

Jess wiped a last piece of cornbread across her plate and sighed in satisfaction. 'Trevor, will you adopt me? That was a life-changing chilli.'

'I don't think Dad needs to go quite that far. He can just give you the recipe.'

'Come on, girls. Enough banter! I want to know what's going on at the *Herald*,' said Trevor. 'It all sounds very mysterious, and you were unusually reticent on the phone, Pol.'

'Walls have ears, Dad. And we've been sworn to secrecy. So, obviously, you didn't hear any of this from me.'

Polynesia repeated her story, pretty much as she'd told the police officers. Although, without D.S. Knight's grounding presence, she did allow herself a few insightful comments about Alice's childhood psychopathy.

'It's not as if I'm the only one who thinks she's a psycho.

When the headmistress says that a girl deserved to be punched, that shows there's something seriously wrong with her, doesn't it?' Polynesia finished.

Her father looked at her thoughtfully. 'I know you've got a history with this girl, Pol.'

'A history!' Polynesia broke in. 'I wish it was just a history. Unfortunately it's also a current affair. At least it was, until today.'

And then the realisation struck her forcefully. She hadn't really thought about the consequences of today's events until now. Unsurprisingly, she'd been totally focused on the murder itself. She hadn't considered that if Alice was serving a life sentence in prison, she wouldn't be in the *Herald* offices demanding weasel coffee and organic, spelt, sourdough muffins every Tuesday and Friday. She began to feel much brighter.

'As I said, you've got a history with her,' Trevor went on. 'But as an investigative journalist, you've got to put that to one side and consider the facts objectively. It's no good making your mind up on day one and refusing to budge.'

'But she was holding the knife!' Polynesia said. 'You don't need to be Hercule Poirot to see that if someone's standing over a corpse with a knife in their hand, they're quite likely to be a murderer.'

'Exactly,' said Trevor. 'Quite likely, but not definitely.'

'Your dad's got a point,' Jess said. 'If you start coming across like some revenge-fuelled vigilante, you'll lose credibility. You need to be cool, calm and unbiased.'

Trevor raised his eyebrows. 'Let's just start with unbiased shall we? No point in overdoing it. Remember that all goals should be realistic and achievable.'

'Ha ha. OK, point taken,' Polynesia said. 'Now stop ganging up on me and tell me what you think.'

'There's one thing that's troubling me,' Trevor said. 'And that's the scream. If Alice thought she was all alone in the News office murdering Martin, why did she scream? The last thing she'd want to do would be to draw attention to herself. Of course, if she heard a noise and realised someone else was there, she might have screamed to make them believe she'd just found the body But in that case, why didn't she drop the knife?'

'Perhaps murder turned out to be scarier than she'd thought. She fancied herself as a ruthless assassin. But once she saw the corpse on the carpet, she lost her nerve.' Polynesia gave a humorless smile. 'We used to call them the Blonde Mafia at school, Alice and her friends. They hunted in a pack and words were their weapon of choice. But if you got one of them on her own and moved in to give her a good slapping, she'd scream and run away.'

'Unbiased! Objective! Open-minded!' Jess chanted.

'I'm sure there's an unbiased, objective and open-minded explanation. Let me think about it.' Polynesia said.

That night she lay in bed, thinking hard. Dad and Jess were quite right; if she allowed her dislike of Alice to show, nobody would listen to her. They'd say she was prejudiced because she'd resented being Alice's errand bitch, and no matter what evidence she came up with, it would be dismissed because she had a grudge against Alice.

That mustn't be allowed to happen. This was her big chance. She'd witnessed a murder. Well, practically witnessed it. She knew the accused and the victim, and she was in the perfect position as part of the News team to ask questions, do some general snooping and then solve the crime. And when it turned out – as she knew it would – that Alice was the killer, then Polynesia's happiness would be complete.

7

Chapter 7

The next morning's visit to the police station was frankly disappointing. The duty officer seemed as uninterested as D.S. Knight in Polynesia's theories about the murder and made her stick to a very bland recital of facts. After signing her statement, she sauntered back to the *Herald*, taking in the food stalls of Borough Market on her way. There was no hurry; she was already so late that she was resigned to being left with the worst story of the day – probably the one about celebrities and their favourite brands of vitamin supplements.

As she walked through reception towards the lift, Susie, the receptionist, called her over.

'Joanna asked if you could go straight up to News. She'd like to have a word.'

That sounded ominous. What had she done? Polynesia racked her brains as she went up in the lift. Apart from discovering a body in the News office, calling the police, discussing a confidential matter with her dad and her best friend and accusing the deputy news editor of being a murderer, she really couldn't think of anything at all.

She tapped lightly on Joanna's door. Joanna looked paler than ever, with dark rings under her eyes as though she hadn't slept well, but she sounded unusually clear and determined.

'Polynesia! When you didn't come in this morning I wondered whether the shock had all been too much for you yesterday.'

'I had to go and make a statement at Walworth Police Station. I hurried in as soon as I could.' Polynesia thought guiltily about her slow detour through Borough Market on the way to the office and hoped Joanna couldn't smell the salt beef sandwich nestling in the top of her backpack.

'Of course,' Joanna said. 'We must all co-operate with the police and hope that this unpleasant business will be over as soon as possible. I don't wish to sound unfeeling, but Martin's death and Alice's potential involvement does leave me with a problem. The News team is now very short-staffed and lacking in more senior, experienced team members.'

Polynesia pricked up her ears. 'You know me, Joanna. I'm definitely a team player. If there's anything I can do to help, anything at all, then please ask.'

'I've spoken to Sir Giles,' Joanna said. 'And he'd like me to step up as acting managing editor, and we were wondering whether you might consider taking on the deputy editor's job? Just temporarily, while we put a more permanent plan together. Of course, if it's all too painful for you, I quite understand.'

Too painful? Polynesia would have happily chewed off her left arm to be handed this opportunity, but she didn't want to appear overly eager.

'Well, it has been a very distressing experience,' Polynesia said. 'But the *Herald* must come first. Every journalist knows that.'

She assumed an expression which was meant to convey backbone in face of adversity, but she didn't think it was entirely successful as Joanna didn't react at all.

'I know Alice's mentoring style was more -' Joanna paused, searching for a word, '- holistic and less practical and focused than you were expecting,' Joanna said.

Holistic! Polynesia thought to herself. That was a great way of making sadism sound like on the job training. But she was careful to maintain a neutral expression and keep her mouth shut.

'But you're a good writer and you've got a sound instinct for a story, so I'm sure you'll pick it up quickly.' Joanna finished, with a hopeful half-smile

Yes, I will. Because, unlike Alice, I won't spend all my time focused on scheming and spite, Polynesia thought to herself. But out loud she said, 'Thank you, Joanna. I won't let you down.'

Polynesia settled herself into her new seat. Would she find it upsetting to use Alice's desk, Joanna had wondered? Hell no! This was the deputy editor's desk, and she was going to sit there. The only desk she wouldn't have been keen to use was Martin's. Well, not before they'd got the bloodstains off the carpet, at any rate.

She logged on to the computer and checked her watch. Thirty minutes until briefing. Would Joanna be running it on her own today, or would she expect Polynesia to step up and start delegating the day's breaking news to the various writers on the team? Before she had a chance to send Joanna a message to ask, there was a shout from across the room.

'Hey, Polynesia! I heard that you were joining the team full-time.' It was Ross, the fearless news reporter. Well, fearless as long as there were no catfights in the offing.

'Great news!' he went on. 'Really pleased to hear about your promotion. Hope you weren't too upset by everything yesterday.'

'It was a very distressing day and a terrible tragedy for all of us,' said Polynesia, mindful of her new strategy. 'But I'm determined to overcome my own anguish and do all I can to help the *Herald* in its hour of need.'

'That's very commendable,' Ross sounded rather surprised. He lowered his voice and gave her a small conspiratorial smile. 'But you must be thinking that it's an ill wind, after all the shit you've had to put up with.'

'I've no idea what you mean,' Polynesia said. 'Martin was a highly valued colleague and Alice's temporary absence means that the News team is short-staffed. So I've agreed to step up and fill the gap until Alice returns.'

She ignored his puzzled look and began typing busily

He walked off and Polynesia continued making one of her favourite to-do lists:

- *Talk to Reception – did they see anyone else from the News team arrive early yesterday? Or did they see anyone suspicious get into the lift?*
- *Talk to Pippa and find out as much as possible about Martin.*
- *Discover Alice's motivation. Note to self ... how do I do this?*
- *Talk to members of the News team about Alice. Did Martin really worship her?? And if he did, was it reciprocated?*

She stopped typing. She really needed a bit of help with this.

She messaged Jess: *Drink after work?*

The reply was instant: *Defo. Meet you 6.15?*

Good. They could brainstorm and put a plan of action together.

Polynesia and Jess chose a table in the far corner of the pub, even though they were fairly sure they wouldn't see anyone from the *Herald*. It was a bit too far from their offices and was resolutely downmarket, with no craft beers, artisanal gins or hand-cooked crisps.

'I'll have a double vodka and tonic and a bag of peanuts, thanks,' said Jess, as she took off her coat and unwound her scarf.

'I'm buying, am I?' Polynesia asked.

'Well, you want my help to solve a murder that's going to cover you in glory and relaunch your career. So I think the least you can do is buy me a drink,' Jess said.

Polynesia felt that this was fair enough, although she was seriously considering adding Jess's name to the book she was going to write afterwards. She pictured the cover: *Murder at the Herald*, by Polynesia Henman, with additional material by Jess Taylor. But perhaps a grateful acknowledgement at the end of the book, rather than anything on the front cover would be more appropriate? She'd have to think about it.

'So,' said Polynesia as she put the drinks down on the table. 'I need to get a head start on the police. Luckily, the two detectives in charge are only interested in facts and are blind to the benefits of having a psychological insight into the main suspect. That puts me one step ahead already.'

'Main suspect?' Jess said. 'I suppose that's better than "only suspect". Still sounds a bit biased though.'

'Don't worry. I've thrown them all off the scent today. I

talked about the tragedy and needing to step up and do my bit to help out in the *Herald*'s hour of need. I said I hoped Alice would soon be back in her rightful place as deputy editor.'

'God, Pol! Don't overdo it. If you start behaving totally out of character they might start to think it was you who murdered him! You know, disappointment turned to jealousy. You killed Martin because he gave your job to Alice and then you set Alice up to make her pay for the way she's treated you.'

Polynesia felt a nasty jolt. That would be one way of looking at it, she supposed. And if she had murdered Martin, what better way to try and throw the police off the scent than to accuse Alice and tell them all about her psychopathic tendencies?

'I'm sure they won't think anything of the sort,' she said, more resolutely than she felt. 'If they look at the CCTV from the car park they'll see that I only arrived in the building about four minutes before I called the police. That'll put me in the clear, won't it?'

'It only takes ten seconds to slit someone's throat, you know,' Jess said.

'But Martin was stabbed. She didn't slit his throat!' Polynesia said, feeling panicky.

'I don't know how long that takes. It wasn't in the article I read,' Jess said. Then she squeezed Polynesia's hand. 'Oh, I'm sure they won't think it was you, Pol. I'm just trying to point out that you need to be careful. If Alice tells the police that you attacked her at school, then they might think it's you who's the violent psychopath.'

'But … but …' Polynesia stared at her in horror and found she was lost for words.

'All I'm saying is, dial it down.' Jess said. 'Don't give anyone the idea that you're acting out of character or they'll start wondering what you're up to. Don't accuse Alice. But don't start sounding like the patron saint of forgiveness either. Just behave normally.'

Polynesia thought for a moment. 'OK. I'll stop laying it on so thick on Monday. I'll say it was the shock that made me behave out of character. I'll say that seeing Martin's body brought my mother's murder flooding back and I just couldn't handle it.'

She saw Jess raise her eyebrows at this.

'Oh, don't worry, Polynesia went on. 'Mum wouldn't mind. She was all in favour of a small white lie in an emergency.'

Having satisfactorily parked that worry, Polynesia carried on with her agenda.

'I can talk to reception and see if anyone else came in early. I can talk to Martin's secretary tomorrow, no problem. I'll dress it up as a bit of bonding after our terrible experience yesterday morning. But I also need to get to the bottom of Martin's relationship with Alice and I'm not sure how to go about it.' She leaned forward and helped herself to a handful of Jess's peanuts and chewed thoughtfully.

'Neither of them had been with the *Herald* very long, had they?' Jess said. 'Perhaps you could start by looking at their previous jobs. Or maybe they lived near each other or something?'

'That's genius!' Polynesia said. 'I'll start digging tomorrow. And Pippa mentioned Martin's wife. I definitely need to track her down and have a chat.'

'Do you think she'll want to talk to you? Grieving widow meets news-hungry reporter?' Jess sounded dubious.

'I know she will,' Polynesia said confidently. 'The thing is, Jess, when someone in your family gets murdered other people step away, and you find yourself in a lonely little club on your own. I shall suggest to Mrs Trellis that we form a club of two and we'll be besties in no time.'

'Isn't that called exploitation?' Jess asked.

'No. It's called playing your trump card. For years I've suffered the slings and arrows of outrageous fortune and now it's my turn to sling them back. So fortune had better start ducking.'

Jess rolled her eyes and Polynesia laughed.

'I'd better get home,' she said, finishing her drink. 'I've got a murder investigation to plan.'

8

Chapter 8

On Monday morning the receptionists were irritatingly vague when Polynesia asked if anyone had entered the building early the previous Thursday. Susie had been busy sorting out some visitors and filling in their details in the log book. Rebecca hadn't noticed anyone from the News team arriving, but she couldn't be sure that someone hadn't come in when she wasn't looking, because she did have a job to do, and in any case she wasn't a security guard, was she?

The entrance to the *Herald* building was through a couple of swing doors leading into a large reception area filled with lifts, stairs, sofas and doors into meeting rooms. It would be relatively easy to slip in unnoticed if you waited for a few people to arrive together and then walked in behind them.

Polynesia wished they had the sort of office where everyone had to buzz in with special security tags or a fingerprint. Then there would be a record of everyone who'd arrived and where they went. She was sure she'd seen some offices on TV that had locked doors between departments and facial recognition cameras in every corridor. Although, on second thoughts, perhaps it had been a prison or a high security psychiatric hospital and not an office block. Still a good idea, though.

And now for Pippa, the devoted secretary, thought Polynesia as she got out of the lift. She pulled a small packet of chocolate rabbits out of her bag. They were ridiculously overpriced in her opinion, but Pippa looked like the sort of woman who'd appreciate chocolate rabbits, so it was worth the investment.

She found Pippa standing rather forlornly by the coffee machine, holding a mug of scummy looking foam. She had obviously selected the button that was optimistically labelled Cappuccino. Didn't she know that you should only ever choose the black Americano and then add your own milk?

'Hi Pippa!' Polynesia said, giving what she hoped would pass for a warm and caring smile. 'I just came to see how you are today. I thought you might like these to cheer you up.' And she held out the expensively packaged chocolates.

'Oh, Polynesia, that's so kind! You know, I am feeling a bit down in the dumps.' Pippa perked up immediately as she took the packet. 'Ooh! Chocolate bunnies are my absolute favourite!'

Result! Eat your heart out, D.I. Wilson, Polynesia thought. I bet you've never considered the psychological advantage of offering chocolate rabbits.

Aloud, she said, 'Shall we have a chat, just the two of us? The others don't understand what it was like, do they?' And Polynesia waved her arm to indicate the various members of the team who were tapping away on their computers or talking earnestly on the phone. 'They weren't there, like we were.'

'You're so right,' said Pippa. 'It's not the same for them. They weren't shut in a room just feet away from Martin's body.' She shivered, but there was no sign of tears and Polynesia was thankful for that.

They sat facing each other on either side of Pippa's immaculately tidy desk. Polynesia wasn't sure how she felt about such tidiness. On the one hand, a bare minimalist desk suggested someone super-organised, but on the other hand, it could also look as though you didn't have any work to do. This wasn't an issue that would affect her on a personal level, she knew. Gran had always called her a clutter magnet when she was a child, and the magnetic pull had only increased as she got older. She wasn't untidy, she reasoned, she just felt comfortable when she was surrounded by her own things. She'd learnt early in life that things, unlike people, have a reassuring dependability.

'Choccy bunny?' Pippa was saying, as she held out the packet.

'No, thanks. I bought them for you.' Polynesia smiled again, trying to look as though empathy was a skill that came naturally to her. 'I know how close you were to Martin. I thought it might help to have a chat about him.'

Pippa's eyes began to fill with tears. 'He was such a nice man. I know he hadn't been here very long, but he was so good at his job. The *Herald* was lucky to have him.'

Lucky to have him? Wasn't that what Martin had said about Alice too? Polynesia felt a quickening of interest.

'Is that what everyone said?' she asked Pippa. 'That the *Herald* was lucky to have Martin?'

'It's what Alice said. I heard her say it several times. That's why I just can't believe that she – that she -' Pippa broke off and a tear rolled down her cheek.

'Martin and Alice must have had a very close working relationship,' Polynesia went on, carefully. 'Do you think they were ever more than -' she paused delicately, '- just colleagues?'

Pippa stared at her. 'No, of course not! Martin would never do anything like that. They were professionals and they respected each other's work. What are you suggesting?'

'I'm only suggesting that stabbing someone to death on their office floor is a strange way of showing respect for their work.' Polynesia had decided to abandon the attempt at empathy and to go for a bit of plain talking instead.

Pippa sobbed and fumbled in her desk for a tissue.

'Look, Pippa,' Polynesia went on. 'Martin was killed. He was brutally murdered in his own office and we need to find out why. You want that, don't you? Justice for Martin?'

Pippa nodded mutely as she wiped her eyes.

'So, you wouldn't say that Martin worshipped Alice?' Polynesia persisted, thinking of Ross's description.

'No. He respected her,' Pippa repeated obstinately.

Polynesia decided to move the conversation on. 'You said he was married – to Clare, wasn't it? Do you know where they lived?

'Somewhere up north, I think. Well, north of London. She's expecting a baby next month. They were both really excited about it. Poor Clare.'

'How could I get in touch with her?' Polynesia asked.

'HR must have her address,' Pippa said. 'I'll get it too, I want to send a card.'

'I don't really want to involve HR,' Polynesia said. 'I'd rather keep it between the two of us. You know, part of our Justice for Martin Campaign.'

Pippa thought about this for a moment and then said, 'I do have Clare's phone number. Martin sometimes asked me to call her if he was busy. But with data protection, I don't know whether I should let you have it.'

'Justice for Martin?' Polynesia said in a persuasive tone.

Pippa sat in silence toying with her bag of chocolates, while Polynesia held her breath.

'OK,' Pippa said finally. 'I think you're right. Martin would want us to do this.' She scrolled through her phone and then scribbled a number onto her notepad and passed the page to Polynesia.

Polynesia thanked her, stood up and headed towards Alice's desk . No, *her* desk, she corrected herself. She smiled as she sat down. This was shaping up to be an excellent morning.

Briefing that morning was rather an uncomfortable experience. It's unusual for a newspaper to feature heavily on its own front page. It was rather like a publicity stunt, Polynesia thought. Instead of the usual enthusiasm for writing the top story, interviewing witnesses, or writing a comment piece, the reporters were reluctant to be involved. Perhaps they sensed that any hint of prurience would be badly received and potentially damaging to both the newspaper and to their reputation as journalists. So, as chief witness, Polynesia found herself tasked with writing a first-hand account of her experience.

'Facts only, please. No speculation or innuendo or anything else that could be construed as libellous or in poor taste,' Joanna instructed.

There would be an accompanying piece, written by Sir Giles, expressing shock and sorrow at Martin's untimely death and detailing Martin's many qualities and achievements.

My first headline story, Polynesia thought as she tapped away on her computer. What a pity it wasn't a brilliant scoop that she'd needed all her investigative powers to uncover, instead of a piece that any old hack could have written if they'd practically tripped over a dead body on their way to work.

She finished her article and then sat considering how best to approach Clare Trellis. Would Clare appreciate a call from the woman who'd practically witnessed her husband's murder? She'd blithely told Jess that Clare would welcome her because they'd both lost a loved one to a violent death, but now she wondered whether that was true. Clare had lost her husband and Polynesia had lost her mother and these were very different relationships. Perhaps Clare would feel that Polynesia didn't understand in the least what it was like to lose a spouse. And then she had a brainwave. Although she herself didn't know what it was like to lose a spouse, her dad did. He could make contact with Clare and offer his support – or Polynesia could call Clare on his behalf. Could she do it without asking Dad first? She reluctantly decided that she couldn't. It would definitely be overstepping the mark to offer her father's services as a bereavement counsellor without running it past him first.

'Dad, where are you?' Polynesia hurried into the house, propping up her bike and kicking her shoes off in the hall.

'I'm in the study, love,' came her father's voice.

The room that had once been her playroom had been turned into a study once she'd become a teenager. Bookshelves and a desk had co-existed with the toys for a few years, but now Polynesia's remaining teddies and her set of Disney soft toys lived on top of her wardrobe. These days the study housed an exercise bike and her father's elderly desk top computer that he nursed back to health from time to time by giving it extra memory, or by hoovering the keyboard with the special mini-vacuum cleaner that Polynesia had once bought him for his birthday.

'You're early,' he said. 'I'm just finishing a bit of research on non-fungible tokens and then I'll start supper.'

Polynesia never ceased to be amazed at her father's wide-ranging interests. Retirement hadn't triggered an interest in golf or fishing for Trevor Henman, instead he spent his time following the latest developments in technology and joining online forums to discuss the advantages of investing in Bitcoin, or where to buy reasonably priced virtual reality goggles.

'Actually, Dad, I wanted to ask you something. How do you fancy becoming an investigative journalist's assistant – unpaid, of course?'

9

Chapter 9

Dad was delighted to be on board. Polynesia had never doubted it for a moment. After all, who wouldn't pass up the opportunity to be involved in a murder investigation? Or perhaps he genuinely wanted to offer support to a grieving widow. She hadn't actually asked him why he was keen to help. The only thing that mattered was that he had agreed and they now had a plan.

Polynesia would phone Clare to offer sympathy and explain that her father had suffered the same terrible tragedy and would like to help. He could support her and give her the benefit of his experience as she struggled to come to terms with what had happened. Polynesia felt a slight twinge as she picked up the phone – could this be construed as being callous and using people? No, she decided, it couldn't. Although she had an ulterior motive for contacting Clare, her dad had lived through the same experience and he would be very helpful, so it was a win-win situation.

Two hours later she phoned her dad. 'I finally got through

to Clare,' she told him. 'Apparently she was getting her nails done when I first called. She couldn't answer the phone in case she smudged the varnish.'

'Nails?' Trevor said. 'Well, that certainly wasn't something I thought about doing after your mother was killed.'

'I expect she needs something to do to pass the time,' Polynesia said. 'Anyway, she's agreed to see us. Three o'clock on Saturday at the café in Bedford Park. She says it's quite quick on the train from St Pancras and we can walk to the park from the station.'

'How did she sound?'

'Surprisingly posh. Not at all like Martin. I always thought he sounded a bit *estuary,* to be honest.'

'We haven't all had the benefits of a private education,' her father said. 'Some of us have had to pull ourselves up by our bootstraps.'

'I wasn't judging him,' Polynesia said quickly. 'I just wouldn't have put two people together who sound so different.'

'What I meant was, how did she sound emotionally, rather than where does she belong in the social hierarchy? How much support do you think she'll need? I'll have to prepare for Saturday.'

'I should prepare for plenty of TLC. You can always deliver less, if necessary. But it's hard to deliver more on the spot.'

'Good idea. I'm off to start now,' he said. 'See you this evening.'

Four days until the meeting with Clare, Polynesia thought. What could she do in the meantime to advance the investigation? A bit of research into their previous jobs, she decided. She'd just dash off her article on the new green energy initiative first. The information was nearly all in the press release anyway, she only needed to make a couple of phone calls, get a few quotes and then she'd be done.

She was about to type Martin's name into Google and start a search when Joanna appeared at her desk.

'Have you got a couple of minutes?' she asked and nodded her head towards her office.

'Of course,' said Polynesia, and stood up to follow Joanna back to her office in the corner of the department.

'I was just wondering how your interview with the police went last week?' Joanna asked, as they sat down at the desk in her office. 'I know they spoke to you and you had to make a statement. Did you get the impression they had any leads they were following up?'

'Any leads?' Polynesia said. 'Apart from Alice Smith standing over the body wielding a knife, you mean?' Then, remembering her new resolution, added, 'But of course, that could be purely circumstantial.'

'So the detectives didn't tell you anything?'

'No. I got the impression that they didn't know anything, and they didn't really want to know anything. I tried to give them a few helpful insights and they just brushed me off.'

'What sort of insights?' Joanna asked.

'Oh, a few perceptive comments about Alice's character. Things that happened when we were at school. But they weren't interested,' Polynesia said.

'That's strange, isn't it?' said Joanna. 'Because, after all, if it wasn't Alice who killed Martin, then who was it?'

'Exactly,' said Polynesia. 'But I expect the police want to extract a confession from her themselves, to use in court. They're probably grilling her in a police station cell right now.'

'No, they aren't. They've released her,' Joanna said, and

Polynesia stared at her in surprise.

'Released her? But she's the prime suspect!'

'I know. But that's not enough, it would seem. Sir Giles told me this morning that she's been released while the investigation goes ahead. The post mortem was carried out on Friday. But we're not likely to be told the results until the inquest according to Sir Giles. He says the forensics might take months to come through. The police have said she's not allowed within a hundred metres of the *Herald* offices, but apart from that she's free to do anything she wants.'

'She won't be coming back to work then?' Polynesia asked, a little anxiously.

'Oh no. We can't employ someone who's under suspicion of murder, not even working from home. It wouldn't go down at all well with the shareholders,' Joanna said.

Feeling reassured Polynesia returned to her desk, typed *Martin Trellis* into Google and started scanning the results.

An hour later she had a fairly comprehensive CV for Martin, from his days at Colchester Grammar, through his university studies at Nottingham and his rise through the ranks at the *Morning Post,* eventually becoming foreign editor three years ago. His final move, to the *Daily Herald* as managing editor, had happened four short months previously. OK, she thought, the best place to find out about Martin and anything shady in his past would be from the foreign news desk at the *Morning Post.* The next step was to find a way in.

She sat pondering this. She would need to be discreet; she could hardly march up to his former colleagues and ask if they'd killed Martin, or if they thought his wife might have killed him. And if it got back to the police that she was questioning possible suspects ... well, the thought of what might happen then made her feel slightly queasy. As she grappled with this problem, the phone on her desk rang.

'Polynesia Henman, Deputy News Editor,' she said into the receiver, still feeling a bit of a thrill at her new job title.

'Polynesia, I have a Mildred Muppet on the line for you. At least that what it sounds like,' Susie said. 'Will you take the call?'

Polynesia felt goose pimply all over. Mildred Muppet? Surely there couldn't be a real person called Mildred Muppet? She hadn't heard that name for years; it had been their nickname at school for the evil French teacher, Mademoiselle Mupart. An even worse thought occurred to her – perhaps it was Mademoiselle Mupart herself on the phone? She could be ringing to say that she'd finally tracked Polynesia down and was demanding compensation for the distress caused by her nickname. She gave herself a little shake. That was ridiculous. How could the Muppet possibly know that it was Polynesia who had coined the nickname, and even if she did know, who on earth bears a grudge for twelve years?

'Thanks, Susie. I'll take the call,' she said, trying to sound brisk and professional, and not like a terrified schoolgirl.

'Putting you through,' said Susie.

Polynesia stood up. She'd heard that you sound more authoritative if you stand up when you speak.

'Polynesia Henman,' she said, a trifle louder than she'd intended.

'Oh, Polynesia,' said a tearful voice. 'I'm so glad to have got through to you.'

There was no French accent, so it couldn't be Mademoiselle Mupart. What's more, the Muppet never been tearful in her life Polynesia was willing to bet. If there was ever any weeping and wailing at school, the Muppet had definitely been the cause rather than the victim.

'I'm sorry, but who is this?' Polynesia asked.

'It's Alice,' she said, and Polynesia's stomach did that flippity thing as though she'd just gone over a hump-backed bridge at 90 miles an hour.

'I couldn't think what name to give that would get you to take the call,' Alice went on. 'And then I thought of the Muppet and just hoped you'd twig that it was me.'

'Why couldn't you just say who it was?'

'I've been told by the police that I'm not allowed within a hundred metres of the *Herald* offices while the investigation's going ahead. And I don't know if that means I can't contact anyone directly either. So, I thought I'd better play it safe and give a false name.'

'I see,' said Polynesia. 'I suppose the next question is, why do you want to speak to me so badly?'

'Because I really, really need your help,' said Alice.

10

Chapter 10

Polynesia found it difficult to settle back to any serious work after speaking to Alice. She'd intended to research Alice's background and career history, but there wasn't much point, she reasoned. As she was going to see Alice tomorrow, she could simply ask her about it. After all, Polynesia had the upper hand now. Alice was begging her for help, so she'd be only too pleased to answer a few background questions truthfully … wouldn't she?

That was the trouble with someone like Alice, Polynesia mused. She was so used to manipulating people to get what she wanted, that she was probably incapable of telling *the* truth. Everything would be about *her* truth, which was not the same thing at all. Polynesia remembered the occasion when Alice had been accused of taking another girl's homework. There had been vehement denials, until a prefect said that she'd seen Alice putting something down the back of a radiator. When the missing homework was found, screwed up, behind the radiator, Alice said that she must have been sleepwalking and had no recollection of putting it there at all. She then pretended to faint dramatically and was sent to the sick room for the rest of the day, missing a maths test and escaping punishment. I'm glad I decked her when I had the chance, Polynesia thought. At least Alice hadn't always had everything her own way.

Will Rowe was walking back towards his desk carrying a large envelope as Polynesia sighed and leaned back in her chair. He stopped and smiled. She noted that he was wearing a blue shirt which matched his eyes perfectly, and she was surprised because she didn't usually notice this sort of thing at all. If one arm of his shirt had been torn off, or the front had been covered in treacle, she would probably have registered it, but shirts and eyes matching was way off her usual level of observation. Perhaps it meant that she was getting middle-aged. Now there was a depressing thought.

'How are you doing?' Will perched on the corner of her desk. 'It hasn't been an easy week, has it?'

'Well, it's been easy in one way,' she said, with a raised eyebrow. 'At least I haven't got into any catfights.'

Will groaned. 'You don't take any prisoners, do you? Are you ever going to let me forget that?'

Polynesia considered this. 'I suppose that a lot of positive input from now on, might eventually blot out any earlier negative experiences. But on the other hand, I do have a distressingly good memory.'

Will stood up, and leant his arms on the desk, moving his head slightly closer to hers. His dark hair flopped down untidily across his forehead. Oh no! Was that another middle-aged thought?

'Perhaps we could make a start on the positive input, then?' he said. 'How about a drink after work?'

Blimey, I'm being chatted up, she said to herself. And Will's not actually that bad when you look closely at him – tall, nice hair, good teeth.

Aloud, she said, 'I'm really sorry, but I've got an important interview tomorrow for a potentially huge story. I have to prep for it this evening.'

Will looked impressed. 'Whoa! Your first full week here and you're already onto something big. Any hints what it's about?'

'If I tell you, then I'll have to kill you,' Polynesia said. Then, realising the implication of this, stammered, 'Oh God! I mean - obviously not actually kill you, it's just an expression ...'

She trailed off and could feel herself blushing.

Will gave a shout of laughter. 'Polynesia, I think this is the first time I've ever seen you on the back foot.'

She glared at him.

'OK,' he said. 'I'll leave you to your murderous thoughts and perhaps we can reschedule that drink when you're not so busy?'

He gave her a smile and sauntered back to his desk.

Well, that was cool. She'd managed to sound off-putting, dangerous, embarrassed, and angry, all in one 90-second conversation. But she couldn't brood about that now, she had far more important things to think about, like how to get Alice to confess to the murder.

She hurried home at 6 o'clock promptly, keen to get started on preparing the questions for her interview with Alice. Jess hadn't needed any persuading to come round for one of Trevor's suppers and to help with the interview planning, so they met at Putney Bridge Station and Polynesia wheeled her bike home as they chatted together.

'I really think I should come with you tomorrow, Pol,' Jess said, not for the first time. 'I mean, meeting a murderer on your own just isn't safe.'

'Come on!' said Polynesia. 'Even Alice isn't stupid enough to kill me in a crowded coffee shop, when she's the chief suspect in another murder case and is busy telling everyone she's innocent.'

'All the same,' Jess said. 'She might get fits of uncontrollable rage. Perhaps Martin's murder was just a spur of the moment thing and she couldn't stop herself. If that's the case, then it could easily happen again.'

'If she did it on the spur of the moment, where did the knife come from?' Polynesia asked. 'I hardly think that Martin would have had a large kitchen knife lying conveniently on his desk.' She looked at Jess and saw her worried expression. 'Look, let's ask Dad and see what he thinks. If he agrees with you, then you can come with me.'

There was a strange smell as they opened the front door.

'Dad?' Polynesia called.

'I'm in the kitchen. Don't open the door, I'm just trying to get rid of the smoke.'

Polynesia hurried into the study, opened the French windows, and dashed along the terrace towards the kitchen. Her father was standing in the open doorway leading from the kitchen onto the terrace, wafting a newspaper and trying to get a bit of airflow into the kitchen.

'I forgot that it was Tuesday,' he said.

'Oh? Which day do you normally set fire to the house then?'

'Very funny,' her father said, continuing to waft vigorously. 'I just meant that as it's Tuesday, we should be at the Peking

Palace, and then none of this would have happened.'

'What actually did happen?' asked Polynesia, as Jess joined her outside the kitchen.

'When you asked if Jess could come for supper, I popped out to Waitrose. I know Jess appreciates my home cooking, and I wanted to make something nice.'

He gave Jess a smile and she responded with a thumbs up.

'I spotted some Merguez sausages, so I thought I'd make a couscous. An authentic one, like we used to have in Paris on our mini-breaks, Pol. But I'd forgotten how fatty they are and when I was grilling them, they started spitting and the cooker caught fire. A sheet of flames shot up the wall as high as the ceiling. It's just as well we've got that fire blanket, and that your old dad isn't too doddery to sprint across the kitchen and grab it.'

'Never mind, Trevor,' Jess said. 'I'm sure we can salvage the rest of it.'

'The fire blanket fell in the stew,' Trevor said sadly. 'So I don't think that'll be very nice either.'

'Let's get a takeaway,' said Polynesia. 'I'll phone the Peking Palace now. We've got a busy evening ahead and I need to eat something more sustaining than cremated couscous.'

They sat at the table and unpacked the foil cartons from two bulging carrier bags, separating them into starters, duck pancakes plus accessories, and main courses.

Polynesia smiled as Jess took in the quantity of food on the table.

'We always over order,' she explained. 'Dad loves a bit of leftover Chinese for lunch. So, we can dip into everything this evening, and whatever's left Dad will mix together to create his famous Leftover Surprise. No two mouthfuls the same.'

'Sounds, umm, interesting,' Jess said.

'Oh, you don't need to be polite,' Polynesia said. 'It sounds revolting. We Millennials want hand-crafted, vine-ripened, carbon-neutral lunches. But the wartime generation needs a fridgeful of little pots of leftovers or they get twitchy and start talking about famine.'

'I'm not quite that old, thank you very much,' Trevor said. 'And if you want my help with this investigation of yours, I suggest you show your elders a bit more respect, my girl.'

Polynesia pulled a mock contrite face and her dad smiled. She was glad they had such a comfortable relationship and could enjoy a bit of banter without worrying about offending each other. She'd noticed over the years that quite a few of her friends came from what she called 'polite families'. That is, the children spoke politely and distantly to their parents, as if they were acquaintances or newish colleagues. And then they either complained incessantly about their parents behind their backs and said how much they hated them, or else never mentioned them at all. She couldn't imagine feeling like that about her dad, she loved spending time with him and had no problems about introducing him to her friends or taking him out as her plus-one in the evening if she thought he'd enjoy it. She was proud of having such an interesting, fun-loving dad, but she was aware that she also felt responsible for him, in a way that anyone with two parents or with siblings wouldn't feel. It was just her and her dad and she would do anything for him, and she was equally sure that he would do anything for her; it was a comforting thought.

'Right,' she said, picking up a piece of prawn toast and dipping it in the chilli sauce. 'I need a list of questions that will lead cunningly to a point where Alice is backed into a corner, gives herself away, and has no option but to confess to the murder.'

'You need to be careful of people who are backed into corners,' Jess said. 'They may come out fighting. Or stabbing in Alice's case.'

'Jess wants to come with me tomorrow,' Polynesia told her dad. 'She thinks Alice might try to murder me in Starbucks in broad daylight. I've told her that's ridiculous, but she wants your opinion before she agrees to let me go alone.'

Trevor considered this for a moment. 'I think you'll be perfectly safe, Pol,' he said. 'If Alice is innocent then she's not a risk. And if she's guilty, her defence seems to be that she was in the wrong place at the wrong time. She's unlikely to jeopardise her chances by claiming to be in the wrong place twice in the same week.'

'No, it would be extremely bad luck to stumble across two brutally murdered colleagues in such a short space of time. And very difficult to persuade a jury that you had nothing to do with either of them,' Polynesia agreed.

'All right,' said Jess with a sigh. 'You win. Go on your own. But you've got to promise to call me as soon as you're home. And why are you going to Starbucks in Wandsworth? You could go to Gino's, it's much closer and the coffee's better.'

'I'm going to Starbucks for a bit of petty revenge,' Polynesia said. 'I'll make Alice wait in the queue and get me a Venti Caramel Frappuccino with three extra shots of espresso and some steamed tiger nut milk on the side. That should cost her at least a tenner, I hope. And then I'll leave most of it and say, "Oh, I couldn't possibly manage a whole one of these, I don't know how people do it. I have such a tiny appetite."'

'Not very edifying behaviour,' said Trevor. 'If I were you, I'd concentrate on getting to the bottom of this murder. If Alice is guilty and gets a life sentence, that's better than some petty revenge. It's nemesis and justice all rolled into one.'

'True,' said Polynesia. 'Let's talk about the questions.'

Two hours later, with a list of eighty questions, typed and ready to print, Polynesia felt as prepared as she would ever be to try and snare a murderer.

11

Chapter 11

Wednesday seemed interminable. Will was out on an assignment, so there was no chance of a bit of banter to make the time pass more quickly. At briefing, she allocated herself a small but interesting story about a group of pensioners who were clubbing together to buy a campsite in Essex where they could recreate the camping holidays of their youth: ex-army tents, billycans, gadgets made of sticks and string, freezing showers. It reminded her a bit of her dad and his enthusiasms. She was staring into the distance, trying to come up with a headline ... *An Introduction to the past tents? Under canvas on Canvey? Carry on Camping?* ... when the phone on her desk rang.

'Polynesia, I have Detective Inspector Wilson on the line. Will you take the call?'

'Yes, put her through please.' Polynesia felt a stab of alarm. She hoped the Detective Inspector hadn't somehow found out about her meeting with Alice.

'Good afternoon, Polynesia. I'm sorry to disturb you at work, but I've been going through your statement. There are a couple of points I'd like to clarify, if you wouldn't mind.'

Help! This was exactly the tactic Polynesia was planning to use on Alice. Surely D.I. Wilson didn't think Polynesia was a suspect and was trying the same trick on her?

'No, of course not. That's fine,' Polynesia said, as calmly as she could manage. 'Anything to help catch a murderer. What exactly do you want me to clarify?'

'You said that when you heard the scream, you went over to Martin's office and his door was shut. Do you remember if it was firmly closed on the latch or just pushed to?'

Polynesia tried to picture the scene in her head. 'I'm pretty sure it was firmly closed. I remember how scared I felt as I stood in front of the door and put my hand out to open it. I wouldn't have had to do that if the door had been pushed shut but not latched. I could have just shoved it open with my foot.'

'That's very helpful –' D.I. Wilson began.

'Oh,' Polynesia broke in. 'And after I heard the scream, I remember wondering for a moment if it was coming from Martin's or Joanna's room. But if Martin's door had been open, I would have known immediately. As it was, I only realised which room it was when I saw Alice's outline moving behind the frosted glass.'

'That's answered my second question as well,' D.I. Wilson said. 'Both doors were shut when you arrived. Thank you, I won't disturb you any longer.'

'How's the investigation going?' Polynesia couldn't resist asking. 'Are you close to making an arrest?'

'I'm sure you know very well that I can't discuss the case with a witness.'

'I thought I'd just ask,' Polynesia said. 'It would be an awful pity,' she added in a wheedling tone, 'if another paper got the scoop, when it's one of our team who's been so tragically killed.'

'Well, if you want to be the first to break the news, you'll have to keep your ear to the ground,' said D.I. Wilson and she ended the call.

Thanks a lot, thought Polynesia. Didn't Confucius say that people who keep their ear to the ground end up with a very stiff neck? She was smiling at this idea, when she had a sudden brainwave about her headline: *Pensioners keep their ear to the ground with new trend for retro-camping.* And she typed away, feeling relieved that D.I. Wilson didn't appear to know that the chief witness in her murder case was about to have a secret meeting with the chief suspect.

Polynesia made sure that she was five minutes late for the meeting. She was the one doing Alice a favour, so let her sweat for a bit and wonder whether Polynesia was going to turn up. She looked around the coffee shop and saw Alice sitting at a table with two drinks in front of her. Damn! Alice was already one step ahead of her. How was she going to demand her Venti Frappuccino now? She'd probably have to choke down a decaf oat milk latte and try not to gag.

She walked across to the table, edging past a couple of women with several large shopping bags, and sat down opposite Alice.

'Sorry, I'm late,' she said with a breeziness she'd been rehearsing all the way there. Then she looked at Alice, and the rest of her manufactured excuse was forgotten as she took in the change in Alice's appearance. She seemed to ooze misery. Dressed in jogging bottoms and an old sweatshirt, she looked small and hunched, her blonde hair was lank and lifeless and her pale face with dark circles under her eyes suggested sleepless nights. Devoid of her red lips, red nails and sooty eyelashes, she looked vulnerable. Polynesia, who was geared up to duel with her arch nemesis, felt slightly cheated. It was like arranging a showdown with Cruella de Vil, who then turned up wearing a plastic mac, declaring that she was now a vegan animal rights activist.

'It's fine, don't worry,' Alice said. She pushed a drink across the table towards Polynesia. 'I got you the Chocolate Cream Cold Brew. The barista said it's their top seller at the moment, so I hope you like it. I didn't think you'd want to join me in an oat milk latte.' And here she attempted a small smile, which wobbled a little and then her eyes filled with tears. 'Sorry,' she said. 'It's just been so awful, like a nightmare. Worse actually, because I'm not going to wake up.'

Polynesia studied her. Was this an act ? Was this manipulative Alice in control, as usual? If it was an act, then Polynesia was impressed. It was definitely Oscar-worthy and put Alice firmly back into the category of arch-villainess. But if it wasn't an act, then what the hell was going on?

Forgetting about her list of carefully crafted questions, she said, 'Did you kill Martin? I mean, maybe it was an accident or something?'

'Polynesia, I swear to you that I didn't kill him,' Alice looked pleadingly at her. 'It was just like I told the police. I went into his room and he wasn't there, which was odd as we had a meeting arranged. But his jacket was on the back of his chair so I walked around to see if his phone was in his pocket. Then I saw him lying on the floor with the knife sticking out of his stomach. It looked so unreal and so ridiculously gruesome that I thought it must be a joke, a trick knife. I said something like, "It's not Hallowe'en yet, Martin" and I grabbed the handle and pulled. Then I realised that it wasn't a joke and I began to scream.'

'And what happened next?' Polynesia asked.

'The next thing I knew, you were in the room, backing away from me and telling me to put the knife down. Like you thought I was a murderer.'

'Well, it was an easy assumption to make,' Polynesia said. 'You were standing over his body, covered in blood and wielding a knife.' She took a sip of her drink. 'This is delicious, by the way.'

'Look,' said Alice, ignoring Polynesia's verdict on the cold brew. 'The only reason I was the one standing there next to his body, is because it happened to be me who went into his room. If I'd arrived five minutes later, it would have been someone else who found him.'

Five minutes later it would have been me, thought Polynesia, going into Martin's office to complain about Alice. But if Martin hadn't been sitting at his desk, she would have left and come back later, she wouldn't have gone round the back of his desk to look through his pockets.

'It sounds a bit weird,' Polynesia said, 'that you decided to go through your boss's pockets when he wasn't in the room. What did the police say about that?'

'I didn't tell them. I just said that I'd gone round to see whether he'd left a note that had fallen on the floor.' Alice's cheeks turned pink, which made her look much healthier, but also extremely guilty.

'So why are you telling me what you wouldn't tell the police?'

There was a long pause.

Finally, Alice spoke. 'Look. I know you don't like me,

Polynesia. You didn't like me at school and we haven't really got off on the right footing at the *Herald*, have we? I know that's partly my fault -'

'Partly your fault!' Polynesia broke in, unable to help herself. 'And how exactly have you managed to convince yourself that you're not wholly to blame?'

'You are quite spiky sometimes, you know. You're so sure of yourself, and quick to dismiss anyone you feel is your intellectual inferior. I know that's what you think of me, so I decided to get in first and make it clear that I was in charge. I got the job, and you didn't. That way, I knew that if you started bitching about me, everyone would think it was just sour grapes.'

'Ingenious,' said Polynesia. 'I don't know about you being my intellectual inferior. If Cambridge had a degree in Manipulation and Intrigue, I'm sure they'd have given you an unconditional offer.'

'You see what I mean,' said Alice. 'That's exactly the sort of arrogant comment I'm talking about. You're reminding me that you went to Cambridge and I didn't, just to make me feel inferior.'

'Given the fact that you've spent the past five months making me feel inferior, you can hardly blame me, can you?'

They glared at each other for a moment.

Then Polynesia said, 'You know, Will and Ross were always terrified that we'd get into a catfight and they'd have to separate us.'

'A catfight?' Alice raised her eyebrows.

'Exactly. Catfights are so last year. It's all handbag hostilities now.'

'Is that what you told them?'

'No, but I wish I had.'

They smiled, and the tension relaxed slightly between them.

'If we could try not to argue for the next ten minutes,' Alice said, 'I'll tell you the truth about what happened.'

'I'll do my best,' Polynesia said.

Alice sat for a few moments stirring her coffee, with her eyes on the spoon, then she looked up and met Polynesia's gaze.

'Martin and I both worked for the *Morning Post*. He was the foreign editor, quite important really, and I was one of the receptionists. He was always friendly and polite, but a bit distant. And then one day he was waiting in reception for a visitor and there wasn't much going on so we started chatting. I told him I really wanted to be a journalist. I don't actually know why I said it. Maybe it was because I didn't want him to think I was just some dumb blonde who was happy in a dead-end job. Anyway, he was so helpful – gave me a few books to read and helped me with my CV when there were a few jobs going at the *Post*.'

She stopped and shrugged her shoulders with a wry smile. 'But at the *Morning Post*, once a receptionist always a receptionist. I didn't get any of the jobs. Ironically, once they'd turned me down I realised that I really did want to be a journalist. Then Martin left and came to work for the *Herald*, and so I thought that was that. But a couple of weeks later he contacted me and said he thought he could get me a job. He asked if I'd meet him one evening to discuss it. I suggested going to the pub, but he said that a friend of his had a flat in Kennington he could borrow. He told me it would be nice and quiet there, and we could have a discussion without being interrupted.'

Polynesia gave a disbelieving snort. 'I can't believe you fell for that.'

'I didn't fall for it. I knew exactly what I was doing. Don't judge me, Polynesia. Just because my way isn't your way, it doesn't give you the right to criticise me.'

'I'm criticising you because you cheated me out of a job!' Polynesia said. 'I knew that interview process was rigged. It just stank.'

'Martin offered,' Alice said. 'I didn't force him. I never threatened to tell his wife or anything.'

'Well, she'll find out at the trial, won't she?' Polynesia said drily.

'No, don't say that! I haven't told the police, surely they won't find out?'

'For God's sake, Alice! The prosecution will take about five minutes to discover that you were a receptionist at the *Post* and that six weeks after Martin started at the *Herald* he employed you as deputy news editor. And with zero previous experience. I'm sure Joanna will happily confirm that Martin insisted on employing you, even though I was the stronger candidate.'

Alice turned pale and shrank visibly once more.

'And,' Polynesia went on remorselessly, 'I think the police might be onto you already.'

'What do you mean?' Alice whispered.

'D.I. Wilson phoned me this afternoon and asked me rather an odd question. She wanted to know whether the door of Martin's office was firmly closed or just pushed to. I couldn't work out why it was relevant, but now I think she's wondering why you shut the door. If you had a meeting with Martin and he wasn't there, surely you'd leave the door open for him?'

'I always hurry in and shut the door immediately, just in case anyone's around,' Alice said. 'I didn't register that he wasn't there until I turned away from the door and looked over at the desk. I waited a few minutes and then thought I'd check his jacket to see if his phone was there. If it wasn't, then he probably had it with him and I could call and find out where he was.'

'So you walked around the desk,' Polynesia said.

Alice nodded.

You know, I think I actually believe you,' said Polynesia. 'I didn't think I would, but I do. So, the obvious question is, if you didn't kill Martin, then who did?'

'That's why I wanted to talk to you,' said Alice. 'I remembered how you solved your mum's murder when we were at school and got your dad out of prison.'

'You called me Little Orphan Polly, do you remember?' Polynesia said. 'You told me that I was an orphan even though my dad was alive, because I'd never see either of my parents again.'

Alice lowered her eyes. 'I do remember and I'm still ashamed of what I said. I deserved that punch you gave me. Mrs Milsom told me as much, after she'd picked me up off the floor and checked my jaw wasn't broken.'

Polynesia gave a small smile. 'Not bad for a novice boxer.'

Alice leant forward on her chair. 'So, will you help me?'

There was a short, tense silence.

'Yes, I will,' Polynesia said finally, and put her hand up to forestall Alice's reply. 'Look, I'm an investigative journalist and this is a good story. If I help you, then I get the exclusive afterwards. Is that a deal?'

'Of course,' said Alice. 'Thank you, Polynesia.'

'And you need to be totally honest with me,' Polynesia said, giving Alice a hard stare.

'I will, I promise.' Alice said.

'We need to keep this on the DL for now,' said Polynesia. 'And for God's sake don't tell D.I. Wilson.'

'She thinks I'm guilty,' said Alice with a shudder. 'My solicitor says the only reason she hasn't arrested me is because of the knife.'

'What about the knife?'

'My fingerprints aren't in the right position on the knife to have used it to stab someone. And the forensics have shown that someone wearing gloves held the knife before me. But the police couldn't find any gloves anywhere, so there wasn't enough evidence to charge me.'

'Just as well it's June and not January, or we'd all have been arrested,' said Polynesia, picking up her phone. 'Let's swap numbers and we can communicate that way. I don't want any more calls from Mildred Muppet.'

12

Chapter 12

Polynesia walked home in a reflective mood. She hadn't intended to believe Alice. She'd been prepared to be spun a good line and had firmly believed that she would see right through it. But Dad and Jess were right, an investigative journalist couldn't make their mind up about a story on the flimsiest of evidence and then refuse to accept any information that didn't fit with their preconceived theory. That wasn't good journalism, and Polynesia was a good journalist. She'd allowed her previous experience of Alice and her profound dislike of the woman to colour her judgement, and that had to stop. The two police detectives had insisted on sticking to the facts when they interviewed Polynesia; no amateur psychology about the significance of childhood behaviours was allowed. And from now on, she would do the same. The facts, the whole facts and nothing but the facts, she vowed.

She knew that she could be impetuous, but she was also honest, and her gut reaction – that Alice was telling the truth – couldn't be ignored. This meant that the only way forward for an ambitious investigative journalist was to go out and find some facts that pointed to a different killer, and then get the scoop for the *Herald,* and write it up with her own byline.

When she got home, there was a note from Dad on the table:

> *Gone to British Computer Society lecture about Dark Web. Might come in handy for tracking murderers. Fish pie in oven.*

She helped herself to fish pie, and sent Jess a quick text to let her know that she'd survived her meeting with Alice unstabbed. Then she sat down to think about how to explain her U-turn regarding Alice's guilt, without sounding flaky and suggestible. It was a classic you-scratch-my-back scenario, she concluded. Alice needed someone to investigate the murder and prove her innocence, and Polynesia already had form here, with one solved killing under her belt. What Polynesia needed was a major scoop that would launch her career as a brilliant investigative journalist, and Alice had promised her an exclusive interview.

> *'I owe Polynesia everything, I can never repay the debt. She'll always be my hero,' said Alice Smith, 30, as she stood on the steps of the Old Bailey, elegant in a pale blue linen L.K. Bennett dress. As she spoke, she clasped the hand of her saviour, the gifted and intrepid journalist Polynesia Henman.*

Polynesia frowned slightly. Her daydream had a nasty flaw. How could the article praise and applaud her if she was writing it herself? She could hear Sir Giles now, *'we don't blow our own ... err ... trumpets here at the Herald. Modesty is the best ... umm*

...err.' Oh well, she could worry about that later. She needed to solve the case first, and then she could start thinking about the front-page article.

The next morning was beautifully sunny and it was already warm at eight o'clock. Polynesia went downstairs and put the kettle on. She saw Dad's notes from the meeting last night on the worktop and she scanned through them as she drank her tea and ate a slice of toast.

- *The Onion Router – wraps messages in layers of encryption, like an onion.*
- *V difficult to track who sent a message and where it started.*
- *Hidden Services have anonymity protected by Onion.*
- *Often used to sell weapons or drugs, to promote terrorism or access indecent images.*

Sounded more like Dad was interested in committing a crime than solving one, she thought with a smile.

She wheeled her bike out onto the path and put on her helmet. It was just as well she wasn't particularly vain, as a cycle helmet does nothing to improve a person's appearance. The helmet's tear-shaped design coupled with the thick chinstrap made her feel part extra-terrestrial and part Little Bo Peep. And when she got to work, her hair would emerge sweaty and even more unruly than usual. But cycling was convenient, green, healthy and it saved her a load of money. Jess's flat in Leytonstone just squeaked into Zone 3, but even then, the monthly travel card was nearly £175, a fact that she never stopped griping about.

Polynesia had offered to source a second-hand bike for her,

but Jess had refused, saying that the medical bills after she fell off would be much more expensive than the travel card.

'You're built for cycling, Pol,' Jess had explained. 'You're tall and anyone can see how powerful your legs are. On the other hand, curvaceous shorties like me are more suited to public transport or a chauffeured limousine.'

'Thanks - you make me sound like a kangaroo,' Polynesia had grumbled at the time.

Now, as she slowed down for traffic lights in Wandsworth, she heard a shout.

'Polynesia, hey!'

She looked up and saw Will Rowe on the pavement, his arm raised to attract her attention. He was wearing a linen shirt, she noticed, in a rather flattering shade of pale blue.

'Hey, Will,' she said, briefly wondering what he thought of her in her helmet. Although if he'd recognised her so easily, she couldn't look that different to normal, which was a depressing thought.

'How was the important interview?' he asked.

'It threw up some very interesting points,' she said, noncommittally.

'I see. "Ask me no questions and I'll tell you no lies,"' he said, with a grin.

'I didn't know you lived round here.' Polynesia changed the subject.

'Yes, we've been in Wandsworth for about six months now.'

We? Did that mean he was living with someone? With someone significant?

As if he could sense her question, he added, 'I share a flat with my sister. Well, I'm her lodger, really. She bought the place and needed someone to help pay the bills. And I fancied moving out of a shared house where nobody ever did any cleaning or washing up, and moving in with a neat freak.'

'So, you've got yourself a cleaning lady free of charge, then? Polynesia said.

'Not at all. Rebecca would -' he broke off, searching for the right phrase. 'Let's just say she encourages me to maintain the same high standards of cleanliness and tidiness that she sets for herself.'

Polynesia laughed.

'Look, I'd better dash for my train,' Will said. 'See you at work.'

That was interesting, Polynesia thought, as the lights turned green and she pedalled off. Why had he stopped her in the street if he was going to see her at work in less than an hour? Maybe he was worried that it would sound stalkerish if he told her later that he'd seen her cycle past and hadn't said anything.

She sent a text to Jess:

Pub after work? Need to get you up to speed.

And got a thumbs up reply by return.

Just before morning briefing, Will stopped by her desk.

'Now that your important interview's over,' he said. 'How about going for that drink this evening?'

'I've got a debrief with a member of my investigation team at six o'clock,' she said. 'But I could meet you later, say half past eight?'

Will raised his eyebrows. 'Investigation team? I can't compete with that! Eight-thirty sounds good. Where shall we go?'

'Tequila Mockingbird in Putney,' she said promptly. 'Anyone who dreams up such a brilliant name for a bar gets my loyal custom for ever. Plus, I can walk there in less than fifteen minutes.'

She sent Jess another text:

btw – I have a date ...

OMG – who with??? Let's meet at lunch – I can't wait till this evening.

Sorry – too busy.

She wanted Jess in an agony of suspense and six hours should just about do it, she thought, looking at her watch.

As she'd expected, Jess was waiting for her in Reception.

'So?' she asked eagerly, as soon as she saw Polynesia.

'I need to get my bike. Meet you on the road in five minutes.'

They headed for the dingy journalist-free pub they'd found the day after the murder. Was it really only six days ago? The place was as empty as they'd hoped, and they settled themselves at a table in the corner.

'It's definitely your round this time,' said Polynesia. 'I've let you join my investigation team, and –' she paused for dramatic effect, 'I'm going to tell you who's invited me out this evening. Double gin and tonic, please.'

'OK, but you'd better hurry up with the big reveal. I can't stand the suspense.' Jess picked up her wallet and went to the bar.

'Here's to successful investigations!' Polynesia raised her glass. 'Now, where shall we start, date or murder?'

'Ooh, date definitely,' said Jess. 'Love trumps death every time.'

'You know you'll never make it as an investigative journalist with that attitude,' said Polynesia. 'Death is our raison d'être, our lifeblood, our –'

She broke off as Jess gave an anguished cry.

'OK,' she took pity on her friend. 'It's someone in the News team, you probably won't know him. His name's Will Rowe.'

'Dark hair, blue eyes, plays rugby, lives with his sister in Wandsworth,' said Jess promptly.

Polynesia started at her in amazement. 'How do you know all that?'

'Pol, I'm a normal girl. I take notice of eligible men. You know, potential partners. And I file them away in my head.'

'But you've got Dan!'

'It's always a good idea to have a back-up.' Jess sounded as practical as ever. 'Did you know that in the nineteenth century in the mining communities up north, a family would always rent a room to an unmarried miner? Even though they lived in a tiny back-to-back house, they'd all squash in somehow. Apparently it was often the husband's brother or cousin. It meant that if the miner was killed, his wife could marry the lodger and she wouldn't be turned out of the house and made destitute along with her children.'

'Well, I hope the wife got some say over who moved in as the lodger,' Polynesia said.

'I expect anyone is better than no one in that situation.'

'Yes, I suppose so,' Polynesia agreed. 'If the only criterion is that you're not dead, it makes the selection process much easier.'

'Will Rowe,' said Jess reflectively. 'And where are you going to meet?'

'Tequila Mockingbird.'

'Good choice, I approve. Now, tell me about your meeting

with Alice.'

Jess listened in silence.

'So he *was* shagging her,' she observed finally. 'And she isn't a proper journalist after all. You were dead right there, Pol. I should have listened to you.'

'Yes. But she wasn't actually targeting me as some form of revenge for childhood slights. That was just me being paranoid. It was coincidence that we both ended up going for the same job.'

'Do you really believe her story? Or are you just pretending you do, to get the exclusive?'

'Jess Taylor, you appalling cynic! How can you even suggest such a thing?' Polynesia feigned outrage.

'I just thought I'd ask. We Lifestyle reporters have very high moral standards, obviously. But I know what it's like in the News team. Sometimes your lot go so deep undercover they marry people, just to get a story.'

'I think that's policemen, not journalists,' Polynesia said.

'As long as you're being straight with me,' said Jess.

Polynesia looked at her friend for a long moment, and then finally said, 'I have been straight with you. I mean, everything I've told you is true. The thing is there's something I haven't told you. I haven't deliberately withheld it, it's just that it hadn't really struck me until this evening . Although maybe it had, subconsciously ...' and she tailed off, chewing her lip and gazing into the middle distance.

'Stop being so mysterious, Pol. Tell me what you're talking about.' Jess was wide-eyed with curiosity.

'The thing is,' Polynesia began slowly, 'when I found Alice with the knife, it was just the same as last time.'

'Last time?' Jess echoed. 'You mean, your mum?'

'Yes, that's right. When I heard all that commotion and got out of bed to see what was going on, I went into my parents' room and found my mum lying on the bed. She'd been stabbed.'

Jess gasped. 'I knew you'd solved your mum's murder, but I never knew you were the one who found her!'

'Well, I wasn't really. I saw the body on the bed and I knew at once she was dead. Even though I was just a kid. Then I heard a noise in the corner of the room. I looked around and my dad was there. He had blood all over his shirt and he was holding a knife. He'd found her, but everyone assumed he'd killed her.'

'Everyone except you?'

'Yes, I was certain he was innocent and that was why I started investigating the murder. So, I know that a person holding a knife and standing next to a dead body isn't necessarily the killer. And that being the case, why have I been so determined to prove that Alice is guilty?'

'Well,' Jess began, 'that experience must have affected you really badly as a child. You probably wanted to block out anything that reminded you of your mum's murder.'

'It's a nice try, but don't let me off the hook.' Polynesia shook her head. 'No, it wasn't that. I had loads of therapy, plus a lot of TLC from my grandma when I was a child. I was probably the least screwed-up teenager in South West London. The truth is that I wanted Alice to be found guilty because I don't like her, and because it would be very convenient for me if she lost her job at the *Herald*.' Polynesia sighed and slumped back in her chair. 'They're both awful reasons for investigating a story. They make me biased, unreliable and a bad journalist. I know you and dad told me to be objective and open-minded.

And I was going to pretend that I was, while still doing my best to pin this murder on Alice. But now I can see that I've been completely wrong. What I need to do is to find the murderer and bring them to justice, regardless of whether or not it suits my goals and ambitions.'

Polynesia took a deep breath and slapped her hand down on the table, as if to add emphasis to her declaration.

'You're amazing Pol. This is one of the things – many things, obviously – I admire about you. You're not afraid to admit you're wrong. And once you've admitted it, you'll go full tilt in the other direction to try and put it right.'

'Justice for Martin,' said Polynesia. 'I made that up to persuade Pippa to talk to me but now it's my mission.'

'So, what's next?' Jess finished her drink and put the glass down on the table.

'Next is the meeting with Clare Trellis on Saturday. Dad and I are going up to Bedford to see her. And that meeting's just got a whole lot more interesting.'

'Has it?' Jess asked. 'Why?'

'Because,' said Polynesia, 'if Clare Trellis knew that her husband was sleeping with Alice, it gives her a cracking good motive for murder.'

13

Chapter 13

The train to Bedford left from the first floor at St Pancras. As they waited, Polynesia and her dad watched the Eurostar trains the other side of the barrier.

'Remember our holidays in Paris, Pol?' Dad asked. 'How you loved sitting and sketching Notre Dame for hours at a time.'

'Yes, it's a pity my artistic talent never came to anything,' Polynesia said. 'I could have rented a garret in Paris to sit and starve in. And you could have come and visited me for lovely holidays.'

'And then there was that time you said you could see the sea from the top of the Samaritaine building. You refused to believe me when I said that Paris is over a hundred miles from the sea,' Trevor chuckled.

'I was only a child, Dad,' she reminded him. 'What about the time you drank that complimentary Calvados and then fell off your chair?'

'The floor was very uneven,' her father said with dignity. He looked up at the departures board. 'Ah, here we go. Platform one.'

They had both agreed that it would be difficult to plan exactly how to approach Clare as they knew very little about her, so they would begin with the sympathy and empathy, and then play it by ear. This meant that Polynesia was free to daydream on the train and she started thinking about her evening with Will on Thursday. They'd chatted about work, the general gripes of any journalist working for a daily paper, and about their respective domestic arrangements. Her dad sounded a lot easier to live with than Will's sister, with her OCD cleaning regime. They'd also discussed the plus and minus points of living in South West London and concluded that Putney was more affluent and respectable, whilst Wandsworth was much more hip and eclectic. But it had all seemed very impersonal, like a couple of strangers passing the time by chatting on a train. And the one thing they hadn't mentioned at all was the murder, which was really odd.

As they walked through Bedford, Polynesia wondered what it had been like in its heyday. You could see from the architecture that the town had seen better days but now, with the garish shop signs advertising cut-price alcohol and cheap fast food, it looked uninspiring and run-down . The park was pleasant enough, though and they strolled up the main avenue past the bandstand towards the café.

'It's a pity about all those weeds in the herbaceous borders,' her dad said. 'It spoils the whole look of the place. I should have brought my fork and trowel.'

'Dad, we're here to investigate a murder, not tidy up the herbaceous borders.'

'Hercule Poirot was very keen on gardening, did you know that?'

'Well, I don't recall him doing any weeding on the Orient

Express. Look, I bet that's her, sitting on the bench over there.'

Polynesia had spotted a well-dressed, heavily pregnant woman looking around as though she was waiting for someone. She walked across and the woman half rose.

'Hi, is it Clare?' she asked, extending a hand formally. 'I'm Polynesia Henman and this is my dad, Trevor.'

Trevor moved forward to shake Clare's hand, and he gave her a smile. 'Hello, Clare. Thank you for agreeing to see us, love.'

'That's quite all right,' she said. 'Actually, it makes a bit of a change from the usual round of antenatal classes, maternity yoga and NCT coffee mornings.'

Polynesia, having no idea what an NCT coffee morning was (… nice cakes and tarts, perhaps?) smiled and nodded her head. Clare Trellis was a handsome woman, not pretty but definitely striking. She was tall and broad shouldered with strong legs and shapely, athletic calves, although they may have developed recently from carrying that huge bump around. She was dressed casually in shorts and an oversized shirt, but her hair was well cut, and her make-up was immaculate, right down to her perfectly manicured nails. She looked expensively maintained, in direct contrast to Polynesia and her dad. Polynesia was wearing an old pair of leggings and a t-shirt from her university days, and Dad was in his favourite multi-pocket workman's trousers. 'I like to have a separate pocket for everything, it confuses the thieves,' he was fond of saying.

'Let's go into the café and grab some coffee,' Clare said. 'And the cakes are pretty good if you're hungry.'

'Sounds like just our sort of place, Pol.' said Trevor. 'You girls go and get yourselves settled and I'll join the queue.'

They chatted about the journey up to Bedford while they waited for Trevor. Six trains an hour to London, and two of them only took 38 minutes, so it wasn't a bad service, and you could always get a seat on the slow trains, because they started from Bedford.

Trevor put the tray down with a flourish. 'Flapjack, chocolate cake and coffee walnut. And if we're still hungry, I've arranged with that nice girl on the till that I can skip the queue and she'll reload the tray for us. I've got my eye on a piece of carrot cake.'

He beamed as he sat down.

'You'll have to excuse my father,' Polynesia said. 'If he sees homemade cake, he behaves as though he's just been released from an obesity retreat.'

Clare smiled. She made no move to take a piece of cake, so Polynesia and Trevor helped themselves.

Dad gave Clare one of his best crinkly smiles. 'Pol and I wanted to say how truly sorry we were about your husband, love. We wanted you to know that we've been through the same experience and so perhaps we can help. You know, if you need someone to talk to.'

'I googled you actually, after you contacted me. It was terrible what you went through, murder and then prison. And your wife killed by your own brother, Trevor. What a nightmare for you!' Clare looked at them steadily as she spoke, with no hint of tears.

Trevor shook his head sadly. 'He was insane. Got it into his head that Mary was his wife and she'd been unfaithful to him with me. He's been in Broadmoor for twenty years now.'

Polynesia shuddered as she remembered those grief-filled days and her grandmother's devastation as one son struggled to cope as a widower, and the other was in the dock, accused of murder. Gran always said that it was having to look after Polynesia that stopped her from going to pieces altogether.

'At least you'll soon have a baby to look after,' she said to Clare. 'And it's Martin's baby, so that must be a comfort to you.'

'I don't know that it is,' Clare said, and sighed deeply. 'Look, I need to be honest with you, as you've reached out and offered to help. You see, I never wanted to have a baby at all. It was all Martin's idea.'

'Oh!' said Polynesia. 'It's just that Pippa said how excited you both were about the baby, so I thought – '

'Pippa's very sweet and she thought the world of Martin. But I'm afraid her view of life is very rom-com happy ever after. I'm sure it wouldn't enter her head that anyone could not be excited at the prospect of having a baby.' Clare gave a small, bitter smile. 'And anyway, I'm sure Martin told her how thrilled we were. He was definitely into the idea of keeping up appearances.'

'Keeping up appearances?' Polynesia was intrigued.

'Yes, this was our fresh start. Move out of London, have a baby and hey presto, we'll be a happy family. At least that's what Martin said …' Clare paused. 'I had an affair, you see, someone I met at work. It was all very exciting at the time, and because Martin always worked such long hours it was easy to manage. But then we got careless and we were caught, and I had no option except to resign. Of course I had to tell Martin and he was amazing about it, so understanding.'

I bet he was, the hypocrite, thought Polynesia.

'And because he was so nice about it all, I agreed to his suggestions. When really I should have told him that our marriage was over and we should get a divorce,' Clare sighed again. 'So here I am. I'm living in a place I never wanted to move to and about to become a single parent to a child I never wanted. You've offered to help me with my grief. But to be honest, what I feel now is annoyance and frustration, offset by a small dose of relief that at least my bad marriage is over. Even though I was too cowardly to end it myself.'

'Whoa, that's quite a story!' said Polynesia.

'I did wonder whether I should keep quiet and just go along with your offer of help,' Clare sounded apologetic. 'But in the end, I decided that it would be better all round if I just came clean and told you the whole story. I'm sorry you've come all this way for nothing.'

Clare's clear-eyed honesty was very appealing.

'Well, actually, we did have another reason for coming as well.' Polynesia made a snap decision that she would get more out of this meeting if she put her cards on the table, just as Clare had. Well, some of her cards, at least.

'Oh?' Clare raised her eyebrows.

'I don't know if the Google article you read mentioned it. But when my dad was accused of murder I was the one who solved the case and got him out of prison.'

At this Trevor reached across and squeezed Polynesia's hand.

'I was quite famous at the time,' she added. 'So, when the deputy news editor at the *Herald* was arrested for Martin's murder, she asked me to investigate. We were at school together, you see.'

'I didn't know anyone had been arrested,' Clare said. 'The police didn't tell me.'

'They had to release her due to a lack of evidence, but she's worried that she's still the prime suspect. It's Alice Smith, do you know her?' And Polynesia watched Clare closely as she mentioned the name.

'Alice Smith? No, I don't think so. Martin never really talked about his colleagues. And he hadn't been there long. I've spoken to Pippa quite often on the phone, but that's about all.'

'Martin and Alice worked together at the *Post,*' Polynesia said. 'He got her the job at the *Herald. M*aybe he mentioned that?'

'Not that I remember. He really didn't talk about work at all. He didn't talk about much really. Perhaps that's where the problems started.'

14

Chapter 14

Polynesia felt cross and unsettled as they made the journey home. She'd now interviewed two potential suspects, and as soon as they said 'it wasn't me', she believed them. Was she just too credulous? Of course any suspect was going to say that they hadn't murdered Martin, that was obvious. But it didn't mean that she had to believe them.

Could Clare Trellis have come down on the train and killed her husband? After all, as she'd told Polynesia, there were six trains an hour and two of those only took 38 minutes. So she could have been there and back by lunchtime. But why do it at the office? To deflect suspicion? It was true that the number one suspect was nearly always the spouse, as Polynesia and her dad had learnt twenty years earlier. But she could surely have found some better way to get rid of him that was closer to home and didn't involve a journey on public transport in the rush hour. A heavily pregnant woman doesn't blend into the background very easily and someone would be bound to have noticed her or offered her a seat on the train. Polynesia wondered how she could get hold of the CCTV footage from the station. D.I. Wilson was unlikely to agree to share it with her, she didn't seem like a very collaborative sort of person.

But the real stumbling block was why Clare would have killed him. The theory about the furious cuckolded wife had been blown out of the water by Clare's admission that she'd had an affair. If she had found out about Martin and Alice, surely she wouldn't have killed him? After all, he hadn't killed her.

Another possibility was that Clare hadn't had an affair at all. It could be that she was one step ahead and had invented a clever double bluff to remove her motive and Polynesia had fallen for it. It was all getting so complicated. She sighed with frustration.

'All right, love?' Dad asked.

'I thought it would be easier than this,' she admitted. 'Especially after last time. Back then I think I had the certainty of youth. It didn't occur to me that I could be wrong about anything. But now, I seem to be blundering about in the dark. What did you think of Clare?'

'I thought she was very open and honest with us.'

'Too honest? I mean she didn't need to tell us all that stuff about her affair, did she? I wonder if she invented the story to throw us off the scent. After all, now Martin's dead there's nobody to corroborate it. A pity we didn't ask her where she used to work.'

'Look, Pol, if she invented the story, she did it on the spur of the moment. She didn't know that you're investigating the murder. She thought we were going to help her manage her grief. I think she told us because she feels guilty about not being grief-stricken. And I don't think you can go questioning her colleagues. Not unless you want D.I. Wilson arresting you for harassment.'

'Point taken.' Polynesia lapsed into a huffy silence.

Five minutes later she brightened and turned to her dad.

'I can't talk to Clare's old colleagues, but I can talk to Martin's. After all, I wrote the front-page article about the murder. They'll know my name. I can just say we're planning an in-depth bio for some future date and I'd really like their input.'

'That's my girl,' Dad smiled. 'I'm glad to see Polynesia Henman, investigator extraordinaire, is back!'

Polynesia's positive mood carried on until Monday. Her spirits were always high when she had a plan, something to positive to work towards. And the current plan was to get hold of Martin's colleagues at the *Post* and find out about his time there. Maybe Joanna would buy into the story and let her have some time off to go and interview them?

She phoned Jess mid-morning. 'Time for a quick lunch later?'

'God, yes! Anything to get away from the Lifestyle Wellness Special. I'm on *Emotional Escape Rooms ... spaces to meditate, rage or decompress: essential for self-expression in today's home.*' Jess groaned loudly.

'I feel your pain. Meet you at 12.30 for an emotional escape to Tokyo Express.'

'So,' Polynesia waved her chopsticks emphatically. 'Joanna was all for it. When I shared my theory that the clue to Martin's murder could well lie in his past at the *Post,* she sounded delighted. She even offered to help me set up a meeting with his closest colleagues there. It's funny really. When Martin was alive, I got the impression that she didn't like him much.

But now that he's dead, she can't do enough to help find the murderer.'

'Maybe that's guilt,' Jess observed. 'She probably wishes she'd been a bit nicer to him when he was alive.'

'And it would be a great scoop for the *Herald* if I manage to uncover something significant.'

'Yes, the power of cynical self-interest can never be underestimated,' Jess agreed. 'So, what's the current plan?'

'Talk to the *Post*. He was there for years and I need to find out who his friends were. There might also be people he was close to who've moved on. When I get some names, we can track them down. And I'd really like to talk to Clare's colleagues, despite Dad's dire warnings. If only I could find out where she worked.'

'Wouldn't Pippa know?' Jess asked.

'Good point! I knew there was a reason I took you on as my assistant,' Polynesia grinned at her friend. 'I'll talk to her this afternoon.'

'What can I do? I need something concrete to focus on. All this wellness woo-woo is doing my head in.'

'I should focus on finding a new job, if I were you! But seriously, when I've got names and a story from the *Post* we can decide on our next move.'

The one thing that Polynesia didn't share with Jess was that she had another date with Will. It was a proper date this time, dinner not just drinks. She didn't tell Jess because she didn't want to be forced to think about why their last date had been so polite and awkward. Was she the sort of person who could only get on with men if she was bantering with them, and essentially insulting them? She didn't seem to know how to be herself on her own with Will, she was only comfortable if she had an audience to appreciate all the verbal sparring. Single, but clueless about how to mingle, she thought gloomily.

Joanna called her in late that afternoon.

'I've made a few calls and found three people who knew Martin well and are happy to be interviewed for our article.'

'Three – wow! That's fantastic, and so quickly. Thank you, Joanna.'

'That's no problem at all. I'm really happy to help.' She handed Polynesia a piece of paper. 'As you say, he was at the *Post* for a long time. So it's much more likely that the reason for his murder is somehow connected to his job there. And he was the foreign editor, so lots of scope for him to get on the wrong side of shady people from dubious regimes.'

Polynesia took the sheet of paper and went slowly back to her desk. It sounded as though Joanna was delighted by Polynesia's theory about Martin's life at the *Post* being responsible for his death. Was that just a natural reaction? After all, nobody wants to think that there's a murderer in their own office, much better for it to be in somebody else's. Or was there more to it? Was she keen to deflect interest elsewhere for a more sinister reason?

She chewed her lip as she pondered this. Joanna hadn't liked Martin, and she hadn't approved of the way Alice had treated Polynesia. Joanna had told her as much, in a roundabout way, something about Martin's management style being different, but she couldn't interfere. Had she changed her mind and decided to interfere to the extent of eliminating Martin and his management style for ever? But Polynesia couldn't see how it would benefit Joanna enough to be worth the risk. Everyone has workmates they find annoying, but they rarely go as far as murdering them. Imagine if she'd murdered Will after he'd infuriated her with his comment about catfights. She wouldn't have a date on Friday if she had. Although given the awkwardness of the last date, maybe that would have been just as well.

She looked down at the piece of paper, with three names and contact details, Guy Frobisher, Deputy Editor; Sylvie Lenôtre, Paris Correspondent and Melanie Pridmore, Foreign Desk Assistant. She'd start with Guy, as he was sure to be the busiest, and try to make appointments to interview them all as soon as possible.

By the end of the afternoon she'd created a new WhatsApp group, *Justice for Martin.* She added Dad and Jess, and then chose a profile picture showing Lady Justice with her sword and scales. Very appropriate, she thought, as she sent her first message:

> *P: OK team – I have interviews with 3 people at the Post this week. Let's have a strategy meeting next weekend once I've got their input. Saturday evening? Dad, will you cook?*
>
> *D: Always a pleasure to cook for such an appreciative audience.*
>
> *J: I'll have to check with Dan. Let you know tomorrow.*
>
> *P: Dad, could you make a lasagne? I know it's Jess's favourite. No pressure, Jess ...*
>
> *J: Pol, you swine. That's just not fair.*
>
> *P: All's fair in love, war and journalism.*

15

Chapter 15

Guy Frobisher was much as she had expected, with all her experience of the senior management of national daily papers. She judged that he was in his late fifties, with greying hair, retro style dark-rimmed glasses and slightly jowly cheeks. He was well-spoken with a hearty and confident manner. If his suit had been any less well-cut, he would have looked overweight, but the Savile Row grey pinstripe made him appear prosperous and well-fed.

She was pleased that she'd decided to prioritise her appearance for once, and to travel by train, not by bike. She was looking relatively smart in the navy skirt and jacket that she reserved for important meetings and interviews, and a pair of flat shoes that didn't quite bridge the gap between comfort and glamour, but were better than her Doc Martens.

She was hoping to project an image of cool, calm professionalism, softened by grief at the loss of a much-missed colleague. This would be the best way to get him to open up and tell her the truth about Martin, she felt sure.

'Awful tragedy about Martin,' he said, as they sat down in

leather armchairs in his large corner office. 'He was a first-rate chap, absolutely first rate.'

'Absolutely,' she agreed. 'That's why we're putting together this in-depth bio. It's a tribute to Martin, but it's also to help with the police investigation.' She stopped and looked appraisingly at Guy to see whether he was going to buy into this.

'Oh?' Guy looked a little surprised, but not sceptical, so she decided to press on.

'Yes. The police have hinted that an article focusing on Martin's past, particularly here at the *Post*, would be very helpful. It could jog memories and might well unearth a motive for the murder.' She smiled disingenuously, hoping that Guy wasn't best buddies with the chief constable.

His eyebrows shot up at this. 'A motive? Here at the *Post*? Good Lord – how extraordinary!'

'Well, he was the foreign news editor. So perhaps he uncovered a terrorist cell or a slavery ring or -' here she floundered, '– some foreign master criminal?'

Guy laughed. 'I don't think that's very likely. And if he did, why would they wait until he'd left the *Post* to murder him?'

Good point, thought Polynesia. Dammit.

'Perhaps it might have been something a bit closer to home then?' she suggested. 'Did he ever fall out with anyone at the *Post* or make any enemies?'

'Good Lord, no! Martin Trellis wasn't the type to make enemies, he got on well with everyone. He was a first-rate chap, as I told you.'

'There weren't any ... err ... indiscretions at work?' she asked in desperation.

'You're barking up the wrong tree there, my dear,' Guy said, shaking his head. 'Martin was absolutely devoted to his wife. Have you met the lovely Clare? Striking woman, tall, very interesting to talk to. And she speaks fluent Russian, or is it Arabic? No, he'd never have done anything to jeopardise his marriage.'

Polynesia's shoulders slumped. This was hopeless. She was never going to get anywhere, Martin had been far too good at covering his tracks.

She tried one last tack. 'Sylvie Lenôtre and Mel Pridmore have agreed to talk to me. Is there anyone else you can think of who knew him well and might give me a few personal details?'

'You could try his secretary. She worked for him for years. I believe she was so distraught when he left that she upped sticks and moved away.'

Polynesia perked up . A distraught secretary – that sounded much more promising.

Guy picked up his phone and pressed a button. 'Tash, could you find me Colette's number? Yes, Martin's secretary. That's right. Thanks.'

He stood up and held out his hand. The interview was obviously over.

'Good to meet you, Polynesia. Best of luck with the article. Hope it helps to track down the killer. Pop next door on your way out and give Tash your contact details.'

She tried not to feel frustrated as she made her way back to reception. Martin had been a lot cleverer than her, and even though he was dead he was still managing to be one step ahead of her. She looked at the three girls manning the reception desk, and with sudden inspiration approached the one who wasn't on the phone. She was a pretty, dark-haired girl with a long fringe and heavily kohled eyes.

'Excuse me, but I'm from the *Daily Herald*. I'm writing an article about Martin Trellis's murder, and Alice Smith, who's one of our journalists has been implicated. I know she used to be a receptionist here and I wondered if you knew her?'

The dark-haired girl looked up, putting her head on one side. It was a strange movement, but Polynesia supposed that she had to turn her head like that to stop her fringe from completely covering her eyes. It made her look like an inquisitive budgie.

'Oh, I knew her, all right,' the girl said. She stopped and looked at Polynesia appraisingly. 'If you're writing an article, you might as well know the truth. Alice Smith was a right bitch. To be honest, I wouldn't be surprised if she murdered someone, especially if there was something in it for her.'

Polynesia tried to react casually to this, she didn't want the girl to think she'd gone too far and clam up. 'What do you mean, exactly?'

The girl sighed. 'Oh, you know. She was always sucking up to the senior management and telling them things. Trying to make the rest of us look bad and make her look good. Just generally being a real cow, in other words.' She gave a shrug. 'I haven't got anything specific on her. If I had, I'd have gone to the police myself!'

Polynesia smiled at her, she'd finally found a kindred spirit where Alice Smith was concerned. She fished into her bag and pulled out a business card. 'If you think of anything else, anything at all, please give me a call.'

The girl looked down at the card and then up again at Polynesia, twisting her head for a clear view. She's going to need an osteopath soon if she doesn't change her hairstyle, Polynesia thought.

'Will do,' said the girl. 'See ya.'

Sylvie Lenôtre was as unrewarding to interview as Guy Frobisher had been. She assured Polynesia on the phone that Martin had been an amazing boss and a wonderful human being. She gushed about how she'd looked forward to his trips to Paris so that she could feast off the journalistic pearls of wisdom that fell from his lips.

That left Melanie Pridmore, foreign desk assistant, who had agreed to meet in her lunch hour at a café near the *Post*. This might or might not be promising. Mel might have something to tell her that that she didn't want anyone at work to overhear, or alternatively, she might just be badly paid and looking for a free lunch.

Mel was a plump blonde forty-something, wearing a clinging pink top and pleated skirt that even Polynesia could tell was unflattering. She was waiting outside the Italian café and stepped forward eagerly to shake hands.

'Hi, I'm Mel. This is exciting. It's not often I get invited out to lunch!'

They went inside and Mel filled her tray with a panini, a bag of crisps, a cake, a cookie and a coffee. Then she added an apple as an afterthought. Polynesia got her credit card out, trying to remember whether Joanna had mentioned anything about expenses. They sat down and she delivered her speech about helping the police and getting justice for Martin and then looked at Mel expectantly.

'Wow! This is so unreal. I mean, Martin - murdered! We could hardly believe it! We thought there must've been some mistake. Martin killed? It just doesn't make any sense.' She took a large bite of her chicken pesto panini and chewed energetically.

'So you can't think of anything that happened at work that might have led to this?' Polynesia probed. 'Did he cover any dangerous stories or cultivate any dubious contacts who turned on him?'

'No way! Politics was Martin's thing. You know, elections and campaigns and all that.'

'Politics can be pretty violent at times.'

'Not Martin's sort of politics,' Mel said firmly. 'He covered all the elections in Europe. I can't see some Prime Minister murdering him because they didn't like their election coverage in the *Post*.'

Neither could Polynesia, but she persisted anyway.

'He was the editor for all foreign news though, wasn't he? So maybe it wasn't his story that upset the dangerous characters. It might have been someone else's story and he just okayed publication.'

'Why wasn't the other reporter killed then?' Mel asked, removing a fistful of crisps from the packet. 'If they both knew this dangerous bit of information, why only kill one of them?'

What was wrong with these *Morning Post* people, Polynesia thought crossly. Why did they keep picking holes in her hypotheses?

'You don't know of any other reporters who've died in mysterious circumstances, then?' Polynesia asked, not entirely seriously.

'No, definitely not.' Mel paused for a moment. 'Although there was a girl who died,. Not murdered, obviously. But I know Martin was really upset about it. It was a while ago now. She didn't work for the *Post,* she was some sort of influencer,

I think. She was a friend of one of our receptionists.'

Polynesia held her breath. 'Do you remember which receptionist?'

'Yes. It was the blonde one. Bit of a Barbie-type. She doesn't work here any more. Now what was her name? Oh, I know, she was called Alice. I remember because her blonde hair reminded me of Alice in Wonderland.'

'Alice Smith?' Polynesia's mouth felt dry.

'Don't know, sorry. Receptionists don't tend to have surnames, do they? She was the one who always looked immaculate. Red nails, red lips, artfully tousled hair. And she was always a teeny bit nicer to the men than the women.'

'Well, that certainly sounds like Alice Smith,' Polynesia said. 'Do you know what happened to her friend?'

'No, I'm afraid not. I don't think I was meant to know anything at all. But I overheard Martin talking about it one day. He was having to take time off work to go to the inquest and was rearranging some meetings. He was talking to Colette about it, she was his secretary. He was saying what a tragedy it was and how upset he was. You ought to talk to Colette. She'd know much more about it than me.'

'I'd love to talk to her,' Polynesia said. 'But nobody seems to know where she is. She left the *Post* and hasn't been heard of since.'

The significance of this suddenly struck her and she shivered.

'I'll ask around if you like,' Mel offered. 'Least I can do after this yummy lunch.'

'Thanks,' said Polynesia. 'What did you think of Martin, by the way?'

Mel considered this. 'To be honest, I always found him a bit dull. You know, very earnest and serious. But I think that was because I wasn't really his type. I was too old for a start. He was always much more smiley if he was talking to any of the younger women.'

'He wasn't smiley with me,' Polynesia said.

'I expect that's because you were his intellectual equal,' Mel said with a wryly raised eyebrow. 'And Martin wouldn't have felt comfortable with that.'

Polynesia smiled at her with real warmth and felt better than she had in days.

16

Chapter 16

The interviews at the *Post* added up to a considerable extra workload, meaning that Polynesia was extremely busy and found herself racing to meet deadlines several times that week. Alice called regularly, leaving long, plaintive messages, and in the end Polynesia was forced to send a brief text:

Sorry, can't take calls, work manic. Update you soon as.

That should stall her for a while, she hoped.

There was no time for any gossipy lunches with Jess either, and when Ross tried a bit of friendly banter one afternoon, she treated him to a death stare that made him flush bright red and bend his head low over his computer keyboard for the rest of the day. She knew she needed to build a working relationship with the others in the News team, and that if she got a reputation for being difficult it wouldn't help her progress up the career ladder. But once the investigation was over, she reasoned, there would be time to build bridges and explain her behaviour. Once she'd solved the murder, she'd invite everyone out for a celebratory drink. If there was one thing that was guaranteed to make you popular with reporters, it was offering them free alcohol.

On Friday afternoon, she was just giving her article on sleaze in Westminster a final proofread, when Pippa approached her desk, holding out an open bag.

'Would you like a chocolate badger?'

Mindful of the need to be nice from time to time, Polynesia made an appreciative noise and took one.

'Badgers! Never seen these before,' she remarked.

'They're a limited edition, part of the Woodland Friends range. Ever since you gave me those yummy bunnies I've been addicted to chocolate animals. I think I'll try the squirrels next.'

'Mmm,' Polynesia murmured. She hoped this could be taken to indicate either that the badger was delicious, or that she wholeheartedly agreed that chocolate squirrels were the way forward.

Pippa dipped into the bag herself, pulled out a badger and looked at it. 'With rabbits I always start with the ears. But with a badger I'm never sure whether I should start with the nose or the feet.'

Jesus! Was this woman for real? Polynesia clenched her jaw and forced a smile, then looked pointedly back at her article.

'If you'll excuse me, Pippa. I need to finish this. But thanks for the badger.'

'Oh, I'm not stopping. I just came over to give you the information you asked for.'

'Information?'

'Yes, about where Clare Trellis works. Sorry I've been a bit slow. Joanna keeps me really busy these days. I hardly have a minute to myself. Anyway, I knew she'd been a teacher. When I was planning a trip to Paris with my mum, Martin told me that Clare used to teach French. He said that when they first met he was impressed, because she worked in a really posh school. Of course I couldn't remember the name, so I looked through every list of schools I could find online, until the name jumped out at me. It's a private school in Kensington called Petersham House.'

'That's really helpful, thank you.' Polynesia jotted down the name of the school.

'No problem. Always keen to help.' Pippa raised her hand in a clenched fist and chanted, 'Justice for Martin!'

Then she turned and made her way back towards her desk.

Polynesia sighed. She sincerely hoped that she wouldn't have to ask any more favours of Pippa. Her tolerance level for fluffy chatter had never been particularly high, and she felt herself teetering on the brink of the danger zone every time they had a conversation. A snapped retort or a sarcastic comment would be bound to reduce Pippa to a weeping mess. Banishing an image of Pippa doing the backstroke in a pool of her own tears, she remembered Petersham House and looked at her watch. It was nearly five o'clock and that was much too late to be calling a school, especially on a Friday, and anyway, she needed a plan before she called. That was something she could brainstorm with Dad and Jess tomorrow - how to find someone at the school who would corroborate Clare's story about her affair.

She cycled home through the heavy rush hour traffic focusing on blue cars. It was an old trick she'd learnt from her therapist as a child, if you're feeling anxious, start counting things. It could be anything: pushchairs, pedestrians in jeans, number plates including the letter P. But today she decided to count blue cars. It helped clear her mind and stop the swirls of anxiety that clutched at the pit of her stomach and then worked upwards to tighten her chest every time she thought about her date with Will that evening. She'd avoided speaking to him at work all week, telling herself that if they talked in the office, they'd have nothing to talk about at dinner. But really it was because she was worried that the easy, relaxed banter they'd exchanged as colleagues had now disappeared completely, and been replaced by a permanent awkwardness.

Eighty-six blue cars later, she was wheeling her bike up the front path and wrestling with the front door. Propping her bike up with one leg, she used both hands to wrench the key around in the stiff lock. Dad had insisted on buying the most expensive, most secure lock he could find, which was understandable in London. But why did it have to be so difficult to open?

'Alohomora!' she muttered. 'Just open, you bastard.'

One final violent twist and the door opened. She grabbed the bike and wheeled it inside.

'Dad?' she shouted. But there was no answer. A note on the kitchen worktop explained his absence:

> *Met Veronica at Silver Surfers. Gone round to teach her how to use Facebook. And no, it isn't a date. She's nearly ninety.*

That was a relief. She wouldn't have Dad fussing around, and all the time pretending not to fuss around, when she left to meet Will. It wasn't fair, he was very keen for Polynesia to find a boyfriend, but politely rebutted any attempts she made at matchmaking on his behalf. She wondered whether the Silver Surfers had a dating app – they couldn't all be nearly ninety, surely? There must be one or two in their sixties, who'd be jolly glad to have a bit of a romance with a man who could sort out their email problems and back up their hard drive? She made a mental note to investigate this when she had more time, poured herself a glass of water and hurried upstairs to change.

She opened her wardrobe and looked inside without enthusiasm. She was beginning to realise that you can't go from being the sort of person who doesn't really care what they're wearing as long as it's reasonably clean, comfortable and roughly the right size, to being someone who wants to look party perfect, unless you go through the intermediate stage of buying some clothes. Polynesia had cycling clothes, lounging on the sofa clothes, popping to the pub with friends clothes and dull but safe work clothes, and none of them seemed appropriate for this evening. She took a few things out and held them up in front of the mirror, then threw them on the bed. Her university May Ball dress would look ridiculous. And as for the dirndl she'd bought for a trip to Oktoberfest – she could just imagine the sideways glances if she turned up wearing that. Her interview skirt and jacket were just plain boring, and, in any case, she'd worn them to work this week . It would look as though she'd come straight from the office without bothering to change. In the end she decided to mix things up a little and went for a pair of jeans with a relatively new t-shirt and her mum's old, beaded evening jacket, finished off with a pair of tartan Doc Martens. She hoped she looked edgy rather than deranged.

Arriving ten minutes early at the French brasserie, she decided to walk around the block rather than wait inside on her own. She didn't want to give the impression of being overly keen or needy; she wanted to stroll in casually at seven-thirty on the dot and walk confidently up to the table where Will would be waiting for her. She turned left down the little lane past the hardware shop, and headed towards the scout hut, where she would turn left again and make her way slowly back to Chez Pierre. There was someone standing outside the scout hut, reading the noticeboard intently, and as she got closer she could see that it was Will.

Almost without thinking, she called out, 'Hey, Will! Is it the Scouts or the Beavers you're interested in?'

Will turned round with a grin. 'Actually, neither. I've got a bit of man crush on Bear Grylls. As he's the chief scout, I thought I'd just check and see whether he'll be visiting Putney any time soon.'

'I would never have had you down as a Bear Grylls groupie.'

'I'm not, really.' He walked back towards her. 'I just read it on the noticeboard. I was killing time, didn't want to arrive early.'

'Snap,' she said. 'Obsessive punctuality has been drilled into me since I was a child.'

'I think mine's more innate than drilled,' Will said. 'Mind you, with my OCD sister, I think I got out of the gene pool relatively unscathed.'

They strolled back to the restaurant with none of the awkwardness that had marred their previous date. Polynesia was so relieved that she felt like skipping. But that would definitely look weird, so she contented herself with a 'Yay, it's Friday!' as they sat down at their table.

Will looked at her. 'You've cheered up.'

'Aren't I always cheerful?'

'Not exactly,' he said. 'In fact, all week I've been wondering if you were working up to cancelling on me. You've been going out of your way to avoid me all the time.'

'I've been really busy, that's all,' she protested.

'And Ross said the hates vibes coming off you the other day could have penetrated titanium.'

'Maybe I just don't react well to pressure,' she shrugged.

He looked at her quizzically for a moment. 'If there was a problem, you would talk about it, wouldn't you?'

'Of course I would,' she lied. 'Let's not talk about work. I'd much rather hear about your man crushes. Tell me, who else ruffles your truffles, apart from the rugged Bear Grylls?'

It had been a nice evening, Polynesia decided, as she sat on the bed undoing her shoelaces. It had been a fun evening and a jokey evening, but had it also been a romantic evening? She wasn't sure about that. And she also wasn't sure if she'd wanted a romantic evening. Would she have wanted to sit holding Will's hand all evening, looking into his blue, blue eyes and admiring his long eyelashes? OK, so she had admired them anyway, but only in passing – it wasn't as though they were the main feature of the evening. What she wanted, she deduced, was a blokey sort of relationship, with lots of banter and jokes, with a nice-looking man that she could lust after in a sideways, low-key fashion. She couldn't see herself ever greeting a boyfriend with 'hello, gorgeous,' as she'd heard friends doing in the past. It was much too … well … too confident, she supposed. If you called someone gorgeous, it was obvious that you knew you were gorgeous too. But if you told someone they were gorgeous and they thought you were just average – good fun of course, but not gorgeous – what happened then?

Stop overthinking everything, she told herself sternly. This afternoon you were worried that the whole evening would be a stilted disaster, and now you're worried because you think the whole evening was a bit blokey? This is Will we're talking about, and he knows you. If he'd wanted to have dinner with a girly girl, he would have invited one, but he invited you.

She clambered into bed, resolving not to think any more about this until Monday at the earliest. The most pressing need now was to develop a strategy for the next phase of her murder investigation.

17

Chapter 17

Saturday mornings were reserved for a long bike ride. It helped clear her head after a busy week, and getting away from the heavy commuter traffic of her regular weekday rides was a joy. The sun was shining through the curtains when she woke up at half past seven, so she decided she'd better get going early before it was too hot for any exertion.

She pulled on her Lycra shorts and top, filled a water bottle, clipped it to her bike and put on her shoes. She clattered into the dining room, the cleats on her soles sounding like a tap dancer, grabbed an emergency banana and stuffed it into her back pocket. Then she was off, pedalling across Putney Heath and into Richmond Park. She'd do four laps of the park, and with the two miles each way across the Heath, that made 32 miles. Just over two hours if she kept up a good pace, she reckoned and then she could go home for a well-deserved breakfast with Dad. He was used to her coming back scarlet-faced and dripping from a morning ride, and if he found it off-putting to sit and eat pancakes with someone who radiated heat and was squelching in a puddle of her own sweat, then he was far too delicate to mention it. Everyone knows that you have to cool down properly before you shower, otherwise you just end up clean and sweaty instead of dirty and sweaty, which is fairly pointless.

As she leaned forward and powered up the first hill, she began thinking about the task she'd set herself. She wanted to find Martin's killer before the police did, but she had no idea how far the police had got with their investigation. For all she knew, they were about to make an arrest. D.I. Wilson could be on a plane this very moment, heading for Romania to interview a gang of people smugglers that Martin had been about to expose in a front-page article. But somehow, she didn't think so. From the evidence she'd discovered so far about Martin's duplicitous lifestyle, she was pretty sure that the killer was someone much closer to home. The only question was … who?

By seven o'clock that evening the lasagne was in the oven and Polynesia had set the dining room table with notepads, pens and bottles of water.

Dad looked over from the salad he was making and said, 'I thought this was supper, not a board meeting, love. Where are the knives and forks and wine glasses?'

'This is psychology, Dad. The human brain craves completion, did you know that?' She put glass tumblers at each place and straightened all the notepads. 'It's called the Zeigarnik effect. If you don't complete a task, it creates cognitive tension and so you keep coming back to it. Which means that if we start our meeting before supper, we're much more likely to carry on afterwards and come up with a strategy. Whereas, if we start with supper, we may still be making polite chitchat at nine o'clock and have no plan for next week.'

'If I know my daughter, any more than two minutes of polite chitchat and she'll be rolling her eyes and harumphing.'

'I have never harumphed in my life, thank you very much! You make me sound like some fossilised old colonel.'

The doorbell rang.

'Excellent! Now we can start.' Polynesia hurried to the front door.

'This looks very businesslike,' said Jess as she came into the dining room and saw the table.

'It's psychology, apparently,' said Trevor, coming forward to give her a kiss. 'It's got some fancy foreign name, but it's otherwise known as *I've started so I'll finish,* as that dry, old Icelandic stick used to say.'

'Icelandic stick?' Jess was flummoxed.

'Don't worry about it, Jess. Dad's talking about the olden days.' Polynesia patted her father on the shoulder. 'He forgets that we aren't all five hundred years old, with memories of the Sixteenth Century Megadrought when all the sticks in Iceland dried out.'

'I'm talking about Magnus Magnusson, as well you know, cheeky madam,' said Trevor. 'You used to love *Mastermind* when you were little, precocious child that you were.'

'It was the music and the way the room suddenly went dark and silent. It sent shivers down my spine. I couldn't answer the questions, obviously. I was only about seven at the time.' Polynesia moved towards the table. 'Let's make a start and put the Zeigarnik effect into practice. We can eat in half an hour or so, but the important thing is to get our discussion underway before we break.'

She told them about her interviews with Martin's colleagues

from the *Post,* and Mel's revelation that Martin had known a girl who had subsequently died, and he'd been required to give evidence at the inquest.

'Why couldn't Mel have been a bit more inquisitive?' Jess grumbled. 'If she'd only listened a bit harder outside the door, then we'd have more of an idea about what happened to this girl.'

'Yes,' Polynesia agreed. 'And Colette the devoted secretary has vanished. So we can't even ask her.'

'Oh, I don't think that's a problem,' Trevor said. 'We can easily find out what happened.'

'How?' the two girls asked in unison.

'You need to ask Alice. This girl was Alice's friend, you said. So it stands to reason that Alice must know what happened to her.'

'If I could trust Alice to tell me the truth, I'd ask her,' said Polynesia. 'Don't you find it a little odd, that the man she swears she didn't murder was involved in the death of her friend, and she didn't think to mentioned it?'

'Perhaps she was worried that it would give her a motive,' said Jess.

'But she must have known that the police would find out. I mean we've found out, and it looks really suspicious that she's kept quiet about it.' Polynesia said.

'It might not be anything suspicious at all,' Trevor said. 'Alice might not have even considered that there was a connection. Let's say her friend was an epileptic. If she had a fit and died while Martin was with her, that would be why he was at the inquest. There might not have been the slightest indication that her death was anything to do with him.'

Polynesia sighed. 'You're right, Dad. I will have to talk to

Alice about this. But how can I convince her to tell me the truth?

'Oh, that's easy, love. It's all a question of psychology.' And he winked at her.

Polynesia laughed.

'Touché!' she said. 'Come on then, Dad. Let's have the psychological lowdown on how to get a pathological liar to tell the truth.'

'Tell Alice about the piece you're writing on Martin. Tell her that Joanna got you some interviews at the *Post* for a bit of back story. All perfectly true. Then say that Mel mentioned a suspicious death that Martin was linked to.'

Trevor leaned forward with both hands on the table. 'Now, here comes the psychology. You tell Alice that you don't believe a word of it, because you know Alice has told you everything about her involvement with Martin. After all, that was a condition of you agreeing to help her. But Mel is less convinced and is thinking of going to the police. So you feel it's only fair to warn Alice, in the spirit of your mutual full disclosure.' He sat back with a look of triumph.

'Trevor, that's positively Machiavellian!' Jess said in admiration.

'You youngsters aren't the only ones with a bit of psychology at your disposal, you know,' Trevor said. 'And when you've said your piece, Pol, you just sit there in silence until she starts to sing like a bird. As they say in the old detective novels.'

He pushed back his chair. 'Have we triggered enough cognitive tension to be allowed to eat the lasagne now?'

'I hope so,' said Jess. 'I've got cognitive tension and salivary overflow, and I'm finding it difficult to concentrate.'

'So,' said Polynesia ten minutes later, busy spearing a forkful of salad. 'Problem number one sorted. So let's move on to problem number two, how to talk to someone at Petersham House about Clare Trellis. Any ideas?'

'Could we send them a fake request for a reference?' Jess suggested. 'Trevor could mock up some headed paper for a fake school. We could ask the Head for a full reference with any reasons why the candidate wouldn't be suitable for the job.'

'We could try,' Polynesia said dubiously, 'but I'm not sure whether extra marital affairs are the sort of thing that would be mentioned in a written reference. I think it would be more likely to be mentioned in a phone call. You know, no paper trail.'

'Well, we could write first and then Trevor could phone them and pretend to be a headmaster.'

'No, thank you,' said Trevor. 'I don't think I'd be at all convincing as a headmaster. One phrase in jargon and I'd give myself away immediately. Besides, where's this fictitious school supposed to be? If we put our address here in Putney, they'll know that there's no such school a mere five miles away from Kensington. I suppose we could make the address somewhere at the other end of the country, like Durham. But then how are we going to get any replies they send?'

'Oh! I hadn't thought of any of that.' Jess looked crestfallen.

'It's also quite likely,' Polynesia added, 'that someone from the school might contact Clare to wish her good luck with the new job, or just to say that they'd completed a reference for her. We've got her onside at the moment. But if she finds out that we're investigating her story, she won't be onside for much longer.'

'Dammit!' said Jess. 'What else can we try?'

They all stared at the table, but inspiration eluded them.

'Rome wasn't built in a day, love,' Trevor said. 'I'm sure that if we all sleep on it, someone will come up with an answer. It's a well-known psychological strategy.'

Polynesia groaned. 'I'm beginning to wish I'd never mentioned psychology in the first place!'

'What about Will?' her dad continued. 'Did he have anything to say about all this last night?'

Jess pounced. 'Last night? Why were you talking to Will last night?'

'Oh, we just popped out for a spot of supper,' Polynesia said airily, trying to glare at her father without Jess noticing. 'Just a spur of the moment thing, you know.'

Her father opened his mouth and she kicked him under the table.

'Honestly,' she went on, 'it was nothing, just a quick meal. We were back home and in bed by 10.30. I was, I mean … in bed, on my own. I don't know about Will, obviously. He went home and …' she felt herself reddening.

'Pol, you are funny,' Jess hooted with laughter. 'You seem to think that having a boyfriend is like having herpes. It's something you need to hide from people.'

'He's not my boyfriend,' she said. 'It was just a quick supper. And to answer your question, Dad,' here she felt more comfortable and on firmer ground, 'I didn't talk to him about this at all. Will has no idea that we're investigating Martin's murder.'

'Perhaps you should tell him,' he said. 'The more brains on this the better, in my opinion.'

'I'll sleep on that one too,' she said, in an ending-the-conversation tone. 'Any more lasagne going?'

18

Chapter 18

Polynesia slept on both the problems. She slept very well actually, which may or may not have been down to the excellent Chianti that Dad had served with the lasagne.

'It's all about locale and terroir,' he was fond of saying. 'You have to trust the locals to know which food and wine go well together.'

And she had to admit that he was right. The Chianti had been spot on with his lasagne al forno, in the same way that his chilli con carne went so divinely with an ice-cold Corona. With hindsight, it had been a blessing in disguise that her mother had been such a terrible cook. It meant that Dad had got into the habit of doing all the cooking right from the start of their marriage. So, after her mother died there had been no abrupt change to a diet of beans on toast while he frantically read cookery books and learnt to roast a chicken, because he was the one who'd been roasting the chickens all along. Equally importantly, he was used to women who didn't cook, so Polynesia felt no shame and happily took on the mantle of being hopeless in the kitchen. She wondered briefly whether

Will could cook – in all their discussions of domesticity, they'd never talked about cooking. She wasn't sure that his OCD sister would let him loose in her kitchen. If she didn't trust him to load the dishwasher in the right way, she would surely get very twitchy if he started scraping cast-iron pans back and forth on her ceramic hob or using a metal spatula in a non-stick wok. These were two crimes that Polynesia had committed as a teenager, and her grandmother's subsequent wrath had forced her to rethink her ambition to become a famous TV chef. In fact, she'd rethought it so thoroughly, that she'd barely used a saucepan since.

After all their talk about the power of psychology yesterday evening, she was disappointed to find that she had no light bulb moment when she woke up. She hadn't the slightest idea how to approach Petersham House for the lowdown on Clare Trellis, and she was still undecided about whether or not to tell Will about their investigation and rope him in to help. Oh well, perhaps tricky issues required more sleep and she'd have her answer tomorrow morning. In the meantime, however, she did have one avenue of enquiry to pursue, she needed to ask Alice about her friend.

Strike while the iron's hot, she said to herself, as she got out of bed. What did that even mean? Everyone knew that the whole point of an iron was to use it while was hot. But did you actually strike the clothes? Surely it was more of a firm glide across the surface? She made a mental note to research this idiom when she had more time, but now, she needed to speak to Alice.

She sent a quick text:

Sorry for radio silence ... frantic week. Have news – can we meet?

The reply pinged back almost immediately:

Yes. Free today. Free every day .. lol! When good 4 U?

Three o'clock today, Starbucks?

Ok c u there.

Polynesia looked at the messages and shuddered. She could hardly believe that a former pupil of Putney Bridge Girls' School would embrace textspeak so wholeheartedly. She wondered what Mrs Milsom would say about this. She remembered only too clearly the headmistress's lecture about the falling standards of written English and the evils of the greengrocer's apostrophe … or should that be greengrocers' apostrophe?

She resolved to be tolerant. At least Alice hadn't written *c u l8r,* which would have been comparable to having *I'm a moron* tattooed across her forehead, in Polynesia's view..

She cycled slowly to Wandsworth; it was another hot summer's day, and she didn't want to arrive scarlet and sweaty. She was sure that Alice would be looking cool and dewy fresh, as though she'd stepped straight out of an air-conditioned limousine and into the coffee shop, and Polynesia didn't want the contrast between them to be any more marked than it usually was. She was wearing a pair of cut-offs with a plain navy t-shirt that was only slightly faded with wear. And in deference to the hot weather, she'd swapped her Doc Martens for a pair of baseball boots. She was just locking her bike to the railings when Alice arrived, looking like a girl in an advertisement for something summery, in a green linen dress and a straw hat.

'Hi Alice! You're looking very Duchess of Cambridge today!' She was pretty sure it would come across as a compliment, Alice was so obviously a royalist.

'Thank you. And you're looking very … well … very you,' said Alice, looking at Polynesia's ensemble.

'Yes, vagrant-meets skater boy is a style I've made uniquely mine.'

Alice smiled and Polynesia noticed that she looked a lot healthier than she had the previous time they'd met. Her hair was newly washed, her face had some colour, and the mascara and kohl were back. The usual red lipstick had been replaced by a pale pink which looked nicer, less vampish and much softer.

They sat down with their coffee and Alice dived straight in. 'You said you had news.'

'Yes. Something came up this week and I thought you ought to know.'

She told the story of her interviews at the *Post*, just as Dad had suggested, and watched Alice carefully. When she mentioned the friend who had died, Alice turned pale and began to breathe more heavily.

'Of course I told Mel that she must have got hold of the wrong end of the stick. But she was adamant that she hadn't and she feels she needs to tell the police,' Polynesia finished.

Alice sat perfectly still, except for her eyes which were moving rapidly from side to side as though she was thinking hard. Polynesia waited without speaking.

'I did have a friend who died,' Alice said eventually. 'She was my flatmate, and her name was Rosa.'

'I see. But how was Martin involved?'

Alice sighed. 'Rosa was an influencer. You know, people would send her stuff or pay her to review things. She really wanted to be famous and she used to hang around people who might be useful to her.' She said this in a disapproving tone that made Polynesia want to shout something about pots and kettles.

'Anyway,' Alice went on, 'she used to drop into the *Post* quite often, she liked the idea that she might spot a celeb coming in for an interview or something. I'd make her a coffee and she'd sit there as if she was waiting for a meeting. Then one day Martin saw me giving her a coffee and having bit of a chat. He asked me who she was. This was after I'd become friends with Martin, so I didn't mind admitting to him that she wasn't really there on business. I told him she was my flatmate and he asked to be introduced to her.'

It was unbelievable! Polynesia had thought of him as dull old Martin, with his grey suit and flat voice, but really he'd been some kind of monochrome sex machine. So much for her powers of journalistic intuition.

'That was definitely a bad move,' Alice said. 'Rosa wasn't exactly pretty, but men were always attracted to her. She was tall with long dark hair, and those Slavic cheekbones – her dad was Serbian. Martin used to call us Snow White and Rose Red. He said it was a fairy-tale his mum used to read to him when he was little about two princesses, and one was blonde and the other was dark. Anyway, he told Rosa he interviewed a lot of important people and maybe he could get her a few introductions. She was really excited about that. They started meeting up after work, sometimes in a pub or restaurant, but usually at our flat. They couldn't go to his place, of course, because of his wife. Even though they were separating, they still lived together because he couldn't afford to move out until they'd sold up. And he didn't want to upset his wife because of her mental health issues. He was so thoughtful.'

If Alice had told her that Martin was, in fact, an alien

who had ended up in Essex because his UFO had crashed-landed beside the Colchester bypass, Polynesia wouldn't have found the story any more unbelievable. Here he was, a forty-something gamma male, spinning ridiculously corny lines to young alpha women, and succeeding! He had an attractive, intelligent wife, plus two girlfriends who were both potential trophy wife material. Here was a man who was winning at life – or at least he had been until he was murdered.

'How did Rosa die?' she asked.

Alice shifted in her seat and bowed her head. 'Martin and I had been getting closer. We talked a lot at work, and one day he told me his feelings towards me had changed. He realised that I was the one he loved, and not Rosa. That evening he took her to a pub on the river for a drink and he told her it was over, that he wanted to be with me. She stormed out of the pub and left him there on his own. After a while he came back to the flat to tell me what had happened and he spent the night with me.'

'He didn't believe in wasting time, did he?' Polynesia couldn't stop herself.

'It was true love. There was no point in waiting,' Alice said.

Polynesia remembered once reading a story about a girl who thought that the stars were God's daisy chain and that every time a fairy sneezed a baby was born. She wondered now whether that girl had been called Alice.

'So she stormed out of the pub?' Polynesia prompted.

'Yes, and she didn't come back to the flat all night. We thought she must have gone to stay with friends. You know, couldn't face seeing Martin and me together.'

'That would have been understandable.'

'But she hadn't gone to see friends.' Alice's shoulders sagged.

'When I got back from work that evening the police came round to say that they'd found her body in the river. She'd fallen in and drowned. It was such a shock. I mean, we hadn't reported her missing or anything, we just thought she'd turn up once she'd calmed down.'

'So Martin was the last person to see her alive. That was why he had to appear at the inquest,' Polynesia said thoughtfully. 'What was the verdict?'

'That it was an accident, a tragic accident. Nobody was to blame. The coroner said she died around two o'clock in the morning. She must have been wandering around by the river for several hours before she fell in. It was ten o'clock when she rushed out of the pub and Martin got back to the flat an hour later. He waited for ages to see if she'd cool down and come back so he could give her a lift home. He didn't like the idea of her being out on her own so late at night.'

'Such a gentleman,' Polynesia said.

If Alice noticed Polynesia's scathing tone, she gave no hint of it.

'The whole thing was terribly traumatic for both of us,' she said. 'And Rosa's parents were awful. They practically accused us of conspiring to get rid of Rosa. Her mother called me a tart in the coroner's court, in front of everyone! I think that's why I didn't tell you. It would have been too stressful for me to rake it all up again. And after all, it had nothing to do with Martin's murder.'

Polynesia lost her cool. 'Nothing to do with Martin's murder!' she almost shouted. Then, getting control of her anger, she hissed, 'How can you possibly say that? What pea-brained logic leads you to that conclusion? Supposing Rosa's mother murdered him because she believes he caused her daughter's death, and she's framing you because she thinks you're the tart who started it all!'

Alice didn't look so healthy any more, her skin developed a grey tinge and she began to shiver. 'I never thought of that,' she whimpered. 'Please, Polynesia, you have to believe me. If I'd thought Rosa's death had anything to do with Martin's, of course I would have told you.'

Polynesia looked at Alice appraisingly. Alice had previous form when it came to being devious and dishonest. But on the other hand, she wasn't very bright either, so perhaps she hadn't seen the possible link between the two deaths. Alice sniffed pitifully and fumbled in her bag for a tissue.

'Right,' said Polynesia. 'So we've now added another two suspects to our list. Are there any more bombshells that you've forgotten to mention?'

Alice smiled weakly, 'No, nothing. I promise I've told you everything.'

'You told me before that there was nothing between you and Martin until after he'd left the *Post.* That wasn't true, was it?'

'What I meant was that there was nothing *much* between us until after he'd left the *Post.* Hardly anything at all, we were too shocked by Rosa's death. Things cooled off for ages until he moved to the *Herald.* Then said he could get me a job and it all started up again.'

'And by then his wife was pregnant and they'd moved out of London to make a fresh start,' Polynesia said acidly.

'I didn't know that,' Alice said. 'He didn't tell me and I've never been to his house. I don't even know where he lived.'

Polynesia looked at her closely. It sounded plausible, but then Alice always did sound plausible, that was the problem.

19

Chapter 19

Polynesia's article on Westminster sleaze in Saturday's paper garnered her a few plaudits from her colleagues and even generated a couple of copycat articles in the tabloids. Sir Giles was very pleased and sent her a congratulatory email and suggested she follow up with a series of interviews with members of the Opposition. This kept her busy for the next few days, researching, interviewing, and then writing her articles until late into the night, hindered by demands from Joanna or Sir Giles for more details or yet another rewrite. By Friday the series of articles was over, and Polynesia hoped that she never had to talk sleaze with anyone ever again. But it did seem as though she was finally getting somewhere in the News department; Sir Giles had even called one of her articles 'insightful'.

At Friday's briefing, she allocated herself a story about new research into gut health, reckoning that she could write it on autopilot after her years in Lifestyle, when probiotics, pre-biotics, biomes, psyllium husk and colonic irrigation were all regularly analysed and either extolled or pilloried, to reflect the zeitgeist. This would give her a bit of time to get her thoughts back on the murder trail.

She arranged a quick drink after work with Jess and was already waiting with her bike when Jess came out, blinking in the bright sunshine, to join her friend.

'Hello, stranger, how's Sleazegate going?' Jess asked, hitching up her shoulder bag and falling into step with Polynesia.

Polynesia groaned loudly. 'If I have to listen to one more politician saying they had absolutely no idea ... blah, blah blah ... I might do something drastic. Honestly, you'd think they all went around blindfolded the whole time.'

'I've heard that some of them quite like it blindfolded,' Jess said. 'Handcuffed too.'

They both laughed.

'How about a Prosecco in Borough Market as it's such a nice evening?' Jess suggested.

So they walked past the Old Operating Theatre Museum and across the road towards Borough Market. Squeezing into an outdoor seating area, they waited for their drinks.

'This is the trouble with London,' Polynesia grumbled. 'There are just too many people. On a nice evening, everywhere's packed. If this was Italy, we'd be sitting in the charming village square with a couple of the locals enjoying a tranquil aperitif. Not packed into an outdoor seating area under a railway bridge like a couple of inner-city sardines.'

'But if this was a village in Italy, you'd be working in the local supermarket stacking shelves. You wouldn't be writing for a national paper,' Jess pointed out.

'Stop being logical. I'm cross because I'm tired.'

'You've had a successful week! You're a rising star, Pol. You should be feeling sorry for me. I've spent the last few days writing about colour psychology.' Jess began to speak in a breathy voiceover style. 'What does your wardrobe say about you? Are you getting the right message across at work and at home? Follow in the footsteps of Isaac Newton and Carl Jung and use this fascinating study to ensure that you always create the right impression.'

Polynesia looked Jess up and down. 'So I'm guessing that your red polka dot dress says *kill me now ... just use any one of the white spots as a target.* Am I right?'

'Pretty much. Whereas your white shirt says *I'm honest* and your blue trousers are backing that up, saying *yes, and I'm loyal and competent. So trust me to do a good job!'*

'Pity about the Doc Martens,' Polynesia said, looking down at her feet. 'I'm pretty sure they're saying *and if you don't trust me, I'll kick your head in.*'

She raised her glass to Jess, good humour restored. 'Here's to the psychology of catching a murderer.'

'I'll drink to that,' Jess said, and they clinked glasses.

'So what's the latest?' Jess asked. 'I slept on the problem of Petersham House. But I'm afraid I didn't get a flash of inspiration in the morning.'

'Me neither,' said Polynesia. 'But I did manage to winkle the truth out of Alice.'

'Well,' said Jess, when she'd heard the full story. 'She really is a slippery customer. I understand why you'd never trust her further than you could throw her. I thought you were being a tad paranoid at first, but now ...' She raised her eyebrows and shook her head in mock despair.

'Leaving the perfidious Alice to one side, we now have two more suspects to interview. How are we going to get hold of

Rosa's parents?' Polynesia mused.

'There should be a report of the inquest in the papers. I'll track it down and see if I can find the parents' names,' Jess offered. 'There can't be that many girls called Rosa who've drowned in the Thames.'

'And I think I'll talk to Will. Dad's right, we need all the brains we can muster to solve this.'

'Ooh! So have you got another date this weekend?'

'Nothing planned.' Polynesia was determined to play it cool from now on whenever Will's name was mentioned. 'I'll send him a message and see what he's up to.'

'I'd better go,' Jess finished her drink and stood up. 'Dan's cooking tonight, I don't want to be late. See you Monday. Have a good one!'

She disappeared in the direction of the station and Polynesia wondered what it would be like to be part of a couple, to have someone at home waiting for you and cooking for you. Sure, she had Dad, but it wasn't the same. She didn't feel obliged to consider him before she made any plans. They lived together, but they weren't committed to each other. Polynesia wasn't sure if she would find commitment reassuring or stifling.

She messaged Will, who suggested Saturday brunch before he headed off to a stag party. She agreed, thinking that his brain power would be infinitely superior before the party than after it.

Generally speaking, Polynesia wasn't a great fan of brunch and its breezy assumption that you were quite happy to replace two meals with just the one. Given the option, she would have gone full-on Hobbit and had breakfast, followed by second breakfast and then elevenses, but she knew when she was sailing against the wind. So whenever anyone suggested going out to brunch, she agreed – after all, who was going to know how many breakfasts she'd already eaten at home?

On Saturday morning she opened the curtains to reveal a cloudless blue sky – definitely a day for an early bike ride. Later, after porridge and raspberries – so good for the blood sugar levels – she had a cooling shower and then wondered what to wear. Would it be worth tapping into the psychology of colour? She wanted to project the right image when she talked to Will.

She wandered downstairs in her towel and found Dad still reading the paper at the dining room table, with the remains of their breakfast all around him.

'Can I have the Lifestyle section? I want to look at Jess's article on the psychology of colour.'

'Course you can, love. Don't tell Jess, but I'm not much of a lifestyle man myself.'

Polynesia looked at his workman's trousers with their unflattering lumpy pockets and his tatty old sweatshirt which was unravelling at the neck. 'I think she knows that, Dad.'

She took the page upstairs and scanned it as she went through her wardrobe. She could wear her blue denim cut-offs – *trust, loyalty and competence* – with a black t-shirt – *sophistication and security*. Or how about her brown linen trousers – *dependability and trustworthiness* – with a pink shirt – *compassion and sincerity*? What she really wanted to project was confidence, success, and bravery, and that was orange, but she didn't have any orange clothes … dammit! In the end she went for khaki shorts, hoping that the hidden mix of yellow, green and brown would suggest that she was creative, dependable and nurturing. A white t-shirt proclaiming her honesty and innocence completed the look.

'This had better work, Jess, after all the trouble I've gone to,' she muttered as she went downstairs to find her shoes.

The Shak Shack was a hipster magnet in Wandsworth, famous for two types of shakshuka, the red and the green. They also served a variety of other Middle Eastern dishes, suitably reworked to appeal to well-travelled Millennials who wanted a meal to remind them of their holiday in Turkey, but wanted it to be a whole lot nicer than anything they actually ate there. At least that was the conclusion Polynesia had come to. Why else would they serve free range duck eggs? Whoever remembered eating those in Turkey? And the range of coffees: chemex, pour-over, nitro, was equally rose-tinted. There was nothing on the menu that resembled the black, gritty, bitter-as-hell drink she remembered gagging on in Istanbul.

Will was waiting in the queue when she arrived, so she joined him. He was wearing a grey t-shirt – *focused, neutral, calm and careful.* Was that a good sign or a bad sign? He bent down and they brushed cheeks. It was a friendly almost-kiss, not a romantic one. But still, it was a step further along the road than last time they'd met. Although, to be fair to Will, she had set a fairly unromantic tone on that occasion by shouting loudly about boy scouts and beavers. Oh well, perhaps one day she'd learn to be ladylike, despite a lack of suitable role models in her life.

They ordered shakshuka with Turkish bread, and Will asked for toast and jam and a selection of breakfast pastries.

'I need the carbs. This evening's going to be all about survival,' he explained.

'Sounds grim. Let's hope the groom survives, or it will all

have been a liver-trashing waste of time.'

'He's a prop forward. If anyone survives, he will.'

'Well, I'm glad I've got you pre-hangover, because there's something I want to ask you,' she said.

Will smiled. 'Sounds interesting, ask away,' he said.

Polynesia took a deep breath. 'Did you know that my mum was murdered when I was eleven?' she asked.

He sat back in his chair and met her eyes. 'Yes, I did. Alice told us when you first joined the News team on secondment. But she said not to mention it to you.'

Polynesia was surprised. 'I wouldn't have expected Alice to elicit sympathy on my behalf.'

'No,' Will agreed. 'I don't think it was the sympathy angle she was going for. It was more that she wanted to give the impression you might be a little unbalanced. You know, PTSD or something. She probably wanted us to be a little wary of you, and not take anything you said about her at face value.'

'What a scheming bitch!' Polynesia fumed. 'I can't believe I'm trying to help her!'

Will stared at her. 'What do you mean, you're trying to help her? You were delighted when the police led her away!'

'I know I was,' she said. 'But let me explain what's happened since then.'

The food arrived and they dipped bread into egg yolks as Polynesia told him about Alice's plea for help and her multiple confessions to pretty much everything except the murder. She then moved on to Clare Trellis's affair, Rosa's death, and the three-strong murder investigation team that she had put together to try and solve the crime.

'So that's where we are,' she said finally. 'Moving forward at a snail's pace, with no idea what the police are up to. We can't think of a way to get to talk to the Head of Petersham House. And if we do find a way, and the Head can't corroborate Clare's story, what then? How likely is it that a heavily pregnant woman travelled to London to kill her husband, when she could quite easily have done it in the comfort of her own home?'

'This whole thing sounds insane,' Will said. 'How can you possibly think you'll solve the crime before the police do?'

'I've done it before,' she said obstinately.

'Yes, but last time it was your mum who was killed, your dad who was accused and your uncle who was the murderer. You didn't exactly have far to look, did you?'

'I suppose not,' she said glumly. 'The real problem is a lack of suspects. To be honest, it's not very likely to be Clare or poor Rosa's parents, is it? But who else is there? I mean, I was the first on the scene and there was no one else in the place. Then you and Ross and Pippa arrived, but he was already dead by then, so it couldn't have been you.'

'Phew! I'm relieved to know I'm not a suspect.'

She ignored his attempt to lighten the conversation.

'So that's the situation.' She jabbed dejectedly at a congealing egg yolk with the last piece of bread. 'Everyone else arrived much later, which means they're in the clear. There are literally no suspects!'

'There was someone else who arrived early,' Will said thoughtfully. 'Joanna.'

'No, that can't be right!' Polynesia thought back to that morning. 'She arrived quite late. I remember Sir Giles had already got us into the downstairs office for a pep talk when she turned up.'

'She must have gone out again and come back later,' Will said.

'I know because I saw her going in through the main doors at about quarter past eight. She was only a few yards in front of me and it was definitely her. I walked straight past because I wanted to get a coffee from that new Australian place first. But there was a huge queue, so it was a good twenty minutes before I came back, maybe a bit longer.'

Polynesia stared at him. Joanna! It was true that her behaviour had been rather odd in the days before the murder. Polynesia had sensed a certain shiftiness, and Joanna had made a few comments suggesting that she wasn't happy with Martin's management style. But was that sufficient reason to commit murder? You'd have to be abnormally career-focused to get so upset about your boss's poor leadership qualities.

'What do you think of Joanna?' she asked.

'I haven't thought much about her at all,' he said. 'She seems quite quiet and very self-contained. She's obviously good at her job, but a bit characterless really.'

'Funnily enough, that's pretty much what I thought about Martin, and look how wrong I was there,' Polynesia said with a wry smile.

Will laughed. 'Yes, he was a dark horse. Whoever would have guessed what was hidden behind that dull exterior!'

'Maybe Joanna did guess,' Polynesia hazarded. 'And she murdered him to stop him bringing the *Herald* into disrepute.'

'That sounds a little far-fetched,' Will said.

'You're right,' said Polynesia. 'Any self-respecting journalist loves a bit of disrepute, that's what sells papers.

'There might be a perfectly innocent explanation. Joanna might have gone into the building, realised that she'd forgotten to pick up some lunch, or some paracetamol and gone out again,' Will suggested. 'When she got back, Martin's body had been discovered and she kept quiet because she didn't want the police to label her as a suspect.'

'But surely it wouldn't take her an hour to buy lunch,' Polynesia objected. 'And how would she know that nobody had spotted her arriving earlier? It would look super-suspicious if she didn't mention it and then the police found out.'

'Maybe she did mention it. After all, we don't know what everyone else said to the police in their interviews.'

No, I suppose not,' she sighed. Then she brightened as a thought struck her. 'Hey, do you think she was having an affair with Martin too? She might have killed him in a fit of jealous rage when she realised that he was two-timing her with Alice.'

'It's possible, I suppose. I'm beginning to realise that where Martin was concerned, we need to expect the unexpected.'

'A man with the grey exterior of a middle-ranking civil servant, but the red-hot interior of a living sex legend,' said Polynesia, shaking her head in wonder.

'If only I'd realised while he was still alive, I could have asked him for his secret,' Will said, and she gave him a playful punch on the arm.

'Sorry, I've got to go,' he went on. 'But I'll ask Rebecca about that school if you like.'

'Rebecca?' she asked.

'Yes, my sister. Did I tell you she's a teacher? She might have some ideas. I'll let you know on Monday.'

He bent down and kissed her on the cheek, a proper kiss this time. Then he picked up his bag, gave her a smile and threaded his way out of the busy restaurant. Polynesia watched him go but made sure she didn't put her hand up to her face to touch the place he'd kissed until he was out of sight.

20

Chapter 20

Will phoned on Sunday afternoon and she was glad of the distraction. She'd been making notes and thinking of ways forward, only to meet a dead end every time.

'How was the party?' she asked.

Will groaned. 'Don't ask. Well, you can ask if you like, but as I've very little memory of what happened, you won't get much of an answer.'

'That good, eh?' she said.

'Never again. As I remember saying last time as well. Anyway, I'm calling because I have some interesting news for you.'

'Oh, yes?' Polynesia sat up straighter, her notepad of scribbled thoughts slipping off her lap.

'I spoke to my sister this afternoon, and I seem to have tapped into a vein of rule breaking, and exposed a fondness for criminal behaviour that I had no idea existed!'

'You mean about Petersham House?'

'Exactly! She was thrilled at the idea of making bogus calls to elicit confidential information. I didn't know whether to be shocked or impressed.'

Polynesia felt a momentary panic. 'Did you tell her why you need this information?'

'Only vaguely. She thinks it's all connected to a hush-hush news report. Which it is, in a way.'

'In a very tenuous way,' Polynesia said. 'We'll have to make sure she knows that anything she finds out is strictly confidential. Could we cobble together some secrecy agreement and get her to sign it?'

'This is my sister we're talking about. She doesn't need to sign anything, we'll shake hands on it. And then if she blabs, I'll smash her favourite mug and put jam in her shoes. That's the way siblings deal with each other.'

Polynesia laughed. 'Makes me glad I don't have any. If anyone put jam in my shoes, I'd probably shove their head down the loo.'

'Yep, that's another favourite,' Will said, and then he paused. 'Look, I was wondering if you wanted to come over this evening. We could put a script together for Rebecca and then talk her through it? And maybe order a takeaway? There's a Thai place that isn't bad.'

Polynesia thought of Dad downstairs in the kitchen, peeling the potatoes and carefully bringing the meat up to room temperature before he cooked the Sunday roast, his favourite meal of the week. She pictured the dining room table, covered with steaming vegetable dishes, a gravy boat, a large carving platter – and then at one end, a single place setting and a solitary wine glass.

'I'm really sorry, but I can't make it this evening. I'd love to, but …' she trailed away.

'Don't worry,' he said hurriedly. 'It was just a thought. Bit short notice really.'

'How about lunchtime tomorrow,' she said. 'If you're free? We could put the script together then. I'd like to get going on this as soon as possible.'

'That's fine. I'm in the office all day tomorrow.'

'Great! I'd like to meet your sister, obviously, and thank her for her help. It's just a bit difficult this evening,' she said.

'Of course. Some other time. See you tomorrow.' And he ended the call.

Polynesia bent down and retrieved the notebook. She stared at it moodily for a while and then began to scribble a few notes.

They chose a table outside a large, busy café. She didn't think that what they were doing would automatically lead to a prison sentence if they were caught, but there was no point in taking any chances. The customers here tended to grab a quick sandwich and a coffee and then get back to the office or to their sightseeing. They weren't hanging around listening to the people at a neighbouring table planning to prank call a headmistress.

'How was your evening?' Will asked.

'Good, thanks.' She didn't elaborate. 'How was the Thai takeaway?'

'Oh, I didn't bother in the end. It didn't seem worth it, just for one.'

Great! Now she felt guilty about two men sitting eating alone.

Will was looking down at the chicken Caesar baguette in his hand with more concentration than she felt it warranted, and she decided to be bold.

'I'd love to try it,' she said. 'Pad Thai is one of my absolute favourites. How about next weekend?'

'It's a date,' he said, looking up and smiling.

She grinned back, suddenly feeling ridiculously happy, and pulled out her notebook. 'I've had a few ideas ...'

Half an hour later they had a plan. Rebecca would introduce herself as the head teacher of a brand new school in Bedford, as yet totally unknown in the small world of private education. Clare has applied for a job there, and she sounded lovely in an informal chat but mentioned something about some issues at her last school that may mean she's not a suitable candidate. Rebecca, the head teacher, thinks Clare looks an excellent candidate on paper (Polynesia hopes this is true, and Clare certainly gave an impression of competence when they met) so Rebecca would like to know, off the record, if there's anything in Clare's past that would make her application a non-starter.

'Rebecca can't wait to get going on this,' Will said, as he put the notes he'd made in his pocket. 'I think she sees herself as some sort of undercover crusader for justice.'

'Don't disillusion her yet,' Polynesia advised. 'If she finds out that all this is designed to get our unpleasant boss off a murder charge, she might have second thoughts.'

They walked slowly back to the office, dodging the endless number of people posing for photos on the bridge. Everyone has their own photo pose these days, Polynesia thought as she watched them posturing for the camera. Back in the day, you just stood and smiled as the photographer snapped away, but now you have to pout and look down, or muss your hair and turn your head to one side. How do these people know what their best photo angle is? Do they experiment and find the perfect one for themselves or is there a website that gives you a body scan and then sends you the results?

Dear Polynesia,

The results of your scan indicate that you should put your right hand on your hip, tilt your head coquettishly to the left, and then look at the camera with an enigmatic smile.

She noticed that Will was looking at her, expectantly.

'Sorry, just daydreaming,' she said.

'I was asking if you'd like to come round tomorrow evening, so Rebecca can give us her report on the phone call? It might be easier if you hear it directly from her. Then I could make my famous carbonara.'

'Sounds awesome,' she said. Carbonara? Did she like that? She was sure she'd heard of it before. It sounded burnt, but hopefully that was just the name. Foreign words could be deceiving, as she knew from her French lessons at school. 'Remember, girls, that your *ancienne professeur* must never be translated as your ancient teacher,' Mademoiselle Muppart would say, chuckling as though this was the best joke she'd ever heard. Polynesia would have to ask her dad about carbonara, he'd be sure to know.

She left home the next evening armed with the knowledge that carbonara is a pasta dish made with eggs, bacon, and cheese, and that the name derives from the charcoal burners who'd first enjoyed this artery-clogging feast. So she was partly right; it did sound burnt, but only in the same way that pigs in blankets sounded cute and toad in the hole sounded repulsive. It was poetic licence, rather than a culinary description, she decided.

Will and Rebecca lived in a street of large Victorian semi-detached houses. You could tell which houses had been divided into flats, because the small front gardens were neglected. Nobody wants to spend money on a garden if they only have a one-third share in it, she supposed. Rebecca's was the first floor flat in a house with three large wheelie bins and a patch of weed-choked gravel filling the space between the low front wall and the house. The red front door looked newly painted, and there were three bells, all clearly labelled. She rang the middle one, which said *Rebecca Rowe* on a neatly typed label, and then *Will Rowe* was scrawled underneath in biro. They must be chalk and cheese, she thought.

She heard thudding footsteps and Will opened the door, his hair damp and his shirt clinging to his torso, as though he hadn't dried himself before getting dressed.

'Hi, Pol,' he said, and she noticed the abbreviation with pleasure. 'Sorry, just got out of the shower. I went out for a run. It was a bit too hot really, but I need to keep fit if I want to play for the Batterers again next season.'

'The what?' She pictured men in chain mail charging forward with battering rams. Was that ever considered a game?

'Battersea Rugby, better known as the Batterers. More for the similarity of the two words than for our fearsome reputation, I have to admit. Anyway, come up, Rebecca's just finishing her yoga.'

The rather tatty carpet on the stairs and landing gave way to beautiful wood flooring as Will ushered her into the flat. She looked around her and the whole place exuded expensive tranquillity. There were white plantation shutters at the windows, and two large sofas which screamed high-end chic. At the other end of the room was a glass dining table with a polished steel base and six matching chairs covered in what looked like padded, grey suede. Of course it was immaculately clean and tidy, she'd been expecting that, but it also looked like something out of a glossy magazine.

'Wow!' she said as she took it all in. 'I can see why Rebecca's houseproud. I didn't know teachers lived in such luxury these days.'

'Rebecca got a generous divorce settlement and sank it all into this place,' Will said. 'She needed a sanctuary after a few turbulent years. I help out by paying rent, and that gives her a bit of money to indulge her passion for interior design.'

A door opened and Rebecca came into the room. She was tall and extremely slim, wearing bright pink leggings and a strappy Lycra top. Her dark hair was held back with a wide stretchy band, her feet were bare and her toenails were electric blue.

'Polynesia, this is my sister, Rebecca,' Will said.

'Hi, there,' Rebecca lifted a hand in greeting, and then pulled off her hairband and shook out her long, straight, sleek hair.

Polynesia put a hand up to her own hair which was curlier than usual, thanks to the humid weather, and just as boringly light brown as ever. I'm a poodle, she thought glumly, and Rebecca's a beautifully groomed Afghan hound. For the first time she saw that being high maintenance wasn't always to be derided - you get what you pay for, after all. She paid for very little when it came to aesthetics and it was beginning to show, now that she was thirty. She was very much afraid that she was starting to go to seed. Get a grip, she told herself severely. You've got a good brain, and that's worth a lot more than beautiful hair.

'Hi Rebecca,' she said. 'Thank you so much for helping us

out, I do appreciate it.'

'Oh, my pleasure. Any time,' Rebecca said. 'I really enjoyed it, and it made a change from teaching Shakespeare to teenagers who've watched the film and don't see why they should read the book too.'

'I loved Shakespeare,' Polynesia said enthusiastically. 'I liked the insults best, I collected them. I used to go around calling people a cream-faced loon or a lump of foul deformity.'

Then, aware that this made her sound slightly weird, she changed the subject hurriedly. 'As Will explained, this is a potentially explosive story we're working on. Your input may well make the difference between success and failure.'

Will rolled his eyes, but Rebecca looked impressed.

'I recorded the conversation,' she told Polynesia. 'Then I made notes and deleted the recording, just in case my phone ever gets into the wrong hands.'

'A wise decision,' Polynesia said gravely.

Rebecca pulled a handful of A4 lined paper out of a large tote bag and sat down cross-legged on the geometric patterned rug. Polynesia perched on the edge of the sofa, hoping there was no bike oil on the back of her shorts.

'I made an appointment to ring Dr Webb, the Head, at lunchtime,' Rebecca began. 'Her secretary bought into my story completely and said she'd make sure Dr Webb was back at her desk. Apparently, she sometimes wanders around the school making her presence felt during the lunch hour. I decided to call myself Rebecca Rowan. Almost me, but not quite me, if you see what I mean.'

'Good thinking, Bex,' said Will.

'Anyway, Dr Webb was terribly nice. She congratulated me on my headship at a new school and said it must be wonderful to start with a clean slate and be able to put my own stamp on everything. I said yes, it was a fantastic opportunity. And you know, for a moment I almost believed I was Rebecca Rowan, brand new headteacher. It was surreal.

'Then Dr Webb said, "Actually Mrs Rowan, I'm glad you've phoned me because there is something you should know about Clare Trellis, and I wouldn't have felt comfortable putting it down in writing."'

Rebecca looked up triumphantly from her notes, and Will gave Polynesia a smile and a thumbs up.

'You were right about that. Well done, Pol!'

Polynesia glowed.

Rebecca went on, 'So I asked her if she could be a little more specific, and she said ... hang on a minute, I've got it here somewhere ... ah yes. She said "Mrs Trellis was unfortunately found in flagrante." She actually said that! Oh, and did I say she was Scottish? So she really rolled the r ... in flagrrrrante.' Rebecca started to laugh and then stopped abruptly. 'Actually, I think poor Dr Webb was rather shocked. She could hardly bring herself to say it.'

'Did she tell you who was in flagrante with Clare?' Polynesia asked, hoping Dr Webb had confided that it was a seventeen stone, ex-SAS, PE teacher, given to jealous rages and often seen with a murderous glint in his eye. That would make their investigation so much more straightforward.

'Yes, and it's too clichéd for words.' Rebecca shook her head in mock disapproval. 'You know Clare taught French and Russian? Well, it was the Russian language assistant. A moody Slav called Dmitri with soulful eyes and - best of all - he was twenty-two! They were caught *in flagrrrante* in the Modern Languages office after school one day. Dr Webb said she was thankful it wasn't a pupil who found them, or the police would have been involved. As it was, Clare resigned immediately, Dmitri went back to Russia and they managed to keep a lid on it.'

Rebecca looked up at Will and Polynesia with a gleam in her eyes. 'So, have I uncovered a disreputable gang of cougars, bringing young men over to England for sex?'

Without waiting for a reply, she went on, 'Only, if I have uncovered the gang, I do hope I'll have time to get myself a stud-muffin before you bust the whole thing wide open.' And she gave a snort of laughter.

Polynesia felt herself warming to Rebecca. Despite her obviously insane level of self-discipline and high standards of cleanliness, she sounded as though she had a good sense of humour.

'You'll have plenty of time. We're in the very early stages of the investigation,' Polynesia promised with a grin. She fished around in her bag and brought out a bottle of wine. 'I brought this to go with the carbonara.'

'Thanks,' said Will. 'I'll get a couple of glasses.'

'Oh, only two?' Polynesia asked.

'I don't drink, I'm afraid,' said Rebecca.

'And she won't be joining us for carbonara either,' Will added, 'because she's vegan.'

Of course she is, thought Polynesia. A teetotal vegan. Was there a better example of an iron will and self-discipline of steel?

21

Chapter 21

And another one bites the dust Polynesia hummed to herself as she sat at her desk the next day, pretending to be busy with some research about housing benefit fraud, but actually thinking hard about possible suspects. Now that her affair had been confirmed, Clare was off the list. She hadn't really considered Clare a prime suspect though, not since she'd met her, and she was glad to have her instinct backed up by evidence for once. She wondered whether it was Clare or Dmitri who had started the affair. But it would be a bold 22-year-old who made a move on his boss. Then she remembered how she and dad had once seen an immaculately turned out older woman with a scruffy young guy on holiday. He looked like a student in old jeans and a baggy t-shirt, and she behaved like his mother in the daytime, paying for everything and telling him he should be more adventurous in his eating. But when they got on the dance floor in the evening, nobody would have mistaken them for mother and son, he had his hands all over her and she obviously loved it. If you wanted youth and vigour, you had to sacrifice a certain amount of suavity and sophistication, she supposed.

She was interrupted in her musings by Joanna stopping at her desk.

'Sorry to interrupt, you look deep in thought,' she said. 'But I was hoping you could spare me five minutes for a quick update.'

Joanna gestured with her head towards her office and Polynesia obediently rose to her feet and followed her.

Joanna closed the door carefully and they sat on either side of her large well-organised desk. Polynesia noticed that one of the baskets of papers was labelled *pending* and she stared at it thoughtfully. Pending was a good word to describe her investigation so far. At every turn she found she needed something else to happen before she could progress, and it was very frustrating. Perhaps she should get herself a filing basket labelled *pending*? Then she could put all the unresolved stuff in there on separate pieces of paper and stop stressing about them. Once she'd got the information she needed, she could then update each piece of paper and move it out of *pending* and into the next basket, labelled *results*. She was sure this would be psychologically beneficial. But equally, it did sound like a lot of tedious work, and much the sort of thing that Bob Cratchit used to do as he sat on a high stool in his fingerless gloves, scratching away with his quill pen. She made a mental note to find a high-tech equivalent to the pending basket.

'So,' Joanna clasped her hands together on her desk and looked intently at Polynesia. 'I just wondered where we are. You know, vis-à-vis the article?'

'Well, as you saw, I was busy looking into the figures for housing benefit -' Polynesia began.

'Oh no, sorry. I meant the article about Martin,' Joanna

interrupted her. 'It's been at least two weeks since I found you those contacts at the *Post.* I was wondering how you were getting on? Is it ready to go? And more importantly, did you find anything shady in Martin's past that might explain his murder?'

Polynesia stared at her in surprise for a moment. She'd forgotten that Joanna didn't know there was never going to be an article about Martin, it was only a pretext for the interviews. Joanna had no idea that Polynesia was investigating the murder, and that Joanna herself was now a potential suspect. It wouldn't be a good idea to mention this either; Polynesia didn't relish the idea of being greeted by a twelve-inch carving knife on her arrival at work one morning.

She smiled brightly at Joanna. 'It's going well, thanks. I haven't finished yet because they're trying to track down Martin's secretary, Colette. Apparently, she knew him best, but she's moved on and they don't know where. So I've been waiting on that.'

'No skeletons in the cupboard, then?' Joanna spoke lightly.

Polynesia was thinking on her feet. Should she mention Rosa? If Joanna was looking for a scapegoat, then it would be a good idea. But if she'd been madly in love with Martin herself, it could be a very bad idea to mention a potential rival. She decided on prudence.

'No, no skeletons. Not even the teeniest fragment, I'm afraid. I thought I'd wait another week and if there's still no word about Colette by then, I'll just have to go with what I've got. Does that sound like a plan?'

Joanna sighed. 'I suppose so. But do let me know if you hear anything before then.'

'Of course.' Polynesia stood up to leave. Dammit, now she'd

have to write the article.

'You know, writing the article could be a good thing anyway,' Jess said, as they sat in Tokyo Express having lunch. 'Maybe someone who didn't even know that they knew something will suddenly realise that they did after all. That happens a lot.'

'You mean,' Polynesia put on her best amateur dramatic voice, 'now that I've read this article, I've suddenly realised that the mysterious, grey-suited man I saw carrying a body bag out of the *Morning Post* offices must have been Martin Trellis!'

'Exactly. You never know whose memory will be jogged. You need to cast your net wide and wait for the fishes to bite.'

'I don't think they bite in a wide net,' Polynesia pointed out. 'You're confusing fly fishing and net fishing.'

'Whatever,' said Jess. 'You know what I mean.'

'And how did you get on with Rosa? Any luck with finding her parents?'

Jess gave her a smug smile. 'You'll be impressed. You're not the only super-smart investigator round here.'

'Come on then. Don't leave me in suspense!'

'When I got home on Friday, I was all fired up with enthusiasm and Dan was busy in the kitchen, so I went online and – boom! It only took about ten minutes to find her, and then I tracked down her parents. It was lucky her dad's Serbian, that narrowed down the search a bit. Anyway, her name was Rosa Markovich and her parents live in Brighton.'

'Good work! I'll call them today.'

'Done it,' Jess looked even smugger. 'I called them on Saturday because I wanted to check they were the right

Markoviches, and they invited us to tea, me and Dan, on Sunday.'

Polynesia felt extremely put out. This was her investigation. Nobody should be going out having tea with potential suspects without her full permission. And Jess had taken Dan with her! What was this - some kind of *Take Your Family to Work* investigation? Not only had they gone to Brighton without telling her, but they'd had their cosy tea party on Sunday and it was now Wednesday. So Jess had held onto the information about Rosa's parents for three whole days.

'Why are you looking so cross, Pol? I thought you'd be pleased! I used my initiative, showed independence, and got results. What's the problem?'

'There are two problems as far as I can see. Why didn't you a) tell me beforehand that you were going, and preferably invite me along? Or b) at least tell me straightaway on Monday that you'd spoken to them?'

Jess looked hurt. 'I wanted to tell you in person. I wanted to impress you! When I suggested lunch on Monday you said you were seeing Will, so I decided you were probably more focused on him at the moment, and I'd wait until I saw you.'

Polynesia was slightly mollified. 'Will and I were planning the phone call to Petersham House. We weren't having a social lunch.'

'Ooh! How did it go?'

They discussed Rebecca's conversation with Dr Webb. Jess agreed that it was highly unlikely that Clare had murdered Martin because of his infidelity, when she was hardly monogamous herself.

Jess was equally convinced that Rosa's parents had played no part in Martin's killing.

'They're absolutely lovely,' she enthused. 'Sue made some scones and the most delicious lemon cake.'

'You can't just assume she's innocent on the strength of her excellent sponge cakes! She's obviously quite fiery. She called Alice a tart at the inquest.'

'I know, we talked about that and she's ashamed of what she said. She was grief-stricken and lashed out. Anyway, Milos has emphysema. He can hardly get up the stairs without help. I just can't see them getting on the train to London to commit murder. They were absolutely broken by Rosa's death and they're hoping some more press coverage might throw up new evidence. They're convinced that something sinister happened to her. They said she wasn't the sort of girl to go drunkenly stumbling around the streets.'

'I'm sure most parents say that about their children,' Polynesia said drily. 'Well, it looks as though I'll have to mention Rosa in the article I'm writing, and just hope that it doesn't provoke a fit of fury from Joanna.'

'Joanna?' Jess was intrigued.

'She was in the office early the day of the murder, Will saw her. But she's kept very quiet about it, and she's super-keen for me to find some incriminating information about Martin's past at the *Morning Post*.'

'Why will she be angry about Rosa?'

Polynesia looked thoughtful. 'Because I'm beginning to think that she's a spurned and jealous psychopath.'

Jess looked amazed. 'But surely you don't think she killed Martin?'

'I'll have more of an idea about that once I've found out what she was doing in the office that morning. I want to know why she arrived early and then left again, and why she hasn't told us that she was there. I just need to find some way of winkling the information out of her.'

'For God's sake be careful, Pol. We don't want a second murder at the *Herald.* Leave the heroics to the police.'

22

Chapter 22

Polynesia mulled over the problem that afternoon, in between banging out her article for the next day's paper and trying to avoid Pippa, who was going round the office collecting money for Melissa's baby. She didn't mind forking out a bit of cash for people she knew, but as Melissa had been on maternity leave for weeks, she felt that she hardly knew the woman and didn't see why she should be expected to part with five pounds just to celebrate someone else's fertility. The single, childless woman was at a real disadvantage in the workplace. She'd saved her colleagues a fortune over the years by not getting engaged, married or pregnant, and yet nobody had ever suggested a whip-round to celebrate her continued spinsterhood.

Feeling uninspired, she resolved to talk to Dad when she got home. Perhaps they could brainstorm and come up with an idea.

But when she got in, the house was empty. There was no note on the kitchen worktop, which was always Dad's favourite way of communicating any last-minute absences, so she wandered into the study to see what he'd been up to. Perhaps he'd been doing some bitcoin trading or researching how to hack into D.I. Wilson's computer, she thought, smiling to herself. The computer hacking had been her suggestion, born of frustration when she couldn't think of a way to discover whether there was any useful CCTV footage from the area around the *Herald* building on the morning of the murder. She didn't think Dad had taken her seriously, but she wouldn't have put it past him to have had a go and somehow succeeded. However, when she clicked on the mouse and the screen came to life, there was a picture of an idyllic tropical beach. Surprised, she leaned closer and read the text: *Rugged, covered with rainforest and endlessly diverse – no amount of superlatives does Costa Rica justice.* Dad hadn't mentioned anything about a holiday, and anyway, he liked going to France or Italy. She'd never heard him express interest in a tropical getaway.

Just then she heard his key in the door.

'Sorry I'm late, love,' he called. 'Been helping out at the library and our session overran. We had twenty people wanting help with getting online, or accessing their emails. And it wasn't just OAPs either.'

He came into the study and saw her standing in front of the computer.

'I didn't know you were interested in going to Costa Rica,' she said, indicating the screen.

'Oh, just doing a bit of general research,' he said. 'I may extend my horizons beyond the Med. And how was your day? Any new developments to report?'

Changing the subject was always Dad's way of indicating that he didn't want to discuss something, and she could understand his reluctance. Going on holiday with someone was a big step, and he might not be ready to talk about it yet. Perhaps he'd decided an older woman wouldn't be a bad bet after all, and was going to invite 90-year-old Veronica on an exotic holiday. And why shouldn't he? She'd been on at him for years to find himself a girlfriend.

'I was hoping we could do a bit of brainstorming this evening,' she said. 'I'm getting a bit stuck with my investigation.'

'How about tomorrow?' he suggested. 'Only there's a few things I need to look up this evening.'

'Silver Surfers keeping you busy?'

'Something like that. We could have another meeting of the Justice for Martin team tomorrow, if Jess is free.'

'Good idea. I'll ask her.'

So Polynesia spent the evening making notes, crossing things out, and making more notes, until she was happy that she had summarised the current situation:

1. Clare Trellis is no longer a suspect - her infidelity confirmed by headteacher.
2. Alice looks less likely as a suspect following confirmation of her story about Rosa.
3. Rosa's parents are probably not suspects, but might have to go back on the list if we run out of other suspects.
4. Colette the secretary is unlikely to reappear before the deadline for my article, and do we need her now anyway, given that Rosa's parents have been located?
5. Rosa's death will have to be mentioned in the article, along with the fact that the verdict was accidental death. But I need to imply that there might be more to it, whilst

being careful not to incriminate myself or the *Herald*.

6. Joanna is now a suspect. How can I find out why she was in the office that morning?

She looked at the page of notes and grimaced. It wasn't a lot for five weeks' work. On the plus side, she'd been hired to prove Alice's innocence, and Alice was still technically innocent. But on the minus side, everyone else was also technically innocent. The only way to prove beyond doubt that Alice was innocent, was to prove that someone else was guilty.

She went to bed, wondering whether the power of psychology would solve her problems as she slept. But she was beginning to think that psychology was like the elves and the shoemaker; you had to be surprised and grateful for any nocturnal revelations. If you started to expect them, and take them for granted, they just melted away and left you to struggle on alone.

In the end the Joanna solution presented itself suddenly and unexpectedly. It wasn't psychology but serendipity, Polynesia thought. She was crossing reception the next morning on her way to the lift when she heard a voice calling 'Hey, Pol!'

She looked around and saw Will coming through the doors and striding towards her. 'Have you got a minute?'

Without waiting for a reply he walked towards the small meeting room and peered inside. Satisfied that it was empty he went in, and Polynesia followed.

'What is it?' she asked

'Rebecca got a phone call from Dr Webb yesterday,'

'What?'

'Exactly. It seems that the Doc did a call back and Bex hadn't thought to hide her number. Anyway, she wanted Clare's address in Bedford to send a card. You know, condolences on Martin's death.'

'Eek!' said Polynesia.

'Exactly! Bex said she was sorry but she couldn't do it, data protection and all that. She suggested Dr Webb look online to try and find it. She also said that she'd decided not to take Clare's application any further, so would Dr Webb please not mention it to her.'

'Thank God your sister's a quick thinker!' Polynesia said. 'Or we could have been in a huge amount of trouble.' She shuddered.

'That's why I wanted you to know. We need to be much more careful in future.'

She was glad he'd said 'we', it made her feel all warm inside.

'Any progress your end?' he went on.

She told him about Joanna, about the conversation they'd had yesterday and her growing belief that Joanna was now the main suspect.

'But I just can't think of a way of find out what she was doing in the office that morning,' she finished.

'That's easy. I'll ask her,' Will said.

'You can't just ask her that!' she was aghast.

'Yes, I can. I'm the one who saw her, after all. I'll just say, very casually and innocently, that I noticed her coming into the building that morning. Then I'll say I bet the police were really pleased to have a witness, as the whole place was so empty that morning.'

She thought about this. If Joanna was the murderer and Will told her that he'd seen her coming into the building, what would Joanna do? Polynesia knew what she'd do in that position, she'd murder Will before he told anyone else.

'I'm coming with you when you ask her,' she said firmly. 'I don't want her bumping you off too.'

A summer's day is not when you see the News office at its frantic, truth-delivering best. Parliament is winding down for the summer recess, there are no marches, demos or protests because everyone's on holiday, and criminals traditionally view the long nights of winter as their peak season. So, with no urgent deadlines, it wasn't difficult for Will and Polynesia to find themselves casually engaged in conversation by the coffee machine and from there to sidle towards Joanna's office, where they could see her sitting at her desk twirling a pencil.

'Hey, Joanna,' Will said, leaning casually on the door frame with the well-practised ease of a reality TV star. 'Polynesia and I were just discussing the article she's writing about Martin. And I said, wouldn't it be great if Joanna had actually seen something significant when she arrived that morning?' He paused. 'I mean you might even have seen the murderer!'

Joanna went white and stared at him. 'Why would I have seen anything?' she said, finally. 'I didn't arrive until half-past nine.'

'I meant the first time you arrived,' Will explained in an innocent tone. 'I saw you come in at about quarter past eight when I was on my way to grab a coffee. I expect you dashed in and then dashed out again to an important meeting. But I thought you might have seen someone or something unexpected.' He gave a shrug that managed to be both elaborate and casual. Playing a role convincingly was obviously a talent that the Rowe siblings shared.

Polynesia was totally unprepared for what happened next. Joanna stood up, strode to the door and slammed it shut, forcing Will to leap out of the way. She stood with her back to the door and glared at them.

'Now, listen to me. If, and I repeat if, I was here early that morning, it was for a reason that I have no intention of disclosing to you. It's utterly irrelevant because I didn't see Martin or that little tart either.'

It was the second time Alice had been called a tart, Polynesia reflected. She wasn't going to like it when she found out.

'I didn't see anyone at all,' Joanna went on. 'Except the electrician doing the PAT safety testing on all the computers, and that cleaner with a limp who barely speaks any English.'

'Esteban,' Will said promptly.

Polynesia looked at him in surprise. How did he know the name of some random non-English-speaking cleaner?'

Joanna continued to glare. 'Whatever,' she said.

It was like watching a wolf suddenly strip off its sheep's clothing. You'd been convinced for years that it was a sheep, and then you suddenly wonder how on earth you could have been so utterly fooled, because this was quite patently a wolf.

'And,' she went on, 'if you breathe a word of this to anybody else, there are some important people in high places who will be very upset. If that happens, I'm afraid, you'll give me no choice and I'll have to sack you both. Is that understood?'

Dumbly they both nodded.

Joanna moved away from the door, wrenched it open and motioned them out.

Dad sat with the lamb tagine in front of him forgotten, as he listened to Polynesia's story. Jess was twisting her napkin round and round in her hands as she shared her friend's distress.

'So what am I going to do?' Polynesia wailed. 'Unless I drop the whole thing, she's going to sack me!'

'If she sacks you and then they arrest her, you're bound to get your job back,' Jess said encouragingly.

'And if they don't arrest her, I won't,' Polynesia said morosely.

'So she was there all the time. But she says she didn't see anything,' Dad said thoughtfully.

Do you think she's lying?' Jess asked. 'Maybe she saw the murderer and wants to get the scoop for herself?'

'If that was the case, why wait?' Polynesia said. 'Why wouldn't she have told her story immediately?'

'Because of the important people she told you about?' Jess hazarded. 'She might have been with the Prime Minister or someone. They wouldn't want to get mixed up in a murder investigation.'

Polynesia snorted. 'Do you really think the Prime Minister would turn up at the *Herald* offices at eight o'clock on a Thursday morning? I don't think the important people were actually there with her, it was more of a threat that they'd get involved if we don't shut up. She says she only saw a random electrician and a Venezuelan cleaner called Esteban that Will knows because he practises his Spanish on him sometimes.'

'But can we believe her?' Dad said. 'Look, Will knows this cleaner chappie. Why doesn't he talk to him and see if he saw anything. Joanna's never going to find out, as she doesn't talk to the cleaners.'

'I'll ask Will. But I wouldn't be surprised if he didn't want to be involved any more,' Polynesia said gloomily. 'He offered to help out and now he's been threatened with the sack.'

'It looks like that's our only avenue for now, love, until the article comes out next week. Then we'll have to hope for some new leads.' Dad patted her hand encouragingly. 'Now, I've made a strawberry shortcake, if anyone can manage a piece.'

'Finally, some good news!' Jess pumped her fist in the air.

23

Chapter 23

News Editor's Violent Death Remains a Mystery.

Five weeks after the lifeless body of Martin Trellis was discovered in his office at the Daily Herald, his death continues to baffle police.

She stopped here, wondering whether D.I. Wilson would be phoning her in a huff to say that she wasn't baffled at all and merely biding her time. Oh well, if she did, it would give Polynesia the opportunity to pump her for information. She looked down at her notes and began to type rapidly.

She sketched a picture of Martin's adult life from university right through to his time at the *Morning Post*. There were plenty of quotes from colleagues about what a good chap he'd been - nobody could understand why – such a senseless waste - etc etc.

Then followed a carefully worded paragraph about Martin's connection with Rosa.

Rosa Markovich was an influencer looking to partner with high profile individuals, both to deepen her understanding of the British press and to pass that knowledge on to her many Instagram followers.

Polynesia hoped this didn't sound too unbelievable. She wasn't convinced that many Instagram users had a burning desire to understand the mechanics of the free press.

Like Martin's murder, Rosa's death remains shrouded in mystery. However, the police and the Daily Herald continue to hope that new evidence will come to light to explain both the tragic chain of events which led to Rosa drowning, and the reason why a well-respected news editor was stabbed to death in his office at eight o'clock on a Thursday morning.

She had her own byline, *Polynesia Henman Deputy News Editor,* but no photograph. And after her recent contretemps with Joanna, she didn't think it would be wise to request one. She added her email address, hoping that it would encourage people to contact her directly, then sent it Joanna for approval. Barring any major inaccuracies requiring a rewrite, it would appear in tomorrow's paper.

Apart from the article, her investigation was in the doldrums. Will, infuriated by Joanna's threats, was delighted by the idea of getting one over on her, and he was all in favour of covertly continuing the investigation. He came in early to interview Esteban, ready to do it in Spanish if necessary, only to find that the cleaner had gone away on holiday and wouldn't be back for another ten days.

'It's a bit suspicious, isn't it,' he said disconsolately to Polynesia. 'The fact that he's gone away just when I want to talk to him about the murder?'

'I don't think there's anything suspicious about someone going on holiday in July,' she said. 'If we start suspecting everyone and everything, we won't be able to see the wood for the trees. Talk to him when he gets back. In the meantime, fingers crossed that we get some information after the article's published.'

Polynesia's phone gave a soft ping and she glanced down at the screen. It was a text message from Clare Trellis:

Hi Polynesia, wondered if it would be convenient to have a quick chat?

Oh God! Her pulse quickened. Had she found out about the phone call? Had Doctor Webb told her after all? Calm down, she told herself sternly. Even if Clare knew that the phone call was a set-up, she didn't know that Polynesia had anything to do with it. The only details Dr Webb had were Rebecca's phone number and a false name, there was nothing there to tie in with Polynesia or the *Herald*.

She took a deep breath and replied:

Fine.

Almost immediately the phone started to ring.

'Hi Clare, how are you?'

'Feeling like a walrus at the moment. Not long to go now though.'

'That's good.' Polynesia hoped this was a suitable response despite Clare's ambivalence about the baby.

'Anyway,' Clare got straight to the point. 'I thought I'd call because you told me you were helping an old school friend to prove her innocence, and I'm pretty sure you said her name was Alice Smith.'

'That's right.'

'Well, something rather odd has been going on. I don't understand it, but I thought you might.'

Polynesia felt a stab of excitement. 'What's happened?'

'This week I finally felt up to sorting things out. You know, getting rid of his clothes, filing away his old papers and so on. I want to get it all done before the baby's born. Yesterday I started filing away all Martin's bank statements, which were stuffed into an old envelope at the back of his desk. But when I looked at them, I could hardly believe it. Martin had virtually no money at all!'

What was she trying to say, Polynesia wondered. Had Martin had a gambling habit or a drug problem?

'Well, the cost of living is going up,' she began. 'And if you weren't working -'

'Oh no! I have my own money. Martin hadn't been subbing me. We always paid our own way and he was very careful with his money. He liked to have a contingency fund. A solid financial cushion, he called it.'

That sounded like the Martin Polynesia knew from the office.

'He could have transferred it to a savings account or bought shares,' Polynesia suggested.

'I've checked all that and there was nothing. Just his ISA and a few Premium Bonds. You might think this sounds silly. But it was so unlike him to have run his bank account down to almost nothing, that I wondered,' Clare paused for a moment, 'well, I wondered whether he'd had a premonition that he was going to die and had decided to splash out for once.'

'So what had he been spending it on?' Polynesia was intrigued.

'That's the thing. When I looked closely, there were large sums of money going out every month and always to the same person. The description on the bank statement just says *payment to A Smith*. So I thought about Alice Smith and wondered if it could be her?'

Polynesia's mind whirled. On the one hand, she wouldn't put it past Alice to deviously defraud her lover. But on the other hand, Smith was a common name and she mustn't jump to conclusions.

'I don't know, but I'll find out,' she said. 'Send me a photo of one of the statements and I'll talk to Alice and get to the bottom of all this.'

It was all getting very confusing. Her potential culprits were leaping on and off the podium labelled *Main Suspect* with such regularity that it was beginning to look like a step class. Just as Joanna stepped up, with her admission of being in the office early, Alice came steaming back to knock her off pole position. Although, she reasoned, extracting large sums of money out of someone isn't the same as killing them. And if Alice had found a way of parting Martin from his monthly salary, why would she want to kill him? But then again, as far as she remembered, the goose that laid the golden eggs had been butchered with a large kitchen knife just like Martin. Clearly, being acknowledged as a generous provider wasn't enough to guarantee a nice long lifespan.

She sighed and messaged Alice. They arranged to meet after work the next day at a juice bar. Even an oat milk decaf was apparently now poison to Alice's system. Funny that someone so poisonous should be so susceptible herself, Polynesia thought.

The article appeared in Thursday's edition of the paper and Polynesia waited all day for someone to make contact. She was convinced that the missing pieces of the jigsaw were tantalisingly close, she just couldn't see where they were. She remembered going to a lecture about the fourth dimension once at university. A famous scientist had been invited as a guest lecturer and pretty much everyone in her college had turned up to listen to him. Getting their heads around the concept of the fourth dimension was tricky for the non-scientists and the lecturer tried to simplify the concept. He explained that if we lived in a 2-D world we'd all be flat and move along the ground. We'd only be able to look straight ahead of us, and even if there was something enormous dangling just over our heads, we wouldn't be able to see it because we'd have no idea where to look. She hadn't totally grasped the idea of the fourth dimension, to be honest, but she'd always remembered the image of the flat people having no idea what was above their heads, and that was how she felt now. There was something significant and it was practically within her grasp, if she could only work out exactly where she should be looking.

At five-thirty she gave up. She checked her emails one final time, confirmed that nobody had contacted her about the article, and switched off her computer. She grabbed her bag and walked towards Borough Market to find La Juiceria, and then shuddered as she looked at the menu board outside. Inside, she could see small tables with an assortment of unusually dressed people perched uncomfortably on wooden stools sipping lurid green or purple drinks, with no obvious enjoyment. Do people who like drinking kale juice start wearing socks with sandals to fit in with the crowd, or do sock and sandal wearers end up drinking kale juice because this is where their tribe hangs out?

Alice arrived as she was pondering this chicken and egg conundrum, and they went in together. Alice was dressed casually in a cream denim mini skirt and baseball boots but seemed very much at home with the Happy Socks and sliders brigade.

'I've been seeing a nutritionist,' she explained. 'Shona's just great. She ran some homeopathic tests and I have a very delicate digestive system. So many things are just poison to me, it's no wonder I've been feeling terrible lately.'

'I thought you were feeling terrible because you'd been accused of murder and the *Herald* has put you on gardening leave,' Polynesia said sourly.

'Those things are outside my control,' Alice said serenely. 'Shona has explained to me that I just have to let them float away. But I can control the toxins in my diet. So it's clean eating for me from now on.'

'What can I get you?' asked the bearded man behind the counter, the studs in his ears catching the light.

'I'll have the green cleanse,' said Alice. 'Polynesia, I'd recommend the carrot, orange and ginger. It's a good one for beginners.'

'Do you want spirulina with that?' Beardy asked Polynesia.

She looked at him blankly. Wasn't Spirulina a character in a fairy story?

'Spirulina's a type of algae,' Alice explained. 'Very good for the immune system.'

'No, thank you,' Polynesia shuddered. 'Just the beginner's juice for me.'

'... if I have to,' she added silently to herself.

They took their drinks and perched on a couple of the low stools that turned out to be as uncomfortable as they looked. Polynesia took a sip and had to admit that it wasn't bad at all. It was sweet and zingy and gave her a warm gingery glow.

'What's in yours?' she asked.

'Kale, parsley, green apple and lemon,' Alice said. 'I'm detoxifying my colon.'

'Well, I hope you'll keep any toxins firmly inside your colon while I'm sitting anywhere near you.'

'Very funny.'

They both took another sip of juice, and Alice looked expectantly at Polynesia.

'You said there'd been a development,' Alice said. 'What sort of development?'

'Did you see my article about Martin today?' Polynesia asked.

'No, I've stopped reading the papers. It's bad for my mental health, Shona says.'

'Shona's a psychiatrist as well, is she?' Polynesia made a dismissive noise. 'It's a pity you didn't see the article. It was on page two, and I had my own byline.'

'Is this development a result of your article?'

'Oh no, nothing like that. I just thought you'd be pleased to know that I'm doing so well in the News team.'

Alice gave her a tight smile.

'The development has come from Clare Trellis,' Polynesia said. 'She phoned me this morning to say that she'd been going through Martin's papers –' she paused here and watched Alice carefully, noticing the wary look appear in her eyes.

'And she found something very strange,' she went on. 'Large sums of money have been paid out of Martin's bank account every month to someone called A Smith, and Clare knows that the police have been questioning someone called Alice Smith in connection with her husband's murder. So I'd like to know exactly what's been going on, please.'

Polynesia sat back on her stool, folded her arms and looked Alice firmly in the eye.

'Do the police know?' Alice asked in a small voice.

'Not yet,' Polynesia said. 'Clare had only just made the discovery when I spoke to her, she wasn't sure whether or not it had anything to do with the murder .'

'It doesn't have anything to do with the murder, so she doesn't need to tell them.' Alice's expression was part-defiant and part-terrified.

'I suggest you tell me exactly why you think it has nothing to do with the murder,' Polynesia said. 'And if I'm not convinced, we'll tell the police. I'm sure they'll be very interested to learn about large sums of money appearing in your Nat West Super Saver from the man you claim you didn't murder.'

Alice looked defeated. 'OK. I'll tell you the truth.'

'I seem to remember that you've told me the "truth" at least twice before, and neither version included any mention of you syphoning great wads of cash out of Martin's bank account.'

'When Martin and Rosa first started seeing each other, I was a bit … well, a bit pissed off really,' Alice began. 'I'd been working hard to cultivate him. You know, laughing at his jokes, making out I thought he was a good catch.'

'Didn't you think he was a good catch?' Polynesia interrupted.

'God, no! He was a boring grey man in a grey suit,' said Alice, unconsciously echoing Polynesia's own feelings about Martin. 'But I thought he'd be useful because he had a lot of contacts, and he could pull strings for me.'

'Go on,' said Polynesia grimly.

'I was just getting to the point where I felt I could ask him for something, some help to find a job or an internship or something, and then Rosa waltzed in and snatched him.' Alice's face darkened suddenly. 'She always was totally selfish and greedy. Then they started sleeping together at our flat and Rosa kept going on about all the things Martin had promised to do for her, like introduce her to top journalists and politicians. She was planning a podcast and a YouTube channel and all sorts of other things. But after a few months when Martin hadn't introduced her to anyone, she got fed up. She said she'd tell him that unless he did what he'd promised, she was going to contact his wife.'

'And so they went out for a drink together,' Polynesia said.

'Yes, that's right. Then he came rushing back to the flat at about three o'clock in the morning and said there'd been a terrible accident. Rosa had suddenly fallen into the water while they were walking along the Embankment. She must have slipped, he said.'

'I bet he did. So what happened next?'

'He was terrified that someone would find out that they'd been together, and he'd be accused of killing her. "She had too much to drink, she must have lost her balance and fallen in" he kept saying.'

'What? She managed to topple over a chest-high parapet?' Polynesia said incredulously. 'Surely you didn't believe that?'

'I could see that this was a way to get what I wanted,' Alice said simply. 'I told him I'd give him an alibi in exchange for money and a job as a journalist.'

Polynesia stared at her in horror. 'Oh my God, Alice! You've covered up a murder and you've been blackmailing a murderer. Even for you that's good going! It's a criminal offence, you're an accessory!'

'I'm not an accessory if I say I believed it was a tragic accident, am I?'

'If you believed it was a tragic accident, you'd hardly be stiffing him for practically his entire salary every month!'

They glared at each other for a moment, and then Polynesia sighed.

'Why didn't you tell me all this in the first place?'

'I thought you might not want to help me. Look, I know I'm an accessory and a blackmailer. But I'm not a murderer. And why would I murder Martin anyway? He was my golden ticket.'

'Yes, I also came to that conclusion,' Polynesia said reluctantly. 'But what I don't understand is, everyone in the News team said he was mad about you. Apparently he kept staring at you in meetings and asking you to come into his office for cosy little tête-à-têtes.'

'He kept calling me into his office to tell me he couldn't afford to keep paying me so much, that his wife was bound to find out,' Alice shrugged, 'And I expect he was staring at me wishing I'd just drop dead.'

'Yes, this does all seem to be the wrong way round,' Polynesia said thoughtfully. 'If *he'd* killed *you*, then I could understand it. Mind you, if anyone at all had killed you, I could understand it.'

'That's not funny, Polynesia.'

'I'm not joking.'

24

Chapter 24

Alice had found Martin dull. That was a relief. When she'd thought that everyone except her found Martin irresistible, Polynesia had begun to worry that there was something wrong with her, and that was why she'd failed to respond to his magnetic allure. Now that she knew Alice had viewed him as her personal cash dispenser and career coach, she felt a lot happier. Why hadn't she realised before that a girl like Alice would only be interested in him for what she could get out of the relationship? And Rosa too, of course. And then there was Clare, who'd been playing around elsewhere while her husband was being used by two ambitious, scheming women. She started to feel a little sorry for Martin. Did he know that he was being used and two-timed?

Polynesia went back to the *Herald* to collect her bike and cycled home thinking about what to do next. She ought to suggest a meeting of the Justice for Martin team to discuss developments, but she was reluctant to, because Will should really be invited to join since he was now just as involved as the rest of them. The problem was, she didn't want Dad eagerly sizing him up as a potential boyfriend/son-in-law, or Jess looking him over to make sure he was still a contender for her Plan B Contingency Partner, or whatever she'd called it. She wasn't ready for all that yet, and even if she had been ready, who was to say what Will wanted? He might be horrified at the thought of meeting her dad and the implications that went with it. No, she'd just have a quick chat with Dad once she got home and then she really should go to the gym, she hadn't been for ages. Forty minutes on the cross trainer would give her plenty of time to reflect on what to do next. She thought about Rebecca's willowy frame and mentally compared it to her own athletic build. Rebecca's legs were long and sinuous, whereas Polynesia's had solid well-defined calves and powerful thighs from all that cycling. She made a mental note to investigate yoga classes. Perhaps if she stretched everything out a bit, she'd looked a little less, well ... less sturdy. She remembered a short-lived boyfriend at university saying, as he marvelled over her muscled legs, 'I do like going out with a girl who could fell me in a bout of kickboxing. It takes away the stress of having to be a protective alpha male.' She'd thought at the time that it was meant as a compliment, but now she wasn't so sure.

She could smell curry as she opened the front door. Perhaps she wouldn't go to the gym after all, that carrot juice had made her hungry.

'Smells great, Dad!' She went into the kitchen to see him peering into a large saucepan on the hob.

'I'm having a go at a Goan fish curry,' he said, and laughed.

She looked at him blankly. Why was that funny?

He stopped laughing and shrugged. 'Actually it was funnier in the future tense. I told them at Bitcoin for Beginners this morning that I was goin' to have a go at a Goan fish curry, and they thought it was hilarious.'

Polynesia smiled politely. Was this how dementia started?

Her father seemed to read her thoughts. 'No need to look at me so pityingly, love. I haven't lost my marbles yet. I expect you had to be there, as they say these days.'

'I'm glad you've still got your marbles, because I need to talk to you about today's bombshell.'

'What about Jess? Shouldn't we be having a team meeting, then?' asked her father.

'I can't keep expecting her to schlep all the way over here. I'll fill her in tomorrow at lunchtime.'

'I've got some nice cold Kingfisher beer. Let's sit down and have a drink while the rice is cooking.'

Dad looked grim as Polynesia outlined her conversations with Clare and Alice.

'Blackmailing a murderer!' he said. 'Does she have any idea how dangerous that is?'

'Well, it doesn't seem to have done her much harm,' Polynesia pointed out.

'No, but it could have done. Look at what happened to Rosa!'

'Oh, Alice is too savvy to let that happen to her. There's probably a letter in her solicitor's safe which says T*o be opened in the case of my sudden death,* that points the finger directly at Martin. And of course she would have told him about it.'

'So what's the next step?'

She sighed. 'I just don't know, Dad. Investigating a murder isn't as easy as I'd hoped.'

'You mean you hoped it would be Alice and that's why you decided to investigate.'

'Yes. Does that mean I'm a terrible person?'

'Look, love. She made your life a misery when you were at school, and then she started again when you had the misfortune to run into her at work. She's a nasty piece of work, and nobody would blame you for hoping she was guilty of a murder that even the police think she committed.'

Dad squeezed her hand and she felt tears of self-pity stinging her eyes. Get a grip and stop being pathetic, she commanded herself. She took a deep, steadying breath.

'Alice is a bully and a bitch and a blackmailer. I also think she's clinically amoral, if that even exists as a disorder.'

'I think it's called sociopathy,' her dad said.

'Then she's most definitely a sociopath. She's also the most repellent human being I've ever met. But what I don't believe she is, no matter how hard I try, is a murderer. And that's what I'm finding very difficult to come to terms with at the moment.' And she burst into tears.

'Come on, Pol, love, this isn't like you,' Dad moved around the table to give her a hug. 'Whatever happened to my feisty girl?'

'Oh, Dad! The last few months have been so awful. She's belittled me, used me and turned other people against me. And now I'm on her side! She didn't kill Martin and I can't carry on pretending that I think she did without losing my integrity. That means she'll be back as my boss once the police investigation's over, and nothing will have changed.'

Dad laughed. 'Polynesia, you don't seriously think that the *Herald* is going to carry on employing someone who covered up a murder and blackmailed the murderer? She's going to prison, if not for murder, then most definitely for blackmail and for being an accessory to murder. She won't be coming back to the *Herald*.'

She looked at him and suddenly felt much brighter.

'You might have brains aplenty my girl,' Dad said, 'but sometimes a bit of common sense is what you need to see the light at the end of the tunnel.'

'You're right, Dad. I was so focused on the murder aspect that I forgot she's a criminal, even if she's not a murderer.'

'With Alice out of the picture, I reckon that deputy editor's job is yours permanently,' Dad said.

'Only if I stop trying to solve the murder,' she said. 'Because if I don't stop, Joanna's going to sack me.'

'Only if she catches you, love.'

The next morning, a brief scan of the online comments about her article revealed nothing but sympathetic platitudes, and not very many of those either. Martin Trellis was already yesterday's news. She was checking her emails disappointedly, when a new one popped into her inbox and she stared at it.

To Polynesia Henman

From Colette O'Hanrahan

Subject: Martin Trellis

Holding her breath she opened the email:

> *Dear Ms Henman*
>
> *I believe you've been trying to get hold of me. I apologise for not replying to any of the messages sent by Guy Frobisher and his secretary, but I've been trying to put my time at the Post behind me and move on. However, when I read your article in the Herald, and in particular your hope that new evidence would come to light to explain why Martin Trellis might have been killed, my Catholic need to confess got the better of me.*

Well, thank God for the confessional, thought Polynesia, and she read on.

When I heard that Martin had been murdered, my first thought was that there must have been quite a few husbands and boyfriends who would have wanted him out of the way. He was a serial philanderer, I'm afraid. But as he was good at his job, the management turned a blind eye. He wasn't interested in me, I was far too old for him, so I felt it was my duty to stay on in my job and be a sort of gatekeeper, if you like. Perhaps I didn't do it very well, but at the very least I stopped him employing a young secretary and ruining her future happiness.

You mentioned Rosa Markovich in your article, but all I know about her is that she drowned and Martin was the last person to see her alive. That meant he had to give evidence at the inquest. He seemed very stressed about it, so perhaps he had real feelings for her.

The misogynistic culture at the Post was a gift to someone like Martin, and I honestly thought he'd stay there for ever. When he left, I was surprised and relieved. I believed I'd done my duty and I resigned without any feelings of guilt and returned to Dublin to work part time and help look after my parents.

I can't give you any names, unfortunately. But if I were you, I'd look for the pretty girls in the office and question them carefully. Although I must warn you that he was very careful at covering his tracks.

I wish you and the police good luck with your investigation,

With kind regards

Colette O'Hanrahan

Polynesia felt extremely frustrated and explained this at great length to Jess at lunchtime.

'So Colette only told you what you already know. And literally the only lead you have at the moment is Joanna being in the office early that morning and refusing to say why?' Jess asked.

'That's pretty much it,' Polynesia said, removing a piece of red onion from her salad and flicking it onto the tray. 'So we've reached an impasse, as Hercule Poirot might have said.'

'Oh, I don't think so,' Jess said in a matter-of-fact tone. 'I think the next step is very obvious. You need to break into Joanna's office and look for evidence.'

Polynesia goggled at her. 'Have you lost your mind? That's the most insane suggestion I've ever heard!'

'Look, Pol. You think Joanna's guilty, and she's threatened to sack you if you don't stop the investigation. Ergo, there must be evidence somewhere that could convict her, or else she wouldn't be worried. And where is it most likely that the evidence is hidden? In her office, of course.' Jess gave Polynesia a bright smile. She looked as though she was explaining logic to a simpleton, Polynesia thought.

'If it's so obvious that there's something in her office, why don't you search it? She hasn't threatened to sack you,' Polynesia said.

'Oh no, I couldn't possibly do it,' Jess said. 'Firstly, I don't work in the News department. If anyone saw me there, it would look odd. Secondly, if I was caught in Joanna's office, I'd have no excuse whatsoever for being there, unlike you.

And thirdly, if I got caught, everyone knows I'm your friend,so she'd think you put me up to it and she'd sack us both.'

'Dad said much the same last night,' Polynesia told her. 'He told me I need to carry on with the investigation, because she'll only sack me if she catches me.'

'I love your dad,' Jess said. 'The bravery of a lion, the wisdom of Solomon and the passion of a chef.'

'It's very easy to be brave if you're not the one doing the actual burglary,' Polynesia grumbled, 'and what would I be looking for anyway?'

'I don't know ... files, letters, a diary? It'll be obvious once you find it,' Jess said confidently. 'Why don't you ask Will to help you? You'll need an accomplice to act as lookout.'

'You seem very familiar with the vocabulary of crime. Should I be worried?'

'It's the legacy of a childhood spent watching Midsomer Murders with my gran. If you need an investigator because someone's been crushed to death by a giant cheese, or coated in truffle oil and thrown in front of a wild boar - well, then I'm your girl.'

'I'll remember that,' Polynesia assured her. 'And it's not a bad idea to ask Will to help.'

'I'm full of good ideas. You'll have to start paying me a consultancy fee soon.'

Jess had to hurry back to work; her article on spa bathrooms wasn't 'aspirational enough' apparently, so she'd have to find some celebrity bathrooms to to sex it up a bit. Polynesia wasn't in a hurry, she'd only sit there checking her emails constantly if she went back to her desk, so she decided to go for a walk. She was wandering along towards Tower Bridge when she suddenly realised that she'd never rung Clare back to tell her about Alice. She needed to tell her of course, but wasn't sure how much to tell her. It would be a terrible shock for Clare to find out that her husband had been blackmailed, and she knew that pregnant women shouldn't have shocks because it could bring on premature labour. She'd learnt this from the many soap opera storylines she'd had to summarise, while working as an intern on a tabloid many years ago. She decided to be vague about why Martin had been paying Alice so much money ... *a colleague in need...* that sounded suitably altruistic.

She sat on a bench and called Clare, who answered sounding rather out of breath.

'Are you all right?' Polynesia asked.

'I think my labour may have started. I'm just practising my breathing.' Clare sounded remarkably composed.

'Oh my God! I'll call back another time. You've got much more important things to be doing now.'

'I haven't, actually,' Clare said. 'Nothing I do is going to make it go any faster, so I might as well talk to you. It'll take my mind off things anyway. So what did you find out?'

The shock of the truth wasn't going to bring on labour if she was already in labour, Polynesia reasoned. And it might even speed things up a bit, despite Clare's assertions that her childbirth time frame was set in stone.

'You were right. It was Alice that Martin was paying every month,' she said.

There was a silence, and then Clare began huffing and puffing again. Polynesia waited.

'But why?' Clare asked, eventually. 'I mean, I saw your article yesterday. Is it something to do with this influencer he knew who drowned? I remember him going to the inquest. He said it was a colleague who'd committed suicide and he was the last to see her. He didn't mention that they were together at three o'clock in the morning.'

'Look, nothing's certain,' Polynesia said. 'All I know is that Alice saw an opportunity to exploit a weakness. But it does seem as though Martin might have been … err … romantically attached to Rosa Markovich.'

There was silence at the other end of the phone. Then Clare gave a short, bitter laugh.

'All this time I've been feeling guilty for cheating on Martin, and now it turns out that he was doing exactly the same. Only he was better at it than me and he didn't get caught.'

'He didn't get caught by you,' Polynesia pointed out. 'But he did get caught by Alice, and that turned out to be very expensive for him.'

There was the sound of heavy breathing again.

'Go and have your baby,' Polynesia said. 'The police will be in touch about the money. I'm sure they'll be going through Alice's bank accounts.'

She thought she heard a grunted 'OK' from the other end.

'Good luck, Clare!' she shouted over the sounds of panting. 'Let me know how you get on!'

She ended the call and walked back to the *Herald*. With any luck, Will would be there, and she could suggest a get-together. Not a date, just a meeting to further the ends of the Justice for Martin campaign. But all the same, it would be nice to see him away from the office, and to have the chance to make him smile and then admire the dimples in his cheeks. However, thinking about the spot of burglary she was planning, she realised that it was hardly likely to make him smile.

25

Chapter 25

She'd been absolutely right about the non-smiling bit. Will was appalled.

'Break into Joanna's office?' he spluttered, almost spilling his beer. 'We could be arrested!'

'Not if we find something that incriminates her,' Polynesia said, trying to sound calm and reasonable.

'Like what?'

'Files, letters, jewels, briefcases full of money... I don't know! But there's got to be something there. Question - who stops people from trying to solve a crime? Answer - a criminal does!'

She was speaking more loudly than she'd intended, and several people in the pub garden turned around to look at her. She lowered her voice and went on.

'Anyway, I thought you were really keen to carry on with the investigation. You know, one in the eye for Joanna, isn't that what you said?'

'I'm keen to carry on with discretion,' Will corrected her. 'It's one thing to talk to Esteban discreetly in the cleaners' cubbyhole. But it's quite another thing to make a forced entry into our boss's office and search it.'

'That's the whole point,' Polynesia explained. 'We won't need to force anything because the door won't be locked. One of us will be the searcher and the other will be the lookout. The searcher goes inside and then if the lookout signals that Joanna's approaching, the searcher nips out and is back to their desk before she's rounded the corner. I'll do it on my own if I have to, but it would be absolutely foolproof with two of us.'

He looked at her without speaking.

'I bet Rebecca would do it,' she said.

'She probably would,' he said and then he sighed loudly. 'All right, I'll do it. I don't want to, but I will.'

She jumped up, stretched across the table and kissed him.

'Thanks, Will. This is the breakthrough, I know it is!'

'If I'd realised this was what you were looking for in a relationship, I'd have suggested a bit of burglary weeks ago,' Will said, taking hold of her hands as she sat down again.

Relationship ... he'd actually said relationship!

'Are we in a relationship then?' she asked, looking him directly in the eye.

He grinned mischievously. 'Well, it's early days, of course. But if we can survive a murder investigation, fake phone calls, burglary and doubtless other criminal activities yet to come, I think we'll be fine.'

She squeezed his hands. 'I do hope so,' she said.

She cycled home smiling to herself; she was in a relationship with Will. It was a pity she put such minimal personal information on social media. This meant that she couldn't update her relationship status with an electronic *ta-dah!*

Nobody online knew anything about her except her name and her love of cycling. They probably wouldn't even recognise her without her helmet on, as the only photos she posted were of cycle rides, cycle races and cycle meets, along with details of timings, terrain and the weather. People who reacted enthusiastically to her posts about fast white gravel and punishing climbs were unlikely to give a toss about whether or not she was in a relationship.

The pub garden had been a bit too public for any top-secret planning.

'Come round to mine tomorrow evening,' Will had suggested. 'Rebecca's going away for the weekend, we'll have the place to ourselves. We can get a takeaway and thrash out the details of our next mission.'

It was all sounding very promising she decided, as she went inside and parked her bike in the hall. She knew that Dad was out. It was the Silver Surfers' summer barbecue, and he was going to be flipping burgers and filling hot dogs all evening. She hoped they'd have a good turnout and that Dad would meet someone interesting and fun - and a bit younger than Veronica the nonagenarian.

She left him a note on the kitchen worktop before she went to bed:

Won't be back for supper tomorrow – going to Will's to plan the burglary!

There was no sign of Dad the next morning, and she was already at work when she got a text:

D: Sorry I missed you this morning. Barbecue was wild

and I overslept. Why don't you invite Will here for your planning tonight? I could make a lasagne.

P: Next time. We're all set to go to Will's today.

D: I could have given you some useful input from my catburgling days.

P: Hahaha. Don't tell Will, he's already worried about my criminal tendencies.

D: If you're sure, love. Thought I'd offer.

P: Thanks Dad xxx

Next time she'd definitely invite Will to supper at home. She knew Dad would love to meet him. She just hoped he wouldn't suggest inviting Veronica along to make up a foursome.

Briefing that morning was mercifully short and uncomplicated. There was a round of applause at the beginning, when Pippa announced that Clare had given birth to a daughter.

'Let's hope she doesn't call her Rose,' someone called out.

Everyone laughed, except Pippa who looked puzzled.

'Rose Trellis,' Ross explained. 'You know, gardening.'

It appeared that Pippa didn't know, so Polynesia pressed on with the meeting. She tasked herself with attending a briefing, to be given by a government press secretary, that had been in Martin's diary and nobody had thought to cancel. At least it would make the day go more quickly and get her out of the office for a while.

At five-thirty she saw Will start to tidy his desk, so she switched off her computer and gathered up her bags. He picked up his backpack and then, to her surprise, took a cycling helmet out of his drawer.

'I didn't know you were a cyclist' she said.

'I bought the bike last weekend,' he said. 'But today's the first day I've cycled to work. I thought we could ride home together, and you can show me all the clever shortcuts to get back to Wandsworth in super-quick time.'

'As long as you've got the hyperdrive facility that's no problem.'

'It was the first upgrade I asked for, Your Highness.'

'Oh, I'm not Princess Leia, that's such gender stereotyping. I'm Han Solo, every time.'

'I should have known. OK, Han, beam me up to Wandsworth.'

'That's not even the right film! How can you call yourself a Star Warrior?'

'I know it's not the same film, but it's synergy. Imagine if you could be beamed up into hyperspace. It's a brilliant idea.'

'Why don't you suggest it to George Lucas?'

'He can't afford my suggestions.'

Bickering happily they found their bikes and headed off to Wandsworth through the rush hour traffic.

Sitting at Rebecca's gleaming dining room table they thrashed out a plan. Monday would be a good day, they decided. Joanna was on the rota to work on Sunday, so she'd be keen to get off home early on Monday. They'd wait until she left the office and then Polynesia would walk up to Will and say '*Is Joanna around? I need to run something past her.*' And he'd reply '*I think she's just gone to the loo. I should go into her office and wait, if I were you.*'

Naturally, if there was no one else in the News office, they'd dispense with the conversation. But it was best to have a script prepared, just in case. Polynesia would be sure have her phone ready to photograph evidence. It would be hidden under the papers she was carrying that were her pretext to be in Joanna's office. Once inside, she'd work her way through the desk, looking for clues. She wondered if she should wear gloves, but they'd look a bit odd in July, unless she went for CSI gloves. And they'd look even odder in the News office, no matter what time of year. So she'd just have to hope that there would never be an occasion in the future when Joanna's office needed to be fingerprinted, or she'd find herself with some explaining to do.

While she was searching, Will would wait around the corner watching the lift, and if Joanna came back, he'd call out to her loudly and ask for some feedback on his article. This would give Polynesia time to slip out of the door and back to her desk before Joanna reached her office.

'Right,' said Will, putting down his pen. 'I think we've pretty well idiot-proofed the plan. I'm starting to feel hungry. How about ordering Thai?

'Pad Thai is one of my favourites, as you know.'

'I was going to suggest branching out and trying something new. What about three-flavour fish? It's one of their specialities and I think you'd love it. It's good to get out of your comfort zone sometimes.'

'Do you really think I've been cosying around in my comfort zone today?' Polynesia sounded a little cross. 'I'm planning to break into my boss's office and she's already threatened me with the sack. That sounds more like the danger zone than the comfort zone to me. I'll have a nice, predictable pad Thai and let the dangers of the world recede a little.'

'Fair enough, I'll order you a pad Thai.' He pulled out his phone. 'I'll just have to wait for another time to persuade you to explore strange new worlds and boldly go where no unadventurous eater has gone before.'

She smiled. 'I see you missed out the split infinitive,'

'Oh yes! Captain Kirk may not have had the benefit of a university education, but I know better than to use a misplaced modifier. "To boldly go,"' he tutted loudly, 'it's a crime against the English language!'

Despite the turbulence of her life at the moment, Polynesia experienced a sudden moment of total happiness. This man was not only risking his job for her, he could also discuss points of grammar, and he'd even bought a bike! Actions speak louder than words, as Dad was fond of saying, and Will's actions showed that he must really like her.

Then it occurred to her that all the bending and shaping seemed to be coming from his direction, and that she ought to be doing something as well, to invest in their relationship. Women's rugby, perhaps? She'd never been much good at team sports at school and had never felt the urge to take up netball or hockey again, unlike many of her university friends. Being naturally bossy, her ideal role on any team would be the captain. But perhaps a certain amount of skill would also be needed to fulfil that role competently, and this would be where she fell down, probably literally as well as metaphorically.

She waited until Will had finished ordering the meal.

'Do you think I ought to take up rugby?' she asked.

He looked surprised. 'Why? Do you want to take up rugby?'

'Not really. It's just that you've bought a bike and cycling's my thing. So I thought I ought to try something you love. It's only fair, after all.'

'Pol, I love your sense of justice, always trying to be fair, and I think that's something we share. I'm not so sure about the rugby. The women do tend to be rather beefy.'

'I'm not exactly a stick insect! Dad once called me sturdy, and I think that's a pretty good word to describe me. I'm not thin and willowy like Rebecca.'

'Rebecca has issues with food, as you've probably realised. I'd much rather be with someone who has a healthy attitude to eating and who enjoys having dinner with me. Anyway, I don't think sturdy is the right word to describe you at all.' He looked her up and down slowly. 'I would describe you as athletic and strong. I know they're not the traditional words to describe desirable women, but surely we've moved beyond all that Hollywood crap?'

She wasn't sure who made the first move. She just knew that they were kissing, and it wasn't a social, platonic kiss at all.

The next morning Polynesia woke up and, after a moment of panic, remembered where she was. She looked down at Will, fast asleep next to her, and smiled. It really had been a perfect evening. But now it was Saturday morning and she had things to do, so she got up and went into the bathroom. As she showered, she thought about the etiquette of staying over at someone's house. Should she have brought spare underwear, just in case, or would that have marked her out as a hussy when she produced it from her bag this morning? It was an academic question as she hadn't brought any, so she'd just have to put yesterday's back on again, or ask to borrow some of Rebecca's. She dismissed that idea immediately. Unless Rebecca had an unsuspected fondness for large granny pants, there was no chance Polynesia would fit into them. She imagined the sort of wispy thongs that Rebecca undoubtedly wore under her

Lycra, and shuddered at the thought of trying to fight her way into a pair and probably tearing them to shreds in the process.

'You're up early,' Will said as she went back into the bedroom.

'It's Saturday morning, which means it's time for the Richmond loop,' she explained. 'It's only fourteen miles if we go round twice. Come on, we can do it together and then have breakfast.'

'I'm having second thoughts about that women's rugby,' he said, watching her getting dressed. 'If they train on a Saturday morning, I think you should definitely sign up.'

She threw a pillow at him, and they grinned at each other.

By six o'clock on Monday evening there were just three of them left in the News department. Joanna was in her office and Polynesia and Will were both hunched over their keyboards, seemingly engrossed in their work. At five past six Joanna walked out of her office, carrying her handbag, and shut the door behind her. As soon as she'd rounded the corner Polynesia and Will sprang into action. He went to the corner and stood there casually, leaning against the wall, and Polynesia opened the door to Joanna's office and stepped inside. It wasn't as tidy as she'd thought it would be, but that made her job easier since she wouldn't need to do so much rummaging to find stuff. She opened a pink cardboard folder, but inside there was only the draft for an editorial later in the week. She closed it and picked up the papers that were casually strewn across the desk. There were several printed emails about a planning meeting for all the *Herald*'s editors, and a leaflet about colonic irrigation. She must mention that to Jess, it might make a good article for Lifestyle.

The computer was still on, which was also good. Luck was

with her, she thought. She had a quick scan through the emails, and was just scrolling back towards the date of Martin's death when she heard Will's voice.

'Joanna! Just the person –'

'Not now, Will. I'm in a hurry.' Joanna's voice sounded horribly close.

'But I was hoping –' Will sounded desperate.

'Whatever it is, I'll do it tomorrow,' Joanna said, over her shoulder as she walked into her office.

Of course Joanna hadn't gone home! That was why her desk hadn't been tidied and her computer was still on. I'm really not suited to espionage Polynesia thought, as a wave of panic engulfed her. She stood frozen with fear as Joanna turned her head, saw Polynesia and stared at her through narrowed eyes.

'What are you doing here?'

'I thought you'd gone! I mean, I just wanted to ask you about this piece I'm doing,' Polynesia gabbled.

'You wanted to ask me something even though you thought I'd gone,' Joanna said. 'And Will wants to ask me something too. I am in demand at the moment.'

She crossed her arms and put her head on one side as she scanned Polynesia slowly from head to foot, and then back up to head again. She looked as though she was deciding what size coffin to order.

Will appeared in the doorway, looking horrified. 'Joanna! I suggested Polynesia should wait for you. I thought you were just in the loo. I'm sorry if she shouldn't have been in your office.'

'Will, Polynesia has just told me she thought I'd already gone,' Joanna said with a nasty smile. 'How long did you think she'd have to wait for me? It must be something important she wants to ask if she was ready to wait all night.'

Will looked flummoxed.

Joanna turned her attention, and her unpleasant smile, on Polynesia. 'Ask away, I'm all ears.'

'It's just – this piece I'm writing … umm … about …' Polynesia's voice tailed away.

'I think you're writing a piece about the Tavistock North by-election,' Joanna said slowly and calmly. 'Was there something particularly tricky about it?'

Polynesia took a deep breath and got a grip of herself. 'No, there wasn't anything tricky about it. Actually, I finished it a couple of hours ago. I was in here because … well, because I wanted to find out why you were in the office the morning Martin was killed. You said you had no intention of telling me, so I thought I'd find out for myself.'

She stopped talking. She felt herself blushing and she could see that Will was looking equally shame-faced. He was going to get sacked too, and it was all her fault.

'Look, Joanna,' she went on desperately. 'Can I just say that this was nothing to do with Will. This was all my idea and I forced him -'

'Oh, very gallant,' Joanna broke in. 'What is this now, the reversal of the sexes? Weak and feeble men need protecting by strong women?'

'I'm not protecting him. I don't want him to be blamed for something he hasn't done!' Polynesia protested.

'We're both to blame, Joanna,' Will said. 'We're both equally guilty of trying to find out the truth.'

Will had rallied, Polynesia was pleased to see, and had now assumed an air of wounded nobility.

'The truth? How very naïve,' Joanna said dismissively.

'Haven't you worked in journalism long enough to know that my truth isn't the same as your truth. And as for *the* truth – well God knows whether that even exists.'

'Couldn't you just tell us your truth, then Joanna?' Polynesia suggested. 'So we've at least got some idea of what happened.'

'I've no idea what happened,' Joanna said. 'I came in early to catch the lecher and the slag. But all I heard was screaming and Alice shouting that she hadn't killed him. So I waited till you were phoning the police and then I dashed down the emergency stairs and out of the building.'

Will and Polynesia looked at each other, and Will gave her an encouraging nod.

'How did you know they were planning to meet that morning?' Polynesia asked.

'My brother's deaf,' Joanna said. 'Did you know that?'

'Er, no,' Polynesia said.

'I hero-worshipped my brother when I was young,' Joanna went on. 'He was deaf, but he was strong and athletic, and very kind. He was the perfect big brother. When our parents sent him to lip reading classes, I begged to go to. I wanted to do everything that my brother did. Every Saturday morning, I learned to lip read, and all week, we practised together.'

She's really lost it now, Polynesia thought. Aloud, she said, 'I see.'

'It means I could lip read every little thing Martin said as he stopped by Alice's desk about fourteen times a day. "I need to see you later," "I'm worried my wife will find out," "Do you swear you haven't told anyone about us?" God! Men are so pathetic and predictable.'

Polynesia put on her best *sisters-in-this-together* expression and was pleased to see that Will was using his initiative and doing a passable impression of looking pathetic and predictable.

'So you knew Martin and Alice were going to meet that morning?' Polynesia prompted.

'Yes. He said, "meet me here tomorrow at eight-thirty." She had her back to me so I couldn't see her reply, but I knew she'd be bound to turn up. He was her boss after all. So I decided to come in and get some photos of them together.'

'In flagrante,' Polynesia said, without thinking.

'Exactly. Then I could take the photos to Sir Giles and get them both sacked for gross misconduct. Just like I'm going to do with you two as well, incidentally.'

'Why did you want them both sacked?' Polynesia couldn't help herself asking.

'Martin Trellis got my job. I should have been managing editor, I was by far the better candidate. But Sir Giles is such an old dinosaur that he went for the man and not the woman. Then Martin brought that ghastly bimbo onto the team, pretending she was a journalist,' Joanna shuddered. 'Anyone could see that she was a gold-digger, and probably a prostitute as well. Martin undermined me constantly and he overruled me when I wanted to appoint you to the team. I said you'd make an excellent deputy news editor and he disagreed. Although now I'm beginning to think that he may have been right on that one,' Joanna gave a sour smile. 'You're not enough of a team player to be a successful deputy editor. You're more of a wild card.'

Polynesia decided to ignore the slur, as Joanna was in a revelatory mood.

'So you don't know whether or not Martin was already dead when you arrived at eight-fifteen?' she asked.

'No idea. But I didn't hear anything, so he must have died silently if it happened while I was in the next office.'

'Are you sacking us now?' Polynesia asked in a small voice.

'No,' Joanna said. 'Sir Giles is in a gîte in the Dordogne.'

She must have noticed Polynesia's mystified expression.

I'll wait till he comes back to work,' she explained. 'I don't want to bother him with unpleasantness while he's on holiday. He'll be back next week.'

'A week's reprieve,' she said to Will, as they left the building a few minutes later. 'If we solve the murder before then, she might change her mind.'

She wasn't sure that the look he gave her was entirely friendly and supportive.

26

Chapter 26

When she got home, she told Dad the whole sorry tale and his sympathetic response made her feel better immediately.

'Of course you weren't to know that she hadn't gone home, love. Why would anyone take their handbag and shut the door behind them if they were only popping out for a few minutes?'

'She was smoking us out,' Polynesia said, morosely. 'When she saw we were the only two left in the department, she got suspicious. She pretended to leave to see what we'd do if we thought we had the place to ourselves.'

'You've still got nearly a week to solve the murder,' Dad pointed out. 'So let's have an emergency meeting of the Justice for Martin group tomorrow evening and you can invite Will too. I think he's earned a seat at the table, as our American friends say.'

'Good plan, Dad.'

'What shall I cook for everyone?'

'Actually, Will's very keen on Thai.'

Dad looked pleased. 'I like expanding my culinary horizons. I'll do a bit of research online and nip to Waitrose in the morning.'

The next day Joanna glowered at Will and Polynesia whenever she walked past them, and she sat in her office with the door firmly closed the rest of the time.

'I don't know what's wrong with Joanna today,' Pippa remarked to nobody in particular as she waited by the coffee machine. 'I asked her if she'd like a coffee and she practically bit my head off.'

Now you know how those chocolate rabbits felt, Polynesia thought.

'Probably just PMT,' Ross said.

'Catfights and now PMT.' Polynesia couldn't help herself. 'My word, what an unreconstructed view of women. Do you also live in a cave and club animals to death when you're feeling a bit snacky, by any chance?'

She saw Will's mouth twitch into a smile.

'I'm not unreconstructed,' Ross muttered, 'I was just saying, that's all.' And he began typing busily.

'I don't think it's PMT anyway,' Pippa said. 'Joanna told me that she went through an early menopause. Her ovaries shrivelled like walnuts when she was only thirty-five.'

'Eww! Too much information,' said Polynesia. 'And why was Joanna telling you about her ovaries? It seems like an odd thing to be discussing by the coffee machine.'

'It was when I was collecting money for a baby gift once,' Pippa said. 'She told me she wasn't going to contribute to something that was never going to form part of her life experience. She said it was like asking a vegetarian to pay for the ritual slaughter of a few goats to appease the gods.'

This was pretty much Polynesia's way of thinking about baby

gifts, minus the ritual slaughter element, so she just made a non-committal noise and went back to her work.

They gathered in the sitting room for the emergency meeting, while delicious smells of coconut and lemongrass wafted in from the kitchen.

Dad called Will *old son* when they were introduced, and Polynesia started to laugh.

'Dad, you can't call people *old son* in Putney. You sound like a geezer!'

'I'm just trying to find the right vernacular. You know, friendly and not too formal. I've had plenty of experience when it comes to girls, but boys are a different matter. I can't go calling a boy *love*, can I?'

'How about *mate*?' Polynesia suggested.

'I think I'll just stick to Will,' Dad said. 'Now let's all sit down and have a drink. I've bought some Singha beer. You wouldn't believe the things they have in Waitrose these days.'

'Dad doesn't just cook a meal,' Polynesia explained to Will. 'He goes full out on the theme. You're lucky he didn't greet you with an expertly choreographed Apsara dance routine.'

'Trevor's the best cook,' Jess added, pouring herself a beer. 'I only joined the investigation team for the food.'

Trevor beamed at her.

Polynesia tapped on her glass. 'Order!' she said. 'Welcome to the emergency meeting of the Justice for Martin team.'

'And welcome to Will,' said Jess.

'I was just going to say that,' said Polynesia. 'Thank you, Will, for joining the team and for agreeing to be sacked with me. Unemployment will be much less lonely if there are two of us.'

Will grimaced. 'It wasn't exactly what I had in mind when I

agreed to help out. I'm still hoping there's some way to avoid it.'

'To recap then,' Dad said. 'Joanna says she went in to work early to catch Martin and Alice together and gather evidence to get them sacked. She knew nothing about the murder and didn't see or hear anything while she was in her office.'

'Do we believe her?' Jess asked. 'I mean, she's fallen back on the wronged woman excuse. You know, competent woman passed over in favour of less competent man. It's a bit of a tired trope, isn't it?'

'Just because it's tired doesn't mean it's not still happening,' Will said. 'Sir Giles is quite old school, isn't he? And Joanna's a single woman, so maybe her career is all she has. Who could blame her for wanting to get a bit of revenge on the man who got *her* job?'

Jess looked at Polynesia and raised her eyebrows. 'OMG! He's a feminist too!' she whispered.

Polynesia looked smug. She may have taken her time finding a boyfriend, but she'd certainly picked a good one.

'And now,' Dad pressed on, 'Joanna's going to get Sir Giles to sack you next week.'

'That's it in a nutshell, Dad. So where do we go from here?'

'Who gets back first, Esteban the cleaner or Sir Giles?' Dad asked. 'If it's Esteban and he saw something, that could be your best chance.'

'I think they both get back at the same time,' Will said. 'Esteban's a bit of a last resort, to be honest. I don't think it's very likely he would have seen the murderer and then gone off on holiday without saying anything.'

'But he may not have realised that the person he saw was the murderer,' Dad said. 'It could have been someone he saw every day.'

'Someone like Joanna,' said Polynesia. 'I think we should tell the police. I'm sure D.I. Wilson could get the truth out of Joanna. After all, she can hardly threaten to sack a detective inspector, can she?'

'I agree,' said Will. 'And you do seem to have got off on the wrong foot with the police, Pol. So if you go to them with this new evidence, they might be more inclined to look favourably on you.'

'And less inclined to arrest me for breaking into my boss's office, I hope.' said Polynesia. 'Glad you agree with me. I'll go tomorrow morning.'

'Pol, I think the best thing for you to do is to get in first with Sir Giles,' Jess said. 'Go in and see him as soon as he's back and give him a sob story. Give him your motherless child speech, and he'll be offering you Joanna's job and a pay rise in about five minutes flat!'

'I didn't know you had a motherless child speech.' Dad looked taken aback.

'Just a means to an end, Dad. Sometimes you're invited to go in through the front door, and sometimes you have to talk your way in at the back door.'

There was a dinging sound from the kitchen.

'Ah, that means the rice is ready. The massaman's simmering away nicely. I'll just go and check my tom kha gai. If I've pronounced that correctly.' Dad hurried out of the room.

'Your dad's amazing, Pol,' Will said. 'I can see now why you have such high standards and won't take any crap from the guys at work.'

'Are you worried you won't make the grade?' Jess asked him with a grin.

'Something like that,' he said, and squeezed Polynesia's hand.

The next morning, Polynesia didn't have the slightest inkling that the day wasn't going to go well when there was a ring on the doorbell at seven-thirty. So much for feminine intuition she thought to herself sourly later.

But at the time, when Dad shouted 'Pol, can you come down please,' she thought there must be a parcel for her. Hurrying down the stairs, still buttoning her shirt, and expecting to see a delivery driver waiting for a signature, she was startled to see two police officers standing in the hall. Dad was standing there too and so was her bike, which meant that the hall was rather crowded. She stood on the bottom stair and looked enquiringly at the policemen.

'Polynesia Henman?' One of them asked.

She nodded.

'We wonder if you'd be so good as to accompany us to Walworth Police station. D.I. Wilson would like to have a chat.'

D. I Wilson must be psychic. How else would she have known that Polynesia was intending to talk to her that very morning?

'Yes, of course,' she said.

'But she hasn't had her breakfast yet,' Dad protested.

'Don't you worry about that, Sir. We'll give her a nice cup of tea at the station.'

'Bye, love,' Dad gave her a peck on the cheek. 'I didn't realise you'd rung them already. It's nice that they've sent a car.'

'See you this evening, Dad.' She certainly wasn't going to tell him that she hadn't rung anyone and was as surprised as he was.

They parked in the car park at the back of the police station and the two officers led her in through a rear door and showed her into a dingy and depressing interview room. They disappeared, promising to bring her a cup of tea, and she fidgeted on her chair as she waited. Criminal investigations involved a lot of hanging around, and she wasn't a particularly patient person. She liked to make a plan and then get on with it at once, whereas crime involved a great deal of lurking and loitering, which didn't really suit her temperament at all.

Consequently, when D.I. Wilson arrived fifteen minutes later, Polynesia was feeling a touch tetchy.

'They promised me tea, but it hasn't arrived,' she said by way of a greeting.

'Hello again, Polynesia,' D.I. Wilson said, taking a seat at the table opposite her. 'D.S. Knight is just on his way with your tea now, I'm sorry it's taken a while.'

As she spoke, D.S. Knight came in, carefully balancing a cup of tea on a thick notebook, and closed the door behind him. He put the tea in front of Polynesia and she peered into the cup dubiously. She hadn't expected Earl Grey, but had hoped for something in a golden shade of brown, rather than a tanning salon shade of mahogany. Not wishing to appear ungrateful, she took a sip and tried not to grimace as the bitter, stewed liquid hit the back of her throat. Never mind, she'd stop off for a latte on the way to work.

'I expect you're wondering why we've asked you to come in this morning?' D.I. Wilson began.

'Well, it's a coincidence actually, because -' Polynesia began.

'It's not a coincidence,' D.I. Wilson interrupted her. 'It's because someone has made a serious allegation against you.'

Polynesia stared at her, all thoughts of tea and latte forgotten.

'A serious allegation?' she echoed, with a horrible sinking feeling in her stomach.

'Yes, that's right. Do you have any idea what that might be?'

'No, I don't. And if you would just let me tell you why I was coming to see you today -'

'Let's deal with that later, shall we?' said D.S Knight, the nitpicker, as he opened his notebook and took out a pen.

D.I. Wilson looked down at her notes and went on, 'We've been informed that you broke into Joanna Mason's office and ransacked it on Monday evening, is that correct?'

'No!' Polynesia was extremely indignant. 'I didn't break in. The door was unlocked, so I just opened it and walked in. All I did was move a few papers and scroll through her emails, I'd hardly call that ransacking!'

'And did you have permission to go through her private papers and personal emails?' D.I. Wilson went on.

'Well, no. But I did have good reason to do it, which is what I've been trying to explain to you.'

'All in good time,' said the nitpicker, scribbling away.

'Ms Mason has informed us that not only is she your boss, but she had also forbidden you to interfere with the police investigation. She says that you ignored her warning.' D.I. Wilson said.

'Of course I ignored her. I think she's a murderer!'

'Looking back at my notes from the day of the Martin Trellis's death, I see that you were convinced on that occasion that the murderer was Alice Smith,' D.I. Wilson said, with what looked like a pitying smile.

'O.K. So I was mistaken about Alice, I accept that. But she is a blackmailer, even if she's not a murderer. So she's still a criminal. That must make me partly right, surely?' Polynesia was beginning to feel exasperated. Why were these detectives so obtuse? If only they'd listen to her, they'd be within a hair's breadth of solving the case, rather than blundering about taking notice of someone like Joanna wanging on about people reading her emails.

'We did notice some unusual transactions in Alice's bank account history,' D.I. Wilson admitted. 'But Alice informs us that they were for ... ahem ... services rendered. While this may be considered reprehensible, it isn't illegal.'

Polynesia slumped back on her chair in despair. Alice was one step ahead of her again - of course she'd rather be considered a prostitute than a blackmailer. And there was no proof, it was just her word against Polynesia's.

'Look, Polynesia,' D.I. Wilson put down her file and looked almost kindly as she spoke. 'I understand that you have a strong sense of justice, and you want to find Martin's killer, but this isn't Watergate, you know. The journalists aren't going to solve this one. The police are working on it day and night, and we have resources that aren't available to you. So leave it to the police, will you?'

Polynesia sighed. 'Alice asked me to help her.'

'I know, she explained that to us. But Alice hasn't been charged with anything, so she doesn't need your help.'

'But she might,' Polynesia objected. 'Nobody's been charged with anything yet.'

D.I. Wilson picked up her file again. 'Shall I read you an extract from the Theft Act 1968?'

Polynesia shrugged.

'A person is guilty of burglary if, having entered any building, ***or part of a building, as a trespasser*** *-'* D.I. Wilson stressed these last words, looking up at Polynesia as she did so, and

Polynesia looked down at the table.

'- ***if, as a trespasser,*** ' D.I. Wilson repeated, *'he steals or attempts to steal anything in the building or that part of it.'* She put the file down again and looked at Polynesia. 'I know you think that you were only looking at emails, but there is such a thing as intellectual property theft. A good lawyer might argue that this was what you were engaged in, and the maximum sentence for this type of burglary is ten years.'

Polynesia felt sick. Was the detective inspector telling her that she was going to go to prison, for walking into Joanna's office and scrolling through her emails?

'Don't look so terrified. I'm not going to charge you this time. But please take this as a warning. If you're caught in anyone's office again, I won't be so tolerant.'

'Thank you,' Polynesia said, feeling tingly with relief. 'I won't be trespassing again I can promise you.'

'I'm glad to hear it. Now what was it that you were coming in to tell us today?'

Succinctly, Polynesia explained how Will had seen Joanna enter the building early on the day of the murder.

'Make a note of that, Sergeant. Mr Rowe should have mentioned that in his witness statement,' D.I. Wilson said.

'I don't think he realised at the time that Joanna hadn't told you she was there.' Polynesia rushed to Will's defence. 'He told you what he'd seen when he came up to the News Office that morning. But he didn't think to say anything about seeing her entering the building earlier, when he was on his way to buy coffee.'

'Full disclosure,' muttered D.S. Knight, as he continued to write in his notebook.

Polynesia gave him an unfriendly look and carried on with

her story. 'When we asked Joanna what she was doing that morning, at first she refused to say anything and threatened me with the sack if I mentioned it again. And then after she found me in her office the day before yesterday, she told us she'd been trying to catch Alice and Martin together. You know - the "services rendered" stuff that Alice told you about.'

She stopped and looked earnestly at D.I. Wilson. 'But I think that was an excuse she'd had time to think up after I asked her about it before. She said she wanted to get Martin sacked because she'd been passed over for promotion because of him. But what if she didn't want him sacked, she wanted him dead?'

'Let's leave the drama to the BBC, shall we?' D.S. Knight said, as he finished making his notes.

'So now Will and I going to be sacked as soon as Sir Giles gets back from the Dordogne. Couldn't you talk to Sir Giles?' she asked hopefully. 'You could explain to him that I was only trying to help.'

'I'm afraid dismissal isn't a police matter,' D.I Wilson said, almost sympathetically. 'I will be talking to Ms Mason again though. I need to hear her side of the story. But don't worry, I won't mention your name.'

'It doesn't matter if you do,' said Polynesia in a resigned tone. 'She's already going to sack me. What could she do that's any worse than that?'

'I thought you said she was a murderer,' said D.S. Knight.

27

Chapter 27

'How did it go this morning, love?' Dad called out as she opened the front door that evening. 'Those detectives must have been very keen to hear what you had to say.'

She threw her bag on the floor and kicked off her shoes.

'D.I. Wilson didn't send the car because I'd contacted her, Dad. She wanted to talk to me because Joanna went to the police and told them that I'd broken into her office and ransacked it. Apparently the maximum sentence for that sort of crime is ten years.'

'The devious bitch!' Dad was suddenly red-faced with anger. 'She's not content with sacking you, she's going to make sure you go to prison too!'

'Dad!' Polynesia had never heard her father swear before.

'Sorry, love, but some people really do take the biscuit.'

'Anyway, I'm not going to prison. D.I Wilson said they won't be charging me this time, but I'm not to trespass in anyone's office again.'

'And what about Joanna being at the scene of the crime? Did you tell them about that?'

'Yes. But I don't suppose it'll do any good. She'll just say she was there to catch Martin and Alice. And Alice has already told the police that she was sleeping with Martin for money, which neatly explains the bank transfers. It's hopeless, I just can't prove anything.' Polynesia slumped down on the sofa.

'It's just a temporary setback -' Dad was speaking in his soothing a sick child voice, which she hadn't heard for a long time.

'No, it isn't.' She interrupted him brusquely, she didn't want to be humoured like a child. 'Will and I have both lost our jobs and it was all for nothing. And once Joanna knows I've told the police about her being in the building when Martin was killed, I'm sure I'll be next on her hit list. Or first on her hit list if she wasn't Martin's killer. I've had enough, Dad. Let's watch a film this evening and never talk about this again.'

'Good idea. Dinner's almost ready. I've just got a couple of emails to send, you go and choose a film.'

The next morning Polynesia groaned as the alarm went off; the dramatic events of the last few days had turned her normally deep and refreshing sleep into a series of nightmares. She felt heavy with tiredness as she got ready, and then trudged down the stairs, not looking forward to another day of Joanna's barely suppressed anger and her own sense of disappointment that she'd failed herself and Will.

'Book smart isn't the same as street smart,' she muttered to herself as she went into the kitchen. 'I'd better make sure I remember that next time I'm all gung-ho about solving a problem and helping someone out.'

There was a note on the worktop:

Had to go out – Veronica's got a problem with her router. Can you fill the bird feeders before you leave. Nuts and seeds in shed. See you this evening. Dad xx

Fill the bird feeders - he had to be having a laugh! It would make her late for work. Why couldn't he fill them when he got back? Or ask her next week when she was unemployed and would have all the time in the world to be filling bird feeders?

She stomped around the kitchen, making tea and pouring cereal and muttering angrily to herself. Five minutes later she was in a more philosophical frame of mind. Why shouldn't she be late for work? After all, it was her second to last day at the *Herald*, presuming Sir Giles came back on Monday and sacked her immediately. It hardly mattered if she blotted her copybook now, when it was already so covered in blots that it looked like an original Jackson Pollock. And it wasn't as though Dad ever asked her to do much, not compared to the amount that he did for her. It would be brattish and ungrateful to refuse to do this small thing for him, she decided. Anyway, she was so over the *Herald*. She'd turn up for work when it suited her, not them.

Feeling better, she went out to the shed and found the nuts, seeds and fat balls and began filling the feeders. Dad loved watching the birds out of the kitchen window while he was in there cooking. He particularly liked the cheeky parakeets that swooped down in a flash of bright green and commandeered the feeders, chirping loudly and scaring off the browner, more timid birds. They're real playground bullies, she thought, and they get away with it because they're good looking. Attractiveness bias wasn't restricted to people, it was alive and well in the animal kingdom too – how depressing was that?

When she finally wheeled her bike out of the door and clipped on her helmet, she knew she was going to be very late. Tough! She pedalled past Wandsworth park at a leisurely speed, enjoying the views of the Thames and was just coming into Battersea when her phone started ringing. She groaned. It must be Joanna on her case, wanting to know why she was late. She was obviously planning to get her money's worth out of Polynesia before booting her out unceremoniously on Monday. She pulled in to the kerb and took out her phone. She took a deep breath, preparing to be harangued by a furious Joanna, but when she looked at the screen, she saw that it was Will.

'Sorry, Will. Is Joanna ranting? I'll be about 25 minutes, I was a bit late getting going this morning.'

'You're not inside then? Thank God for that!' Will sounded relieved.

'What do you mean? Is the *Herald* on fire?'

'No. It's not a fire. There are police here and an ambulance, but no fire engines. Something's happened, but they're not telling us what. Nobody's allowed in the building, and we're all congregating on pavement wondering what to do.'

'Police and an ambulance? It sounds like an accident.'

'Yes, it does. I looked for you outside and when I couldn't see you, I was worried that you might be inside with …' he paused, '… with whatever's going on.'

'I'm on my way. Meet you at the Aussie coffee bar.'

Filled with a sense of dread, she pedalled hard towards Vauxhall and up past Elephant and Castle, and twenty-three minutes later she was chaining her bike up and hurrying into The Bondi Barista. She usually liked to stop in the doorway and breathe in the delicious smell of freshly roasted coffee and enjoy the friendly banter from the young Australian baristas, but today she strode in and made her way straight to the table where Will was sitting with two lattes in front of him. She sat down and he pushed one towards her.

'Hope it's still hot,' he said.

'Any news?' she asked.

'None,' he said. 'I suppose nobody's really in charge, with Sir Giles on holiday and Martin dead. There's no one to take the initiative.'

'Surely Joanna should be in charge?' Polynesia said. 'She is the acting managing editor, after all.'

'I haven't seen her this morning,' Will said. 'Rosie, the features editor was here, and that new sports editor. But they were just mooching around like the rest of us.'

'How very odd,' Polynesia mused. 'I'll text Jess and see if she knows anything.'

Three minutes later her phone pinged.

'Jess is in the Cotswolds, doing an article on Soho Farmhouse, and currently enjoying a cinnamon bun and coffee before interviewing the staff. She'll then be sampling a Japanese-style working lunch with an Oxfordshire twist, and doing a bit of celebrity sniffing. She says the terrorist attack alarm has probably gone off by mistake.'

'I expect she's right,' Will agreed. 'Let's finish our coffee and head back, shall we?'

As they rounded the corner, they could see people going into the *Herald* building.

'The crisis must be over,' Will said.

Polynesia saw one of the Lifestyle reporters she used to work with just ahead of them, and hurried to catch her up.

'Hey, Nat! Any idea what's going on?' she asked.

'Not really,' Nat said. 'Did you see the email?'

Polynesia shook her head.

'It's from HR, sent about ten minutes ago. It just said for everyone to go back to work as usual, except the News team. They need to go to the conference room and wait for further instructions.'

Will and Polynesia looked at each other. This sounded ominous.

The conference room was on the first floor and had a large imposing table down the middle surrounded by chairs of the imposing but comfortable variety. It was the sort of room that Polynesia associated with crusty old men and cigar smoke, and she imagined Sir Giles presiding over meetings in here, with his glasses pushed up on his forehead, giving him that strange middle-aged man look. The News team weren't sitting at the table, they were standing in nervous huddles around the edges of the room. They had obviously decided that it would be inappropriate to look even slightly relaxed or comfortable in the circumstances, so they shifted anxiously from foot to foot, looking at the door every time someone came in.

Polynesia looked around. Everyone seemed to be there except for Joanna and Pippa. One of them had probably had an accident and the other one was accompanying them to hospital.

The door opened and Catherine, the HR Manager walked in. She was a large woman, and Polynesia privately referred to her as Fat Cat, but would never have admitted that to anyone else. Despite her bulk she had a very springy way of walking, rising up on her toes after each step, as though she was saying, '*See how light I am! I'm practically airborne every time I lift one foot off the ground.'*

Catherine bounced into the room now, her pink and orange floral dress billowing slightly with each step, and Polynesia caught her breath. Behind Catherine she could see the unmistakable geometric bob of D.I. Wilson.

The News team fell silent and Catherine looked around at them all.

'I am very sorry,' she began, 'to be the bearer of yet more bad news for the News team. Sorry, that wasn't meant to be a bad joke. I just mean that, once again, tragedy has befallen you.'

Everyone was staring at her now; the tension was palpable.

'I'm afraid I have to tell you that Joanna Mason has met with a terrible accident.'

There was a collective intake of breath, and Catherine was about to continue, when D.I. Wilson spoke.

'I'm sorry to interrupt, but I do think we need to impart clear information, right from the start. Talking about terrible accidents could be misleading. You need to know that Joanna Mason has been found dead in her office, and unfortunately, there's no chance that it was accidental. So we'll be needing statements from you all in due course.'

There were audible sounds of distress now, several people had started to cry and there were agitated murmurs.

'Not again!' someone said loudly.

'Yes, again,' agreed D.I. Wilson and her eyes seemed to linger on Polynesia before they swept the room.

When they were allowed back in the News office after lunch, Polynesia was shocked to discover that she was now the most senior member of staff, and therefore "in charge" as Catherine had told her. How very ironic, she thought, that the person in charge today was about to be sacked, and on Monday she wouldn't even be in charge of a swivel chair. But as she thought about Monday, she suddenly understood that her situation was now looking much less bleak. Joanna had been going to get her sacked and Joanna was dead. Sir Giles was on holiday and knew nothing about the office burglary, because Joanna had said she would tell him when he got back. So, if Sir Giles got back and nobody told him anything, she and Will had nothing to worry about.

Feeling much brighter, she led a very rapid briefing. They'd have to cover Joanna's death of course, but since there very few details yet, it wouldn't take up many columns. She sent a couple of people out to cover a breaking political scandal and the arrival of a visiting head of state, while others worked quietly on undated stories, every journalist's friend on a quiet news day.

Shortly before five o'clock Will stopped by her desk.

'How's it going, boss?' he asked.

'This is unbelievable, isn't it?' she said. 'I feel as though I was on Death Row and now I've been pardoned, if that isn't a tasteless metaphor in the circumstances.'

'Tasteless or not, we're off the hook, and that feels good,' he said.

'I was thinking about that,' she said slowly.

'And …'

'Well,' she went on, 'the thing is, we're off the hook when it comes to –' here she lowered her voice and muttered, 'Joanna getting us sacked.'

'That's what I meant,' Will said.

'Yes, but I told D.I. Wilson that Joanna was going to have us sacked on Monday,' she went on, still muttering. 'So what if

D.I.W. thinks that we killed Joanna to stop her from talking to Sir Giles?'

'Jesus! Polynesia, you can't be serious? You don't murder someone because they've threatened to sack you!'

'Shush! Keep your voice down! We need to be careful what we say when we give them our statements tomorrow.'

The gossip machine was functioning nicely, and Polynesia learned, as she stood by the coffee machine, that Pippa had found the body and was so distressed that she'd gone home for the rest of the day. Like Martin, Joanna had been found on the floor of her office, but unlike Martin, there had been no blood.

'Different M.O. so probably a different killer,' someone had said knowledgeably.

Great! There were now two murderers at loose in the *Herald* community, just what Polynesia wanted to know.

28

Chapter 28

Dad was waiting for her when she got home, with his shoes on and his car keys in his hand. Of course, they were going to The Peking Palace. After everything that had happened today, she'd completely forgotten.

'Hi Dad, sorry if I'm a bit late. I'll be ready in five minutes.' She hurried upstairs to change. She could tell him about Joanna when they were sitting in the restaurant.

She came down in shorts and a t-shirt. Thank goodness the Peking Palace wasn't one of those restaurants with a dress code. She even remembered eating there in her pyjamas once, when she was going through a particularly rebellious phase. The staff had behaved as though there was nothing unusual about a teenage girl in Spiderman pyjamas with a napkin tied around her neck, eating duck pancakes with gusto.

'Thanks for doing the bird feeders this morning, love,' Dad said, after they'd ordered and were sitting with a beer nibbling at prawn crackers. 'I hate leaving them empty. The birds look at me so reproachfully if they swoop down and there's nothing there for them.'

'Actually, Dad, it's a lucky thing that I did feed the birds this morning,' she said, only half-jokingly, 'if I hadn't, I might have got to work in time to see my second dead body this summer!'

Dad gawped at her. 'Second dead body? You're not telling me that someone else has died at the *Herald*?'

'I'm afraid so. It was Joanna, the bitch boss from Hell. I don't know any of the details yet, other than that she was found on her office floor and there was no blood. D.I. Wilson was there today, and we've all got to give statements tomorrow, so I expect I'll find out more then.'

'Who found her?'

'It was poor Pippa. You remember, she was Martin's and then Joanna's secretary? When Martin was killed, Pippa arrived not long after I found the body, and she was absolutely hysterical. I dread to think what she's like now, after finding the second body herself. She went home and nobody's seen her all day.'

'So Pippa's bosses have been dying off one by one, have they?' Dad said thoughtfully.

'Dad! You can't possibly think Pippa had anything to do with the murders! You've never seen a more unlikely murderer. She's all fluffy bunnies and cute kittens and she talks about choccies.'

'It could be a clever disguise,' Dad said. 'I'm not saying it was her, I'm just saying you can't rule her out.'

'Well, if it was her,' Polynesia said, 'with Martin and Joanna gone, I'm going to be her next boss. So if they find me upended in the recycling bin one morning, you'll know who to accuse.'

'All I'm saying is, forewarned is forearmed,' Dad said mildly. 'Remember what we said about keeping an open mind when you carry out an investigation?'

'OK, OK. I'll talk to her tomorrow,' Polynesia promised. 'But the good thing is that Joanna's not going to sack us now.'

'That's true,' said Dad. 'Although, looking on the less bright side, it does give you a motive for murder.'

'God, Dad, anyone would think you wanted me either dead or behind bars!'

'I just want you to be aware of danger. But, as you say, it's lucky you were late in this morning, so the police can't think you had anything to do with it.'

'As long as they believe me,' she said morosely

'There's bound to be cameras along the road, we're the most snooped upon nation in the world, you know. Did you take the A3025?'

She nodded.

'You'll definitely be on candid camera then. And our CCTV at home will show you sorting out the bird feeders. Good job we had it installed after Pat and Tony were burgled.' Dad saw a waiter approaching the table. 'Oh, good,' he rubbed his hands together appreciatively, 'here's the bang-bang chicken, I've been looking forward to this all day. Let's talk about something more cheerful or you'll put me off my dinner.'

They ate and chatted, but Polynesia couldn't shake off the uneasy feeling that things weren't going to be as straightforward as Dad seemed to think they were.

Pippa was back at work the next morning and seemed undecided as to whether she was a plucky heroine or a tragic victim. The tissues were in evidence, but she wasn't using them as much as she had with Martin. That must mean that she didn't like Joanna as much, Polynesia deduced. Or else it meant that she was getting used to finding dead bodies in the office.

'When I saw her on the floor, I thought she was just messing about, you know, trying to scare me. Then I thought, this is Joanna, she's the boss, she doesn't play tricks on people. So I looked closer and I could see that she was a really funny colour.'

The group clustered around Pippa's desk were listening intently.

'So what did you do next?' someone asked.

'Well, at first I thought I might be sick,' Joanna said, with relish. 'But then I remembered Polynesia when she found Martin, and how she'd rushed out of the room and called the police, so that's what I did. And they were here really quickly, so I didn't have time to do anything else.' She sounded disappointed.

'You didn't search the place then, to see if he was still here, hiding under a desk or in a cupboard?' Ross asked

'Ooh no! If there was a murderer hiding here, I wanted the police to find him,' Pippa shuddered. She was definitely in victim mode now.

'Very sensible,' Polynesia said loudly. 'Come on everyone, back to work please.'

Mindful of Dad's hypothesis that Pippa could be picking off her bosses, one by one, Polynesia had decided to circumvent any further episodes of boss rage by bringing in some chocolates. She handed them over now, giving Pippa the sympathetic smile she'd practised in the mirror – head tilted, eyebrows slightly lowered, an upward lift to the lips but no teeth on display.

'Pippa, I brought you these. I thought you might need something sweet after yesterday's shock. They're not animal shaped, I'm afraid, just round, but I hope you like them.'

'Hotel Chocolat! That's so thoughtful, I love them!' Pippa looked delighted.

'My dad loves them too,' Polynesia said. In fact she'd pinched them from her father's chocolate cupboard before leaving for work. She was sure he wouldn't mind. It would be a sound investment if it stopped Pippa from murdering his only daughter.

'So, you didn't see anyone else up here when you arrived yesterday morning?' Polynesia asked her.

'There was nobody here at all,' Pippa said. 'Well, only Gloria. She was waiting for the lift when I arrived.'

'Who's Gloria?' Polynesia asked, her interest quickening.

'The cleaner. She doesn't usually do our floor, but Esteban's on holiday and she's covering for him,' Pippa explained.

'Do you know where I can find her?'

'She leaves before nine, so she's long gone now. You'll have to come in early on Monday if you want to talk to her.'

That sounded very promising. She made a mental note to arrive early on Monday and track Gloria down, and then if Will managed to speak to Esteban too, maybe one of the cleaners would have seen something suspicious.

D.I. Wilson and D.S. Knight arrived mid-morning and commandeered Martin's office to take statements from everyone.

When it was Polynesia's turn she went in and sat down opposite them, with a horrible feeling of déjà-vu.

'Didn't think we'd be seeing you again so soon,' D.S. Knight remarked, as he turned to a clean page in his notebook.

'No, the *Herald* does seem to be suffering more than its share of bad luck at the moment,' Polynesia agreed, stiffly.

'Perhaps not bad luck for everyone, though,' the sergeant

went on, his ginger eyebrows moving slightly, and reminding Polynesia of a couple of the fuzzy orange caterpillars she'd seen recently on a nature documentary.

She maintained a dignified silence.

'Polynesia, could you please tell us your exact movements yesterday morning,' D.I. Wilson said.

Succinctly she explained about the later than usual breakfast, the bird feeders and Will's phone call.

'So your father wasn't at home to verify the time you left?'

'No, but we have CCTV at home, so that'll show me in the garden. And there must be loads of cameras between Putney and London Bridge.'

The detective inspector nodded. 'We'll be checking everything, of course. I think that's all for now, thank you.'

'Could I just ask one question?' Fortune favours the bold, Polynesia thought.

'I'll see if I can answer it.'

'How did she die? I mean, Pippa said there was no blood, and when I found Martin there was lots of blood, so I was just wondering ...' she tailed off.

'If it was the same killer?' D.I. Wilson finished her sentence for her and Polynesia nodded.

'Joanna was strangled, probably with a length of flex. We'll know more once the post-mortem results are in. As to whether it's the same killer, your guess is as good as ours at this stage.'

Polynesia wished she'd studied forensics instead of English Literature. It was all very well being able to discuss King Lear's motives or analyse confessional poetry, but now she wanted to know whether a woman would be strong enough to strangle another woman with a length of flex, and nothing she'd learnt at Cambridge seemed particularly relevant.

She spent the rest of the day watching Pippa discreetly and trying to determine whether her behaviour was in keeping with someone who'd had a terrible shock the previous day, or whether it was more in keeping with someone who was pretending they'd had a terrible shock the previous day. She finally came to the conclusion that she had absolutely no idea.

Polynesia and Will had arranged to meet for dinner. They wanted to compare notes on what the police had asked them, and brainstorm their next moves. But as Will hadn't been in the office either when the murder was discovered, all they really knew was that Joanna had been strangled and Gloria might have seen something.

They went back to Will's flat, where Rebecca was desperate to hear the latest news and to learn whether there was anything she could do to help the investigation.

'Crank calls are my speciality,' she said.

'If we need any crank calls, you're our go-to,' Polynesia promised. 'But the next step is talking to cleaners, and we can do that face to face, no fake identities needed.'

She went home, feeling unsettled. It was all very well to be in the clear, but when everyone else was also in the clear, it wasn't exactly reassuring. The axe would have to fall on someone, eventually. And D.I.Wilson had said 'your guess is as good as ours.' Surely that wasn't the way the police were supposed to work, was it- guessing?

Dad was icing a large chocolate cake when she got home.

'I've made it for Clare, tomorrow,' he said, as he arranged chocolate buttons in a neat pattern on the top.

'She didn't eat any cake last time we met her,' Polynesia

pointed out.

'No, but she'll want to have some at home to offer guests who come to see the baby,' Dad said.

'I see. Guests like you, you mean.'

'I do like a slice of cake with my coffee in the morning,' he admitted.

Dad had suggested the trip up to Bedford to see Clare and baby Martha, and Clare had been touchingly pleased when Polynesia called her. They'd arranged to go on Saturday morning and now Dad showed Polynesia the route he'd printed out, which ran to four sheets of paper.

'I'll need you to navigate if I'm driving, love,' he said. 'So let me talk you through the route.'

'Can't we just use a sat nav?'

'Oh no, definitely not. They send you off in all sorts of wrong directions. I read about a lorry driver who had to be rescued off the top of a mountain by a helicopter after he followed his sat nav.'

'I don't think there are many mountains between here and Bedford, but I take your point. So how are we getting there?'

'Well,' Dad fanned out the pieces of paper and pointed to the first one, 'lots of people recommend the M25 then the M1, but I think we're going to go M25 and then A1. According to the AA ...'

Polynesia zoned out at this point and simply nodded as Dad pointed to each sheet of paper in turn and spoke at length about them. It must be a man thing, she thought, this obsession with routes and maps. They weren't going to be crossing the Gobi Desert, they'd be travelling on motorways with road signs. Anyone with a halfway decent sense of direction could get within a couple of miles of their destination without any maps at all.

'... and there's free parking by the river. We'll walk from there,' he finished, and handed her the sheets of paper.

'Great,' she said. 'I'm off to bed, see you in the morning.'

29

Chapter 29

They made their way to Bedford the next morning with no wrong turns or angry words, mainly thanks to Polynesia hiding her phone amongst the sheets of route planning and checking Google Maps surreptitiously every now and then.

'This is nice, isn't it?' Dad said, as they parked on the Embankment and watched the swans gliding down the river. 'Look at those lovely flower beds. It a pity we can't have something like this in Putney.'

'The Thames is tidal, you know' Polynesia said.

'Oh, I know that's what they say. Personally, I think it's just an excuse not to bother doing anything, so we have to look at acres of mud and silt instead of something like this.' He waved his hand towards the manicured beds. 'If Nebuchadnezzar could build the hanging gardens of Babylon two thousand years ago, I don't see why Wandsworth Borough Council can't give us a few flower beds.'

'Whatever you say, Dad. Now, where's Clare's house?'

Clare lived in a row of attractive terraced houses. Hers had a neatly trimmed privet hedge at the front and a large climbing rose, with the last blooms of summer adding a few splashes of red to the front of the house.

She answered the door with a small baby and a large muslin square draped across her shoulder, and seemed genuinely pleased to see them.

'I've just fed her, so I'll put her down in her crib and we can have coffee,' she said.

'We have cake!' Dad said, holding the tin up in a triumphant gesture.

They handed over their gifts, a teddy from Polynesia and a pair of bootees from Dad.

'I know it's August, plus nobody's worn bootees since the 1950s,' Polynesia muttered as they sat down with their coffee, 'but Dad's friend Veronica knitted them and she's over ninety, so I don't think she's up to date on baby fashion.'

'They'll be great for the winter,' Clare assured her. 'These Victorian houses are so draughty, and they cost a fortune to heat.'

'Still missing your flat in London?' Polynesia asked

'Not so much now. Martha's keeping me really busy, and I've met a few new mums who are on the same wavelength, so I'm feeling much more settled.'

'I expect you know that we've had another death this week.' Polynesia tried to introduce the subject delicately.

'Yes, that detective woman in charge of Martin's case rang me. She wanted to warn me that there could be media interest in me too. She said it'll happen again and again over the years. Every time a journalist is killed there'll be a retrospective looking at other similar deaths, so it's something I'll have to get used to.'

'I'm sorry, love. That's much more than a lovely girl like

you should have to put up with.' Dad put his hand on Clare's shoulder and gave her a supportive squeeze.

Polynesia looked at him in surprise; he wasn't given to shows of emotion, particularly with people he didn't know well.

'Thanks, Trevor,' Clare said with a smile. 'It was shocking, though. I couldn't believe it when she told me, first Martin and now Joanna, it seems so senseless.'

'If only we could make sense of it, we'd know who the murderer is,' Polynesia sighed.

'You'll get there in the end, Pol. I have every confidence in you.' Dad said encouragingly.

'What about Alice?' Clare asked. 'Could she have killed Joanna as some sort of revenge for being accused of killing Martin?'

'Joanna was strangled,' Polynesia said. 'Alice is quite slight. Do you think she'd be strong enough to strangle another woman?'

Clare shuddered. 'I've no idea. I'm a teacher, and we may fantasise about strangling our students, but that's as far as it goes.'

'Probably not with her bare hands,' Dad said. 'But if she used a silk stocking, she might have managed it.'

'The police think it was a length of flex.'

'Well there you go, then,' said Dad. 'I think you'd better find out what Miss Smith was doing last Thursday morning.'

Polynesia thought hard as they sped down the A1 on their way home. Why would Alice have killed Joanna? What possible motive could she have had? Even with so much evidence pointing towards Alice, Polynesia didn't believe she'd killed Martin, and now she couldn't believe there'd be a scrap of evidence linking her to Joanna's death. Clare's idea of revenge didn't sound plausible to Polynesia. All the same, it would be a good idea to talk to Alice. She'd worked closely with Joanna for several months and might have discovered something that would give them a clue as to why she'd been killed.

She pulled out her phone and sent Alice a text. Six texts later, she'd learnt that Alice had taken up cycling (… another one? She'd never realised she was such a trendsetter …) and they had arranged to meet in Richmond Park at the café by Roehampton Gate on Sunday morning.

Polynesia arrived promptly at eleven, red-faced and sweating from her circuit of the park, and sat down to wait at a table outside. Ten minutes later Alice arrived on a pink bicycle with a basket on the front and a skirt guard on the back wheel. She was wearing a vest top, pink checked pedal pushers and box-fresh white trainers. She climbed carefully off the bike and lowered the kickstand into place.

'Lycra, that's brave,' Alice said, looking Polynesia up and down.

'Yes, well some of us are more serious cyclists than others,' Polynesia said, with a pointed look at the pink bike.

'Will you go in and get the drinks? Herbal tea for me,' Alice said, sitting down, 'only I can't leave Poppy out here on her own.'

'Poppy!' Polynesia stood up. 'I cannot believe you've actually named your bike!' She rolled her eyes in disgust and went into the café.

'How's the investigation going?' Alice asked, as she sipped the urine-coloured brew in her paper cup.

'I suppose you've heard about Joanna?'

'Yes, the police wanted to talk to me about it. They can't pin that one on me though, I've got a cast-iron alibi.'

'Oh?'

'I was staying with Mummy and Daddy in Sussex. Did you know they moved to the country after Daddy retired?'

Polynesia shook her head. She knew nothing at all about Alice's parents, other than the obvious fact that they'd spawned a psychopath. She wondered what job her father had retired from … slaughterhouse manager perhaps, or unbalanced leader of a reclusive cult?

'It's deadly boring down there,' Alice went on, 'there's absolutely no social life. But they've been so worried about me, with all this murder stuff, that I went down for a few days last week, and I only got back yesterday.'

Polynesia looked at her. 'You may not believe me, but I'm glad you've got an alibi. I know we're never going to BFFs, but I don't want to see you wrongly accused of murder.'

'Thanks, Polynesia,' Alice looked surprised, 'I wasn't expecting that.'

'Well, it's hardly going to be justice for Martin if the wrong person's found guilty, is it?' Polynesia said, rather undoing her previous attempt at magnanimity. 'Did the police say whether or not they think it was the same killer twice?'

'They didn't tell me anything, and I didn't ask. I was just so glad that I was in Sussex and not in London.'

'What I really want to know,' Polynesia said, 'is whether you can think of any reason why Joanna might have been killed.'

Alice considered this. 'No,' she said eventually. 'I thought she was a boring saddo who obviously had no life outside the *Herald*. She hated Martin, he was always complaining about the things she said to him, and she hated me too. But as neither of us killed her, I can't think of anyone else … unless it was Sir Giles? If Joanna killed Martin, Sir Giles might have killed Joanna because he was furious with her for ruining the *Herald's* good name.'

'Thereby ruining it even further,' Polynesia said drily. 'It's an interesting idea, but Sir Giles is on holiday in France, so it definitely wasn't him.'

'Why are you worrying about this anyway?' Alice asked. 'I asked you to investigate Martin's death to clear my name. And as I'm in the clear for Joanna's murder, it doesn't really matter who killed her, does it?'

Polynesia stared at her, speechless. Alice stood up and moved towards her bike. Polynesia refused to think of it as *Poppy*.

'I must go,' Alice said. 'I need to get some stuff in Waitrose on the way home.'

'I thought you couldn't leave "Poppy" on her own?' Polynesia's air quotes were unmistakable.

Alice just smiled. 'Oh, nobody's going to steal her outside Waitrose are they? It's not that sort of place,'

Polynesia watched Alice pedal majestically away, and she grinned as she saw the slight wobble when Alice made a right turn.

'Cyclist, my arse!' she muttered under her breath.

Polynesia and Will arranged to meet at eight-thirty on Monday morning to track Gloria down, and hopefully Esteban too, if he was back from his holiday.

'Come on, I'll show you where the cleaners live,' he said, pressing the button for the second floor.

'How come you know where the cleaners hang out?' she asked.

'Esteban was wearing a Pumas shirt one day. You know, the Argentinian rugby team?'

She didn't know, but nodded anyway.

'So I asked him about it, and we started chatting. Because his English wasn't very good at first, and I wanted to practise my Spanish, we used to meet up in the cleaners' cubby hole for a coffee and some rugby talk every now and then.'

The power of tribal identity, Polynesia thought, was remarkable. Will had spotted Esteban's shirt and recognised it as a tribal marker, then they had forged a bond even though they had no common language. It had been the same with Alice yesterday, but in reverse. Polynesia had expected the tribal costume of the serious cyclist, but instead, Alice had turned up in 1950s wholesome-girl-next-door garb, and Polynesia hadn't bonded with her at all.

They walked down the corridor to a windowless room with a few battered chairs, a filter coffee machine and a lot of cleaning equipment. The room was empty, so they stood by the door and waited. After about ten minutes, two women arrived carrying a hoover and a mop and bucket.

One of the women smiled at Will.

'Bom dia,' she said.

'Bom dia, Christiane,' he said.

This wasn't Gloria then, Polynesia thought.

'Christiane and Aline are Brazilian,' Will seemed to read her thoughts. 'I'm afraid my Portuguese doesn't extend much beyond hello. Gloria's from Venezuela, and her English is pretty good.'

A plump woman of about forty-five came trundling down

the corridor, pushing a large trolley of cleaning products.

'This is Gloria,' he said.

'Hi Gloria, I'm Polynesia from the News office,' she said and held out her hand. After a moment's hesitation, Gloria shook it and they smiled at each other.

'I'm looking into Joanna's death,' she went on, hoping Gloria would think it was normal for the News team to investigate their own murders. 'I wanted to ask you about Thursday morning. What did you see?'

'I see nothing,' Gloria spread her hands wide in a gesture of regret. 'I tell the police. I clean the News office at six o'clock, very early because Esteban is on holiday so I do double work. News office is empty, nobody there.'

'Did you go into Joanna's office?' Polynesia asked.

'Joanna's office empty. All offices empty. Then I go down to fourth floor to do my cleaning there.'

'And did you see anybody there?' Polynesia asked, without any real hope.

'No,' Gloria said. 'Only when I finished, I call lift, and there is a man in it when it gets down to fourth floor.'

'A man?' Polynesia asked. She and Will were both staring at Gloria now.

'So the man was coming down,' Will said, 'maybe from the fifth floor?' He gave Polynesia a significant look.

'Who was he? Did you recognise him?' Polynesia asked.

'I seen him once before, nice man. He is engineer, doing special testing on the computers. I said to him "you're here very early" and he said, "no rest for the wicked, love."' Gloria smiled. 'He's a very friendly man.'

'What did he look like?' Polynesia's heart had started to beat faster.

'He was old,' Gloria said. 'Too old to work, I think, but of course I don't say it. Not so tall, grey hair, and wearing those special engineer trousers with many pockets.'

'That sounds like the PAT tester, the one Esteban told the police he saw the day Martin was killed,' Will said. 'Just a coincidence, I suppose. Why would some random electrician want to kill Martin and Joanna?'

'No reason,' Polynesia said, and her voice wobbled slightly as she spoke.

Will looked at her. 'Are you all right, Pol? You've gone very pale.'

'I think I'm just hot. I'll go and sit down for a bit.'

'Thanks, Gloria,' Will said, and he put a hand under Polynesia's arm as they walked back to the lift. 'I'll go and get you some water. It must be a bit of a blow for you, this was our only lead and it's turned out to be a dud.'

She made a monumental effort to pull herself together. 'It's fine. I'm sure something else will turn up. And this was always going to be a bit of a long shot wasn't it?'

30

Chapter 30

Polynesia struggled to maintain a veneer of normality all morning, while her stomach churned and her mind raced. Dad had been out the morning that Joanna was killed. Had he also been out the morning that Martin was murdered? She couldn't remember. But she'd left home especially early that day to talk to Martin, so she'd probably assumed Dad was still in bed if he wasn't downstairs. This was ridiculous! How could she suspect her own father of murder? The problem was that she'd always had an over-active imagination. And it was of the variety that rapidly parts company with common sense, leaps ahead and mentally buries someone with a cough, before they've even made a doctor's appointment.

She knew better than to mention her suspicions to anyone else. If they thought she even remotely suspected her own father of being a murderer, they'd probably have her locked up in the nearest secure facility. So she went through the motions; typing, drinking coffee, running morning briefing, until just before lunchtime when she got a call from Sir Giles's office, saying that he'd like to speak to her if she could spare a few minutes.

Trepidatiously, she made her way up to the sixth floor. Joanna had said that she wasn't going to mention the sacking issue to Sir Giles while he was on holiday, but that didn't mean that she hadn't changed her mind. She might have sent him a brief email:

> *Terribly sorry to bother you on your hols, Sir G. But just to give you a heads up, Polynesia Henman and Will Rowe need to be sacked asap when you return. Hope the weather's good. Regards, Joanna.*

She was debating whether or not Joanna was the sort of person to say 'hols', when the lift door opened and she found herself outside the editor-in-chief's office. She'd never been here before, because Sir Giles was more a man of the people than a remote emperor. He liked to come and see you rather than summoning you to come and see him, which is what made her feel that this must be a serious issue. She swallowed hard and approached one of the two women sitting at computers in the outer office. There was a glass wall separating the outer and the inner offices, and she could see Sir Giles sitting at his desk in the inner office, talking animatedly on the phone.

She approached one of the women.

'Excuse me, I'm Polynesia. Sir Giles wanted to see me.'

'Yes,' the woman looked up and smiled. 'Sir Giles said for you to go straight through.'

She walked towards the door in the glass wall and saw Sir Giles putting down his phone and beckoning her in.

'Ah, yes, Polynesia, thanks for coming up,' he said, as he stood up to greet her. 'Come and sit on the sofa over here and

I'll just close the door.'

This sounded ominous; it wasn't usually good things that happened behind closed doors.

Sir Giles sat at the other end of the sofa. He was looking tanned after his fortnight in France, but hadn't lost his harassed air. If you ran a national paper, you obviously didn't leave your worries behind when you went to the Dordogne, you took them along too.

'This is a terrible business about Joanna,' he began without preamble. 'Absolutely shocking, I could hardly believe it. Well, when I say I could hardly believe it, that's not true. Actually I could believe it after what she told me.'

This is it, Polynesia thought. He was now going to accuse her of murdering Joanna to stop Joanna from sacking her.

'Umm … I don't know what she told you,' Polynesia said hesitantly, 'but can I just say that there are two sides to every story.'

'Yes, of course, two sides. But I don't even know one side I'm afraid. That's why I was hoping you might be able to fill me in.' He looked at Polynesia expectantly.

'I'm sorry, I don't know what you mean,' she said. Surely he didn't expect that she was going to sit there on his sofa and confess to murder?

'Joanna sent me a brief email,' Sir Giles said.

So Joanna had changed her mind about not contacting Sir Giles on holiday. Polynesia's stomach gave an unpleasant lurch.

'Oh, did she?' she asked, trying not to sound like a condemned woman.

'Yes. She told me she'd had a tip off, a really big story, she sounded very excited about it. She said that it would be the scoop of the year. But she wouldn't tell me what it was, she just wanted to pique my interest.'

'Gosh!' Polynesia's surprise was genuine. She hadn't been expecting this at all.

'Gosh, indeed,' Sir Giles echoed. 'So I was wondering whether she'd told you anything at all about it, seeing as you were her second-in-command, as it were?'

'Nothing at all, I'm afraid.'

He sighed. 'That's such a pity. I feel sure her murder must be linked to this story, and the police agree with me. They're going to go through all her files again to see if they can find a new lead.'

'I'm sorry I couldn't help,' she said.

'I didn't really expect it, to be honest,' he said. 'I know what journalists are like, we're not exactly a collaborative bunch.'

Polynesia practically floated down to the fifth floor. She felt as light as air. Of course Dad hadn't murdered Joanna - what a ludicrous idea! She'd been killed by some criminal she was about to expose on the front page, and the police were now on the case. Polynesia's responsibilities were over; there was no way she was going to investigate underworld gangs or master criminals. It was time to go back to being acting deputy editor of the News department, and nothing else.

On the way home, she wondered whether or not she should tell Dad she'd been convinced for a short while that he was a murderer. On the whole she thought not. Dad had a good sense of humour and he might find it funny, *'I'm glad you think I've still got it in me to be a one-man killing machine, love.'* But there had been a bit too much killing in their family already, and with mad Uncle Richard in prison for life, Dad might be deeply hurt that she could ever have considered that he might also be a murderer.

'What did the cleaners have to say?' Dad asked, as he served up the fish pie.

'Nothing important,' she said dismissively. 'Gloria saw the PAT test electrician, that was all. We didn't manage to catch up with Esteban.'

'A dead end then?' he said.

'Sir Giles thinks Joanna was killed to silence her. She was about to expose some criminal or other, apparently. The police are looking into it.' She prodded at her fish pie, trying to find the prawns, and then looked up at her father. 'You know what, Dad? I've had enough. I'm hanging up my magnifying glass and I'm retiring. I thought I was an investigator extraordinaire, but I'm not, I'm a journalist with an over-active imagination.'

'That doesn't sound like my determined daughter,' Dad said, shaking his head.

'I'm sorry, but this is the new me and you're going to have to get used to it,' she said, with an air of finality.

After supper she sent a message to Will and Jess:

> *The Justice for Martin Campaign is hereby disbanded. I'm leaving it to the police to solve the murders. Thank you for all your help. Sorry we didn't manage to crack the case.*

Jess replied immediately: *Gutted ... no more suppers ...*

Will said simply: *I understand.*

Tuesday was wonderful, it was possibly the best Tuesday she'd ever spent. It was so nice not to have any responsibilities other than getting the news section of the paper together. It was lovely not to be wondering whether one of your colleagues was a homicidal maniac, or fretting about how to wangle information out of somebody without getting arrested.

She had lunch with Jess and they chatted about the failure of the Justice for Martin campaign.

'Honestly, Pol, you don't need to feel bad about it. I would have given up ages ago if it was down to me.'

'But I really believed I could solve it! I was so determined at first and now I've just thrown in the towel. I'm worried that I've lost my chutzpah, if that isn't cultural appropriation these days.'

'Carrying on when you've been threatened with a ten-year prison sentence isn't chutzpah, it's insanity,' Jess observed sagely.

'I suppose you're right,' Polynesia sighed. 'Anyway, life is certainly less stressful when you're not Polynesia Henman, investigator extraordinaire.'

'Let's make a plan for this weekend,' Jess suggested. 'You need something to look forward to. We could go out to dinner, me and Dan and you and Will. What do you say?'

'Sounds lovely,' Polynesia smiled gratefully. 'I feel more cheerful already.'

'Hey, Pol.' Will came over to her desk as she sat down. 'I was going to suggest lunch, but you vanished. How about dinner this evening instead? A sort of formal ending to the Justice for Martin Campaign. We could drink a toast.'

'Sorry, Will. I'd love to, but Dad and I are heading to the Peking Palace this evening for our weekly Chinese fix. How about tomorrow?'

'Sounds good to me. Oh, by the way,' he sat on the corner of her desk, 'I caught up with Esteban this morning. We had a brief sports chat and then I asked him about the morning Martin was killed. I know I didn't need to because the investigation's over, but it was just a journalist's curiosity, I suppose.'

'And did he happen to tackle a knife-wielding maniac and forget to mention it to the police?' she asked.

'I wish! It was just an ordinary morning, he said. Although he did see the electrician doing the PAT testing that Joanna told you about, and I reckon it must have been the same one that Gloria saw. Esteban said he was wearing those trousers with all the pockets that workmen wear, and while they were both waiting for the lift, he rummaged around in several of them.'

'That's exactly like my dad,' Polynesia said. 'He can never find anything in his trouser pockets either.'

'Esteban told him that if he couldn't find things, that meant he had too many pockets, and the man laughed and said that he liked having lots of pockets because it confused the thieves. So that definitely sounds like the same friendly bloke Gloria described.'

Polynesia felt a sickening swoop in her solar plexus, and she could hear a strange whooshing noise in her head as the full implication of this new information hit her. There couldn't be another man who used all the same phrases as Dad and also shared his dress sense, could there? The cleaners had described a friendly, smiling older man who wore workman's trousers and called people *love* and joked about confusing thieves with his trouser pockets. How many of those were there in London? Probably quite a few, her rational side said. London had a population of nearly nine million, so that must mean there were over a million pensioners, approximately half of whom would be men. So it was quite likely that there would be several who would share the same characteristics as her dad. But her intuitive side, which was so important to her as a journalist, was screaming at her that this was not a coincidence.

'… don't you think?' Will was looking at her enquiringly.

'Sorry,' she shook her head a little, 'I think I must have zoned out there for a moment. What did you say?'

'I was just saying that it's a bit odd that the same man just happened to turn up to test the equipment on both murder days. It's a wonder that the police haven't questioned him.'

'We don't know that they haven't,' Polynesia said, trying to keep her mind on the conversation.

'You'd think they'd have told Sir Giles that this guy was a person of interest. But they just seem to be focusing on finding Joanna's master criminal.'

'I expect we'll never know now,' she said. 'Look, I really must get on. Speak to you later.'

She forced herself to concentrate all afternoon on the article she was writing. Every time her brain started to ask questions, she forced it back to the deadly heatwave sweeping the Balkans. Finally, when she saw several of her colleagues leaving for the day, she picked up her things and headed towards the lift. She tried to look nonchalant and even smiled at a couple of people as she passed them. She felt an overwhelming need to behave normally and deflect suspicion, which was ridiculous because nobody suspected her of anything.

31

Chapter 31

Dad was in his study when she got home, tapping away on his computer with two fingers .

'Hello, love. All ready for the Peking Palace? Let me finish this email and then I'll get my shoes on.'

'Can I talk to you first?' she asked, trying to keep her voice even.

'Of course. Go and sit in the other room and I'll be there in two minutes.'

She sat down on the sofa. This was absurd. She was actually preparing to ask her father whether he'd brutally murdered two of her colleagues. She wouldn't blame him if he never spoke to her again. She'd have to move out, of course, and find her own flat, and things would never, ever be the same again.

Dad came in and sat down beside her.

'I'm ready now. Fire away,' he said.

She looked at her dad, then looked down at the floor and took a deep, calming breath.

'The thing is,' she began, 'two people at work, two of the cleaners who do the early shift, have both described seeing a man in the News office on the days that Martin and Joanna were killed. He was testing electrical equipment apparently -' she stopped, wondering how to continue.

'I see,' Dad looked at her intently. 'Go on.'

'They both described this person and, well, there's no easy way to say this, Dad,' her voice quavered slightly, 'but the person they described sounded just like you.'

Dad looked at her for a long moment and then he smiled.

'That's my Pol. Didn't I always tell you that you'd solve this case?'

She stared at him, blankly for a moment and then with growing horror. 'Jesus, Dad! You're not actually telling me it was you?'

'Of course it was, love.'

'You mean it was you who dressed up as this electrical tester guy, or you who killed Martin and Joanna?' She was desperately looking for a brighter side to this scenario.

Dad chuckled. 'It would have been an incredible coincidence if I'd taken it into my head to wander around the *Herald* offices disguised as some sort of glorified electrician on the very two mornings that Martin and Joanna were killed, wouldn't it?'

That was it then. Confirmation. No more clutching at straws.

'But … why?' was all she could think to ask.

'I did it for you, Pol,' he said simply.

'For me?' she repeated, feeling dazed.

'Yes, for you. It was your dream job, working on the News team. I know you've always wanted to be an investigative reporter, ever since your mum died. I was thrilled when you got the interview, and everyone said you were the best candidate for the job. But then that slimeball Trellis gave it to

Alice Smith. It made my blood boil, I can tell you.'

The thought of her mild-mannered father's blood boiling was quite astonishing. Perhaps she didn't know him as well as she thought she did.

'When that nasty piece of work, Miss Smith, started bullying you and Trellis did nothing to stop her, it was obvious there was something rotten about the whole set up. That was when I decided to kill him,' her father went on. 'It was quite easy really. I sent him a few emails, clever fakes if I say so myself, about a government cover-up. Then I arranged to meet him and bring proof that he could use in an article.'

'But how did you make sure Alice would be there too?'

'Oh, I didn't, love. That was just serendipity, the icing on the cake if you like. I'd arranged to meet him at quarter to eight and he told me he had a motivational chat organised at half past eight with someone he was mentoring. That must have been her. When I killed him I wasn't worrying about who'd find him, I just wanted him out of the way. I knew she'd lose her sting without her fancy man backing her up.'

'But he wasn't her fancy man, was he?'

'No,' Dad admitted. 'As it turns out, he wasn't. But we do know that they were as bad as each other, so I don't feel guilty about dropping her in it.'

Another thought struck Polynesia. 'But what about Clare? You said you liked her. It was you who wanted to go and visit her. You made a cake and got a present for the baby. And all the time, you'd murdered her husband!'

'She was better off without him,' Dad shook his head. 'I knew he was a wrong'un.'

'A wrong'un?' Polynesia's voice rose. 'How can you call someone else a wrong'un when you're a murderer?'

Dad reflected on this for a moment.

'I consider myself to be more of an avenging angel,' he said.

'Well, just as long as the police share your opinion, that'll be fine, won't it?' she said, pointedly.

'I've been in prison before, remember?'

'Of course I remember. It's hardly going to be something I'd forget. My dad being accused of murder and sent to prison.'

She didn't add that it had been the single most stressful event in her whole life. She didn't feel that there was any advantage to be gained at the moment from making Dad aware that he was adding to her stress load.

'When I thought about it,' Dad said reflectively, 'I realised that I could cope with being in prison. I wouldn't choose it, but I wouldn't go under. So that was that, decision made. It was worth doing because the benefits outweighed the risks.

'But why did you kill Joanna? She wanted to give me the deputy editor's job in the first place.'

'That's true,' Dad allowed. 'She didn't stick up for you though, did she? She didn't give Alice a written warning or tell Martin to rein her in. She did nothing. And then last week she put the frighteners on you and threatened you with the sack. Well now, I couldn't have that could I? I knew she had to go.'

'But the police think she was killed by someone who wanted to stop her breaking a story about them.'

Dad smiled. 'That's because your old dad's as clever as a cartload of monkeys.'

'So there was no breaking story, then?'

'It was all a hoax.' He looked very pleased with himself. 'I reeled her in with some stuff from the dark web, you know, deep fake photos and videos. That lecture I went to was very useful. I sent her a few tasters, from an anonymous email account, and said I had a lot more where those came from. Once she was hooked, I arranged a meeting and … what do they say in those spy films? Oh yes, I eliminated her.'

Polynesia was having difficulty processing all this. In the space of twenty minutes she'd gone from having a father who was a slightly eccentric, food-loving, retired engineer, to having a father who was a self-confessed killer, and who seemed to feel no remorse for his actions. It was the chilling matter-of-factness with which he described what he'd done that frightened her the most. Was this a symptom of insanity? Perhaps it wasn't just Uncle Richard who was criminally insane. Could it be a faulty gene that had tainted the whole family? For the first time, Polynesia felt glad that her grandmother was dead. She couldn't imagine the anguish it would have caused her to learn that her two sons were both killers, and that her only grandchild might well go down the same path, if this turned out to be a hereditary condition.

'Dad, we have to go to the police. You need to tell them it was you, before they arrest some other innocent person.'

Dad thought about this for a long moment.

'I tell you what, love. I'll go to the police tomorrow and tell them everything, if we can have one last evening together at the Peking Palace. It'll be something for us both to look back on fondly when we're not together any more.'

'Fondly?' She couldn't help herself. 'Do you really think we'll have a nice evening? There won't be an elephant in the room, there'll be a whole herd of them.'

'We won't talk about it. We'll just make pleasant chit chat and enjoy our last supper.'

She wondered whether Jesus had looked back fondly on his last supper, after he was arrested. Perhaps he had. He would have needed to eat anyway, she supposed, and a meal with friends would have taken his mind off things. It would be the same for Dad. He loved the Peking Palace, and it wasn't as though the police were going to arrest an innocent person this evening. If he postponed his confession until the morning, no harm would be done.

'OK, then, Dad. Let's go.'

'That's my girl.' He hurried off to find his shoes.

Despite the adverse circumstances, it was a nice evening. They ordered all their favourite dishes, and retold a lot of their favourite family stories, especially those involving her mum and her gran. It was a total nostalgia fest and she felt a lot better for it.

When they got home, Dad gave her a big hug and said, 'Tomorrow morning, you go off to work as normal. I'll stay upstairs and keep out of your way. Then I can tell the police that you knew nothing about it, that I didn't see you before you left for work, and that my decision to confess was made after you'd gone. The staff at the Peking Palace will confirm that we had a lovely evening there, and no one will suspect that you knew anything at all. That way, your reputation remains unsullied.'

'Dad, you really haven't thought this through,' she said, detaching herself from his arms. 'How can I stay in a job after you've killed both my line managers? When the story breaks, I'll have to resign.'

'You'll think of something, love. I have every confidence in you.' Dad put his arms around her again. 'Now, give your old dad one last kiss.'

Unsurprisingly, she didn't sleep well that night, but the next morning she went off to work exactly as Dad had suggested. His reasoning was sound, she decided. It was true that the last thing she wanted was for anyone to think she'd colluded with him, or even worse, to accuse her of being a Little Miss Macbeth, egging her father on to commit evil deeds on her behalf.

She spent the morning on tenterhooks, wondering what time he'd gone to the police station and whether D.I. Wilson was even now trying to get him to admit that he and Polynesia had been in it together.

She saw Will at the coffee machine.

'How was the Peking Palace last night?' he asked.

'Great, thanks,' she said automatically.

'I thought we could go Japanese tonight,' he said. 'I know you love Tokyo Express, but there's a new place near me that's a bit more upmarket. What do you think?'

Tonight? Of course, they'd arranged to have dinner, hadn't they? Well, she couldn't pull out, that would look very suspicious. Just do everything as normal, Dad had said.

'Wow! Yes, good idea!' she said. 'Do they do okonomiyaki? That's my absolute favourite! Mind you, I really love sushi as well.' And she clapped her hands together.

Will looked at her strangely. 'Are you feeling all right?' he asked. 'Only you seem to be a bit hyper this morning.'

'I'm fine!' she assured him with a wide smile. 'Just full of the joys of – err – August. And I'm really looking forward to dinner tonight.'

She scurried back to her desk. Damn Dad! He was turning her into a criminal. Here she was desperately trying to appear normal and worrying about alibis, when she'd done absolutely nothing wrong.

As the afternoon wore on, she began to feel more anxious than she had in the morning, if that was possible. Why hadn't she heard anything?

She wasn't exactly sure of the protocol around being arrested. She didn't know, for example, whether the police phoned the relatives of a suspect to inform them, just as the headmistress had always phoned the parents if a girl was put into detention at school. The circumstances were similar but not identical, so the procedures might not be the same, and she had no intention of googling it to find out. She knew all about not leaving an electronic trail, and was well aware that police experts would know if you'd sneezed on your keyboard two months ago, even if you'd scrubbed it thoroughly afterwards with antibacterial wipes. She wasn't going to incriminate herself by looking online for the rules and regulations of remand.

So she went home as normal, and found that the house was empty, which was a good sign. At least the police weren't there waiting for her, so they must have believed Dad when he said that she'd known nothing about it. D.I Wilson was probably having a good laugh right at this moment. Polynesia had been so confident that she'd unmask the murderer, and it turned out to have been her own dad all along and she'd had absolutely no idea.

She could picture D.S Knight's smirk the next time they met as he said, *'Not really your finest hour, was it? Best stick to the day job and leave the detecting to the police.'*

It managed to be both tragic and humiliating, she thought.

She was past worrying about whether her outfit was creating

the right impression, so she just threw on a comfortable denim skirt and her favourite bamboo t-shirt and headed off to Wandsworth. She met Will outside the restaurant, and he gave her a kiss and a hug.

'I always think PDAs are a big no-no at work,' he said. 'So it's good to be able to let loose in the evening.'

She hugged him back, not just savouring the moment, but also wondering how he'd feel about having a girlfriend whose father was a double murderer.

'Let's go in,' he said. 'I called them to ask about the okonomiyaki, and their recipe is Hiroshima style. How does that sound?

'It sounds perfect,' she said, putting all thoughts of future doom to one side and concentrating on acting normally. She was determined to enjoy this meal, even though it might well turn out to be yet another last supper.

32

Chapter 32

When she got home after dinner she was relieved to see that the house was in darkness and there was no police car waiting outside. A quick look up and down the road assured her that everything was quiet and most lights were already off. She felt sure that if the police had been here while she was out, all the neighbours' California shutters would have been twitching, and someone would have rushed out as soon as they saw her pedalling down the road, to tell her that she was a wanted woman.

She hurried inside and checked the letterbox, but there were no letters. Then she checked the landline, and there were no messages. She'd already checked her phone and that was entirely messageless too. So where was Dad and what had happened to him? She pictured him in a small, dark cell somewhere, bent over a rough wooden table, lit by one flickering candle. He had a quill pen in his hand and was scratching away at a letter:

My Deareft Polynefia, by the tyme ye read thif I shall be

no more ...

Stop it! She told herself sharply and shook her head to dispel the image. This was the twenty-first century, so Dad obviously wasn't going to be in the Tower of London, no matter what he'd done. She knew that really, it was just the lack of news that was making her imagination go into overdrive. She was sure that all prisoners were allowed to make one phone call, that was the linchpin of countless TV dramas. So why hadn't Dad rung her? She had a nasty thought – he might have rung Veronica instead, who was even now busy knitting socks to keep his feet warm on that cold prison floor.

After giving herself another stern talking to, she went upstairs and got ready for bed. She was bound to hear something tomorrow. She had a vague memory of learning about the law of habeas corpus in a history lesson once, and it meant that you couldn't just keep a person in prison indefinitely without telling anyone. The trouble was that she didn't know the exact length of time that counted as indefinitely. It was yet another thing she'd love to google, if only the police weren't going be tracking her every move online once Dad was charged.

The next morning she checked both phones, and even the news on the BBC, but there was nothing. They couldn't still be questioning Dad, could they? He'd gone to the police voluntarily to confess, so they didn't need to do the good cop, bad cop routine to try and break him. At least, not unless they were trying to force him to admit that Polynesia was involved too. She could just imagine D.S. Knight revelling in his role as bad cop:

'You say your daughter wasn't involved, Trevor. But I can't believe that a talented investigative journalist like Polynesia wouldn't have sniffed out your dastardly plot within minutes.'

'I swear that my daughter knew nothing, officer.'

'You're a doddery old pensioner and she's a bossy, cocksure, ambitious Cambridge graduate. Are you really telling us that this was all your idea and not hers?'

'Polynesia wouldn't hurt a fly, officer. Whereas I'm a ruthless, sadistic killer.'

'Tell that to the Marines, old man. We're bringing her in.'

She pictured the scene playing out in a grim little room, lit by a single bare bulb. D.S. Knight was wearing a belted raincoat and a trilby, rather than his usual creased grey suit, but the characterisation was spot-on she felt.

She'd only been at work for about five minutes when she was dismayed to see Sir Giles bearing down on her purposefully. Of course, she should have realised. Dad might not have managed to contact her yet, but the police would have been busy updating everyone on the progress of their investigation, wouldn't they? Sir Giles, who had lost two members of his staff, would certainly be one of the first to be given the good news that the murderer had been apprehended. She vowed that she would be noble and dignified as she weathered this particularly devastating storm. She could say truthfully that she'd had no contact with her father since Monday and had no idea where he was. Then, once Sir Giles disclosed the full extent of his crimes, she would gasp in horror and resign immediately.

'Ah, Polynesia, just the person,' Sir Giles stood in front of her desk. 'I wonder if I might have a quick word?'

She stood up obediently, not trusting herself to speak.

'Let's grab a coffee, shall we?' He indicated the machine at the other side of the office. 'Filthy muck, I know, but it makes us all more productive if we're not running out to Starbucks every five minutes.'

Polynesia thought of Alice and her decaf oat milk lattes. Those trips to Starbucks seemed a lifetime ago.

They stood awkwardly in the corner, clutching their paper cups, and Polynesia waited for the axe to fall.

'As I'm sure you're aware, the News team is short of three key players at the moment,' Sir Giles began.

Yes, thanks a lot Dad, she thought.

'So we're going to start recruiting this week,' he went on. 'The advertisements are going out tomorrow for managing editor, news editor and deputy news editor, and I very much hope that you'll be applying for the deputy news editor's role on a permanent basis.'

He smiled at her as she gaped at him.

'Don't look so surprised,' he said. 'You've been doing a jolly good job as acting deputy, even though you were rather thrown in at the deep end. With a bit of training, I think you'll be first class.'

'I – I – thank you,' was all she could manage.

'Don't thank me, I want the best person for the job.' He looked at his watch. 'Now, if you don't mind, I'm late for a meeting. Perhaps you could dispose of this for me.'

He handed her his untouched scum-topped coffee and headed for the lift.

Bloody marvellous, she thought. Her dream job had just dropped into her lap. Well, dream job for a thirty-year-old, obviously she had bigger dreams for when she was forty and then fifty. And now she'd have to resign before the ink was dry on the contract. Lady Jane Grey had managed to hold on for nine whole days and people still pitied her. What would they think of Polynesia's tenure if she had to resign as deputy news editor after about twenty minutes? She had occasionally, in the past, felt as though she had the sword of Damocles dangling over her head, but never before had the thread seemed so perilously close to snapping.

The rest of the day slipped slowly by. She was almost getting used to being in this limbo-land where terrible things were just around the corner, but she couldn't see them or feel them, she could only anticipate them. And for someone with such a highly developed imagination, it was a particularly refined form of torture.

Jess suggested a drink after work, but Polynesia refused the invitation, giving the excuse that she'd been out every evening this week and needed time at home to catch up on life admin.

Bet you're really dashing home for one of Trev's gourmet dinners, Jess had texted back.

You know my dad! she had replied.

But did anyone really know her dad? She wasn't sure that she did, and she'd lived with him her whole life, give or take the odd prison sentence.

She counted black cars on the way home, but it didn't have the usual calming effect on her tightly-strung nerves, and her stomach was still churning as she walked up the path to the empty house. She went into the study to check for messages and there was a light flashing on the answerphone. At last! She hurried over to press the play button.

> *Hello, Mr Henman, this is Nathan from Ace computers. Just a courtesy call to make sure everything's OK with the new laptop you bought yesterday. If you do have any problems, give us a call back on this number or drop into the shop and we'll be happy to help. Thanks now. Bye.*

That was odd. She pressed the button again, but there were no more messages. It made no sense - why had Dad stopped off and bought a laptop on his way to the police station? Surely he must have realised that he wouldn't be allowed to keep it in prison?

She sat down to a solitary meal of beans on toast. She would have to make more of an effort to learn to cook now. She couldn't live on ready meals for the next fifteen years, or however long Dad was likely to be in prison. She'd have to buy a cookbook and start making detailed lists for the supermarket, and then wheel a large trolley around the aisles. In the past she'd only ever dashed in for a few energy bars and a tub of pomegranate seeds, knowing Dad would sort everything else out. She had essentially been a teenager for the past seventeen years.

Her thoughts were interrupted by her phone ringing. She snatched it up. *Unknown caller,* the screen said – it must be Dad calling from the police station.

'Hello?' she said cautiously.

'Hello, love. Is this a good time to call? I thought you'd probably be at home relaxing by now.'

Relaxing? When her father had been AWOL for the past two

days after calmly confessing to a double murder? What planet was the man on?

'Yes, I'm at home,' she said. She wouldn't get angry about the relaxation comment, it would waste time, and this might be the only phone call he was allowed. 'What's happened, Dad? Why haven't you been in touch? Have they charged you or are you still being questioned?'

There was silence at the other end.

'Hello? Dad?'

'I'm still here.' He sighed deeply. 'Look, the thing is Pol, in the end I decided that it was probably best not to involve the police. I thought about what you said, about me jeopardising your job by murdering your boss and your boss's boss too, and you were right. I didn't think it through carefully enough.'

'But, if you're not at the police station, then where are you?'

'I'm in Costa Rica, love.'

'Where?' She heard her voice rise several octaves.

'Costa Rica. It's in Central America. It seems very nice, a bit wet at the moment but the rainy season won't last for ever.'

'I know where Costa Rica is. What I mean is, why are you there?'

'Oh, that's very straightforward. I'm here because there's no extradition treaty with the UK.'

Polynesia was speechless, so her father went on, 'It makes perfect sense if you think about it, love. Nobody knows that I killed Martin and Joanna, so your job's safe, and I don't have to go to prison. It's a win-win, as they say these days.'

She had a sudden flashback.

'This wasn't a snap decision,' she said accusingly. 'You've been planning this. You never had any intention of giving yourself up. You were researching Costa Rica weeks ago.'

'It did seem like a more appealing alternative to prison,' he admitted. 'You should come and join me.'

'I should go and report you to the police,' she retorted.

'That's my Pol,' he chuckled. 'You go down hard, but you soon bounce back.'

'I'm not joking, Dad. The police need to know.'

'If you tell the police, it won't affect me. They can't touch me here, I've told you. All that will happen is that you'll be tainted by association with me.'

He really had thought of everything. She saw that the stark choice currently facing her was that she could either retain her integrity and watch her career nosedive, or keep quiet and take the new job.

'But what would I tell everyone?' she asked. 'They'd be bound to get a bit suspicious. Old Trevor, who's never gone further than the Med on his holidays, suddenly ups and goes to live in Costa Rica without even saying goodbye. People will probably think I murdered you and this is my cover story.'

'Just tell them the truth,' Dad said. 'Not the whole truth obviously, just the bit that explains the travel.'

'Isn't the travel all part of the same *Escaping the Long Arm of the Law because I'm a Murderer* story?

'Pol, do you remember how I started fiddling about on my computer mining Bitcoin when I first retired?

'Yes, I remember you said you wanted a hobby to keep your brain active.'

'I did, and it has. And when the value of Bitcoin shot through the roof, I became a crypto multi-millionaire. Imagine that, your old dad's practically as rich as Croesus! Although I'm nowhere near as rich as Bill Gates, of course. We need to keep these things in perspective.'

Polynesia was already dazed with disbelief, so she accepted this new revelation relatively calmly.

'You want me to tell people you've gone off to live on a tropical beach, now that you're a multi-millionaire?'

'That's right, love. I knew you'd catch on quickly.'

She had a sudden thought. 'Is Veronica there with you?'

Dad gave a shout of laughter. 'Veronica can't get down the front drive without her walking frame. I don't think she'd cope with the jungle.'

Then he became serious. 'This is a burner phone I'm using, and I'm going to destroy it now, so you won't be able to contact me again on this number. Keep your head down, and when the dust has settled, I'll find a way of sending you a message and you can come for a visit.'

'I might still tell the police, you know, Dad.'

'I know you'll do what you think is best, love. I have every confidence in you, and I always have had.'

He ended the call and she sat there, feeling stunned and trying to process everything he'd told her. Then the phone in her hand pinged and she looked down at the message:

PS Make sure you marry Will. He's definitely not a wrong'un.

And then a second one:

PPS Delete this message.

And a third:

PPPS I meant delete both of the messages – and this one.

She stared into the distance for a long time. Burner phone, crypto multi-millionaire, extradition treaty … she couldn't take it in. The ease with which her father had embraced a life of crime was simply mind-blowing.

As for her, in the space of a few short weeks her life had been irreversibly turned upside down, and now she had to decide what to do next.

My Dad the Serial Killer, she thought. What a scoop that would be for the *Herald.*

Notes for Readers

Dear Reader

I do hope you've enjoyed Murder at the Herald. And if you have enjoyed it, I would really appreciate a brief review on Amazon.

Thank you!

Louise Barden

Printed in Great Britain
by Amazon

17591287R00161